The touch had been casual, yet the stab of desire that followed took Ashe completely by surprise

She leaned into him for a heartbeat, then, as if suddenly aware of what she'd done, quickly stood up straight.

Casey quickened her pace and walked past him, her hip accidentally brushing his thigh. The contact nearly destroyed him. He bit back a groan. The woman was killing him.

The more time he spent around that woman, the more he wanted her. Navajo teachings held that all secrets were revealed when a man and a woman made love. There was nothing he wanted to do more than to put that ancient belief to the ultimate test.

Ashe muttered an oath under his breath. He had to stop thinking like this. A night of passion with Casey, or even several, would never be enough for him. His feelings went too deep for a casual fling. What he wanted from Casey was the willing surrender of her heart....

Dear Reader,

Nothing attracts me more than a man with the guts to pursue what he knows is right, no matter what the odds. In THE BROTHERS OF ROCK RIDGE miniseries, I'll introduce two very special men—Ashe and Travis Redhawk. Like most brothers, they're often at odds with each other, but when the chips are down, they stand together ready to face any challenge. This series is about families like my own, the dynamics that separate us and yet, in the end, bring us together.

The past, and tradition, define Ashe and the beliefs that give him direction and purpose. He never expected to have his life turned upside down by a beautiful outsider with as many secrets as there are grains of sand on the Navajo Nation. His story is about loyalty, to the woman he grows to love and to The People.

Next, you'll meet his brother, Travis. Travis is like the wind, which finds purpose only in movement. A warrior in every sense of the word, he's made a place for himself as an Army Ranger. A promise made one moonlit night years ago, now brings him back to the Rez. Travis is a man who will pay any price to keep his word to the only woman he's ever loved. His story is about honor.

I hope you'll grow to love these special men as I have, and that their stories will linger in your memories long after the books have ended.

To receive a signed bookplate to go inside this book, and a newsletter, write me at P.O. Box 2747, Corrales, New Mexico 87048. Please send a self-addressed, stamped envelope.

Walk in beauty,

Aimée

Aimée Thurlo

REDHAWK'S HEART

HARLEQUIN®

TORONTO • NEW YORK • LONDON
AMSTERDAM • PARIS • SYDNEY • HAMBURG
STOCKHOLM • ATHENS • TOKYO • MILAN • MADRID
PRAGUE • WARSAW • BUDAPEST • AUCKLAND

To Angela C and new beginnings

ISBN 0-373-22506-7

REDHAWK'S HEART

Copyright © 1999 by Aimée and David Thurlo

This edition published by arrangement with Harlequin Books S.A.

Printed in U.S.A.

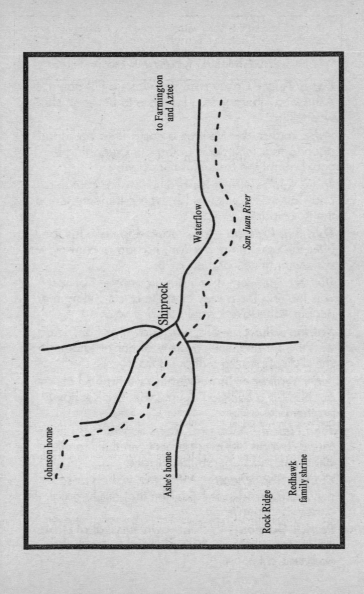

to Farmington
and Aztec

Waterflow

San Juan River

Shiprock

Johnson home.

Ashe's home

Rock Ridge

Redhawk
family shrine

CAST OF CHARACTERS

Casey Feist—Casey said she was an FBI agent. Ashe knew there was a lot more to her than she was telling.

Ashe Redhawk—He was a cop with a personal agenda that included finding out everything he could about the beautiful FBI agent.

Travis Redhawk—If his brother, Ashe, couldn't find Katrina, Travis would, even if it meant tearing the Rez apart.

D.A. Ben Prescott—If he wanted to keep his job after the upcoming election, he had to control two cops with minds of their own.

Delbert Spencer—Now out on parole, Spencer was looking for a way to strike back. Killing the people Ashe loved would be one way.

Katrina Johnson—She was known as Fox, and with the survival skills worthy of her nickname, she'd disappeared without a trace.

Jerry Walker—His interest in Katrina had always put him on a collision course with the Redhawk brothers.

John Nakai—Ashe and Travis considered him a friend, but an old grudge between their families still simmered beneath the surface.

Captain Todacheene—Why was Ashe's boss concealing evidence from him that might break the case wide open?

Patrick Gordon—With his own survival at stake, the ex-schoolteacher had planned to teach the Johnsons a lesson.

Prologue

Ashe Redhawk stared at the stone formations to the west, part of the Lukachukai Mountains. The land of the Diné— the land of the Navajo Nation—was a world filled with secrets; a place of sacred songs, rituals and prayers. Some said those rocks were warriors trapped in stone, guardians of The People.

Ashe appealed to them in silence now, trying to push back the edginess that filled him. There was trouble coming. He was attuned to the rhythms and cadences of the desert, and could feel a change in the air. His ability to sense that growing imbalance was not magic, but part of being a cop and knowing his territory.

As he headed back to town along the empty rural track, his thoughts wandered like the rambling, dusty trail before him. He'd gone to his ancestral shrine at Rock Ridge to leave prayer sticks. They had been an offering to Changing Woman, who had given birth to the Hero Twins—the mighty warriors who had made the land safe for the Navajos. Yet his quest to find the balance that would help him walk in beauty had failed. He had not attained harmony; nor would he, until he found answers to the questions that preyed on his mind.

He thought of Katrina, the daughter of his foster parents.

She'd been twelve at the time his brother Travis and he had come to live with the Johnsons. Katrina, whom they'd nicknamed Fox, had always confided in them, and treated them as longtime friends. The nickname they'd given her had been their gift to Katrina. She'd seen herself as a wallflower, and Travis and he had tried to change her perception of herself. Foxes, they'd explained, could merge with their surroundings and it was that ability to go unnoticed when they chose and observe others that gave them their power.

Throughout the years, the friendship the three of them shared had never wavered. If anything, they'd grown closer. Until a week ago, Ashe would have sworn that there were no secrets between them. But now he knew differently, and that knowledge had taken its toll on the confidence and faith he'd always had in Fox.

As Ashe recalled the police file he'd seen on his captain's desk a week ago with Katrina's name typed on the tab, his hand clenched tightly around the steering wheel. The existence of anything like that had come as a complete surprise to him. His gut wrenched and his chest felt as if a great weight rested on it as he remembered.

Another hard blow had come when the captain had refused to let him examine the file. Ashe was, by all previous standards, a highly regarded member of the tribal police. Yet, for some inexplicable reason, the captain had felt it necessary to lie to him. The captain had quickly put the file away, refusing to let him see it, insisting that Ashe had been mistaken about the name. That obvious lack of trust had shaken Ashe badly. He had done nothing to deserve it.

Ashe tapped his index finger against the steering wheel as he weighed the matter. In the confines of his tribal police vehicle the radio crackled. He was off duty and only half listening, but he was still aware of every word.

In an odd way the police chatter soothed him, much like

the voice of an old, trusted friend. The force was a second family to him these days. His time was divided between the disciplines of the Navajo Way and his work. Though some in the tribe considered it impossible to be both a cop and a traditionalist, Ashe didn't see a conflict. Like the Diné of old, he was a warrior whose beliefs gave him strength.

Ashe concentrated on regulating his breathing, seeking balance within himself. If Katrina did have a darker side, then he'd learn to accept it and help her work through it. Navajo tradition taught that everything had two parts, and that to achieve harmony, both sides of nature had to be embraced. He would do his best to help Katrina find such a balance. He drew on his traditional beliefs now for strength to face whatever lay ahead.

He was just minutes away from his house trailer when he heard a radio call that made his blood turn to ice. There was a 10-39—a disturbance—at the Johnson home. His thoughts quickly returned to his foster parents and Katrina as he spun the vehicle around in the road, switched on his emergency lights, and pressed down hard on the accelerator.

He was certain that this was one source of the imbalance he'd felt. Something was terribly wrong with his adoptive family. A silent cry rose inside him as he raced across the Reservation toward the place he'd once called home.

Chapter One

Ashe drove up to the small, one-story, wood-frame-and-stucco house the Johnsons leased from the tribe. It was set at the base of a hill above the bluffs, about two miles from the school the Johnsons ran.

He scanned the area quickly, but he couldn't see either of his foster parents around, and no other officers had responded yet. That wasn't surprising, considering the tribal police's chronic manpower shortage. As he pulled up and parked beside the Johnsons' faded green van, Ashe caught a glimpse of movement to his left. A figure running from the back of the house disappeared into the tall sagebrush on the hillside.

Ashe jumped out of the carryall, pistol in hand, and identified himself, ordering the running man to stop. Although he must have heard Ashe, he just picked up speed. Ashe's gut knotted as he suppressed the instinct to pursue the fleeing suspect. As a police officer, his priority had to be those inside the house. Fear stabbed through him. He would make sure his foster parents were all right, then go after the fugitive. Fox's car was gone, he noted gratefully. Hopefully, she was attending summer class at the college. He jogged toward the front porch, his gaze darting everywhere, alert to a danger he sensed but could not see.

Everything looked still—disturbingly so. One thing that had always marked the Johnson household was the constant flurry of activity at this time of the year. Alice Johnson spent her mornings gardening, or baking pies for the church and setting them out along the wide porch rail to cool. Nick Johnson was perpetually in the garage, building or repairing furniture. With school scheduled to begin in less than a month, he would be working now to make sure every desk and table was in good condition. Yet, instead, there was only silence.

Fear held him in an icy grip. If anyone had hurt his foster parents, they'd answer to him. He reached the porch steps and noted that the front door was closed. Ashe suddenly heard a car racing up the drive behind him. He turned as an unfamiliar vehicle slid to a stop, throwing a cloud of dust and gravel into the air. Weapon in hand, Ashe crouched behind a post. The new arrival was not a tribal police vehicle but an unmarked, generic-looking sedan that had "government" written all over it.

He'd never seen the beautiful, shapely woman who emerged from the dusty gray sedan before. The sun danced on her shoulder-length reddish-blond hair, making it gleam like melting gold. As she strode up to the house, her movements were graceful and feminine, yet held a hint of challenge.

"Stop where you are," he ordered.

When her gaze met his, he noted the quick, speculative look she gave him. Her eyes were weighing everything. He knew then, without a doubt, that she was some kind of cop, too.

She held up a gold badge. "Casey Feist, FBI," she said.

"A suspect just took off," he said, gesturing uphill. Ashe listened again for sounds coming from inside the house. Either no one was home or… He didn't want to contemplate the possibility. "Check inside the buildings," he added quickly. "A man and woman in their mid-fifties should be at home right now. I'll be back."

Ashe didn't give the woman agent a chance to argue. FBI training didn't generally stress tracking skills and he was certain he could track someone out here far better than she could. After all, he had been trained as a tracker, was at home in the desert, and there were few people who knew this particular piece of property as well as he did. He ran over to where he'd last seen the figure and crouched down, focusing on the boot tracks that led into a drought-hardened arroyo. The suspect obviously didn't know how to avoid leaving a trail. Had he gone around the base of the hill, it would have been far more difficult for anyone to follow because of the rocky ground. Instead, however, the fugitive had stayed on the relatively smooth, softer ground of the arroyo, where he could make better speed.

Ashe increased his pace, and as he broke through an area where tumbleweeds had gathered, he saw the darkly clad suspect about thirty yards ahead, climbing up the steep ten-foot side of the arroyo. The man pulled himself up onto the top, stood, and glanced behind him. Ashe instantly noted the suspect was wearing a ski mask, and that he was armed. His gut turned to solid ice as intuition told him there was death on the man's trail.

Dropping to one knee, Ashe aimed his own weapon. "Police officer! Don't move!"

The man dived away, hiding from Ashe, who couldn't see out of the arroyo from his position at the bottom.

Ashe ran to the arroyo's side, leaped up high, and grabbed on to the top of the vertical bank, pulling himself up and out with the ease of familiarity. As he emerged, the suspect, who'd paused behind a clump of nearby brush, fired two shots.

Ashe rolled for cover, regretting not having peered over the top of the arroyo first to check for an ambush. Anger had clouded his judgment, and now he might pay the ultimate price. He zigzagged in a random pattern as he headed for the cluster of sagebrush to his left. More bullets whined by his head.

Suddenly he heard a burst of gunfire from somewhere behind him. He didn't have to look to know that the FBI woman had followed him. She was giving him covering fire now, forcing the suspect to take shelter.

Trying not to speculate on what she'd found at the house, Ashe dived for safety behind a two-foot-high ridge of hardened sand.

The barrage of gunfire forced his adversary back into the thick brush of the bosque, which paralleled the river not more than a hundred yards away. Ashe took advantage of the moment, jumped up and continued his pursuit, using the tall vegetation to screen himself from view. Intuition told him that catching the fleeing man was imperative.

He was a fast runner with plenty of staying power, but despite his speed and his familiarity with the terrain, Ashe knew he'd lost his suspect for now when he heard the noisy rattle of a motorcycle engine starting up. He caught a glimpse of blue smoke and a dark-colored dirt bike as it roared out of the bosque and disappeared over the hill.

"He got away," the woman said, and cursed softly as she joined him.

Ashe bit back a curt response, wondering why she'd felt it necessary to state the obvious. He gazed down at her, momentarily distracted from his annoyance by the luster of her hair and the way the loose, flame-colored strands caressed her cheeks. As his gaze drifted down, he noticed a dark crimson stain in the center of her chest. His gut turned into a lump of ice. "Were you hit?"

Even as he said it, he knew it couldn't be so. A wound like that would have killed or completely incapacitated her. Another thought pushed in from the edges of his mind. He held himself still, waiting for her answer, but he felt as if something was slowly breaking inside him.

"I'm fine." She holstered her weapon and reached for the cell phone attached to her belt. "More tribal cops arrived at the scene, so I hurried to join the pursuit."

"If you're not hurt, who was?" He felt nothing inside him but horror as the answer came unbidden to his mind, even before she responded.

"The man and woman in the house are both dead," she said quietly. "Did you know them?"

Ashe could only nod. Rage, sorrow and despair ricocheted wildly inside him. The agony that pierced him was overwhelming. Knowing he needed to take action to stay sane, Ashe started running back to the house.

He heard the FBI woman telephoning in a brief description of the dirt bike and the perp as she tried to keep up with him. He was grateful that she was taking care of that, because right now, he knew only one responsibility: He had to see his foster parents for himself and try to figure out what had happened.

Ashe concentrated on putting one foot before the other, never breaking stride until he reached the front porch. There were two Navajo tribal police units parked out front beside his carryall and the FBI woman's sedan. Slowing to a walk, he took a deep breath, then entered the house, waving his badge in the air so the other cops who'd arrived could see it. It was an automatic gesture, but unnecessary. He knew all these officers, and they knew him.

Navajo beliefs had given him a deep aversion to death and anything connected with it but, now, other emotions drove him. A part of him still hoped it was all a mistake;

that no one had died here—or else it was someone he didn't know. He was aware that all eyes were on him as he knelt beside the bodies. One was covered by a handmade orange-and-black-checkered blanket he remembered from his boyhood days. Alice Johnson had finished crocheting it one Christmas. Memories filled his mind, but he pushed them back, forcing the cop in him to come through. Taking a deep breath, he pulled back the blanket.

Alice Johnson's battered face was almost more than he could take. He choked back his grief. A dear part of his world was irrevocably lost. It didn't seem possible. The scene before him became agonizingly surreal.

He pushed back his pain, letting the years of training as a cop come to his aid. It was the only way he had to help her now. He forced himself to do what had to be done, and studied the body for physical evidence.

Her lower arms were bruised and battered. Though now free, her hands had been bound together at some point with electrical cord, probably from the table lamp. Sections of that cord still remained on her wrists. She'd obviously resisted, been restrained, then shot sometime later.

He swallowed the bitterness at the back of his throat, fighting to hold himself together. His hands shook as he pulled the blanket back over the body and whispered goodbye. He had to get through this, and he would, no matter what it cost him.

He stood slowly and went to the other figure. Nick Johnson had also been badly beaten. He had multiple gunshot wounds and lay in a pool of blood. His hands, too, showed evidence that he'd been tied.

Ashe rose to his feet unsteadily. Displaced furniture and broken ceramic figurines suggested a struggle must have taken place. As a cop he was used to dealing with violence, but this was personal. He needed to get some air. He started toward the door when he saw the FBI agent, Casey Feist, enter.

Questions that hadn't occurred to him earlier suddenly crowded his beleaguered mind. What had she been doing here in the first place, and so soon after the killings? The FBI didn't routinely hang around the Rez responding to police calls. They only showed up when they were already working a case, or had somebody to arrest. Her presence disturbed him and filled him with the need to protect the privacy of the family who'd raised him; it was all they had left. He stopped in front of her, blocking her way.

"The rest of us here answered the call because this is our territory and our job. But you're an outsider," Ashe said, forcing his voice to remain steady and strong. "What brought the FBI here so quickly?"

"The Bureau has temporarily assigned me to the Four Corners area. I've been monitoring local police frequencies, trying to become familiar with the Reservation and your department's operations. When I heard this call, I figured I'd come by and observe your officers in action."

He hadn't missed the brief hesitation—a pause right before she answered. It made him suspect she was coming up with an off-the-cuff cover story. But to what end? The badge clipped to her belt was real enough. He gave her a long, knife-edged, suspect-wilting stare, but she didn't flinch or look away.

Ashe dropped his gaze, openly studying her bloodstained blouse and making no effort to disguise the questions it evoked.

Understanding, she nodded and explained. "When I entered the house, I saw the woman move," she said, glancing down at Alice Johnson's body. "She was barely alive. I called for an EMT, then cut the cords on her wrists with my pocketknife and tried to make her comfortable. But it was too late to do much else. She died in my arms.''

Ashe tried to find his voice. ''Did she say anything?'' he managed.

''She asked that I tell her three kids that she loved them all,'' she said in a shaky voice. ''That was it.''

Sorrow and dark despair filled his soul. He struggled against those feelings, knowing he wouldn't be any good to anyone unless he could keep his thinking clear.

Ashe stepped away, letting her pass, then looked outside. Someone was checking the grounds. Recognizing John Nakai, an officer he'd known all his life, Ashe met him near the door. ''Where's Fox?'' he managed, not using her given name as was customary in his tribe. Names were thought to have power that should be safeguarded by avoiding their use whenever possible.

''There's no sign of her,'' Nakai said. ''Her car's not here, either, as you probably already noticed.''

''Call the college. Check and see if she's still around campus.'' Ashe forced himself to concentrate. It was too late to help his foster parents, but there was still Katrina, and that worried him. If the killer was after his entire foster family, she could be in mortal danger.

Ashe walked outside and studied the ground by the garage where Katrina always parked. The tracks here were not fresh. She hadn't been home for two hours or more. That, hopefully, had saved her life.

Casey came off the porch and toward him. Though he hadn't been looking in her direction, Ashe had sensed her approach. There was a vibrancy about her that seemed to charge the air around her. It touched him in a way nothing ever had before. Even now, in the midst of death, she reminded him that life continued and that its warmth would eventually soothe his pain.

"What is it, Agent Feist?"

"I just learned from one of the officers that you're Detective Ashe Redhawk. I need you to tell me everything you can about the victims. Murder on the Reservation is a federal crime, so this case now falls under my jurisdiction."

"I know." It took every bit of willpower he possessed to remain outwardly calm. "The people inside are—were— my foster parents. Their daughter, who also lives here, will be coming home from her college classes, and might be in danger. She's the one I'm worried about now."

The newcomer's hazel eyes shimmered with a gentle softness that stole past his defenses, warming the cold emptiness inside him.

No. He fought against those feelings, struggling to stay focused. Casey Feist was a beautiful Anglo woman, but clearly one who did not belong here. This was the Dinétah, the land of his tribe—a people who had seen too many hardships and whose spirit was tested with each sunrise.

"Do you know who might have committed these crimes? Who were their enemies?" Casey pressed, cutting into his thoughts.

"They had none that would do this," he answered. "There were, of course, those who didn't believe their school belonged here—too many Anglo ways in what they taught. But they were respected. Everyone and everything has a place. That is part of our way."

"Were you close enough to them to have known something about their dealings with the community?"

"Yes. I grew up here. These people gave my brother and me our second chance. We came from Rock Ridge—south of Shiprock—to live with them after our parents died in an auto accident. Our clan is poor and no one could afford to take in two more mouths to feed. My brother and I owe these people," he said, pursing his lips and pointing Navajo-style toward the house. Rage filled him as he thought of the brutality and senselessness of their deaths. They would be avenged. He'd see to that.

Officer Nakai came running up to them, a worried frown on his face. "Fox didn't attend her noon class, but she was at her ten o'clock session."

Ashe nodded, looking at his watch. "Keep checking."

He closed his eyes and cleared his thoughts. For a moment, he concentrated on the way the wind felt against his skin and the heat of the sun against his back. Control. Without it there was no harmony, no beauty. Now, more than ever, he needed to draw strength from the beliefs that sustained him.

Gathering himself, he opened his eyes once again. There were plans to be made, difficult decisions to be weighed and then implemented. And most important of all, there were questions to be answered.

"You were here when I arrived," Casey reminded. "How did you get here so fast?"

Ashe knew where she was heading. She was trying to figure out whether he should be considered a suspect. He bit back his outrage. "When I heard the call, I was on my way to my trailer, which isn't far from here. I'd spent the last few hours at our family shrine at Rock Ridge."

"Did anyone go with you, or did you see anyone this morning?"

Ashe met her gaze with a steely one of his own and held it until she looked down at the notepad she carried. "No. No one can corroborate what I've told you."

"I'd like you to come back inside the house with me now, Detective Redhawk. I know this will be difficult, but I need you to look around the house very carefully. Maybe you can spot something that's not right, or that's missing from the premises. There are no obvious signs that burglary was the motive, and we're going to need some leads. Time's already working against us.''

"The killer will be found," Ashe said, conviction making his voice reverberate. "I'll see to that myself. Right now I'd like to supervise the officers recording the physical evidence, like the plaster casts they're making of the boot prints and the motorcycle treads the fugitive left behind. There should also be shell casings—the shooter used a semiautomatic.''

Her eyes narrowed. "I know you're a cop—"

"I'm a detective. And I know how to work a crime scene." He kept his voice cool and steady. He had no intention of backing off. Things would go more smoothly, however, if he could convince her that he was capable of working this case despite his ties to the victims.

"That may be so, but it's also true that you have a personal stake in this case and your perspective will be skewed. Leave this case to me, Detective. I know what I'm doing, too.''

"Maybe, but you'll still need my help. The procedures you're used to following don't always work here. That's the reality of the situation on the Navajo Nation, and you might as well accept it.'' He strode toward the house, leaving her standing alone outside in the shimmering heat. FBI or not, she was on his turf. Someone had declared war on his family, and he had no intention of letting someone else fight this battle for him.

CASEY FEIST STARED AT Ashe Redhawk as he walked off, then quickly followed him to the house. She knew all about him, though he didn't know that, and he fascinated her. Yet, until now, everything she'd learned had been based on anecdotes and on personnel reports as impersonal as the police jargon that filled them.

Now that she'd actually met the man face-to-face, he intrigued her more than ever. There were obviously many different sides to his nature. With his shoulder-length black hair and powerful build, Ashe Redhawk looked like a legendary Native American warrior from a painting of the Old West.

As the tribal officers examined the crime scene, she noted how the other cops responded to him. Detective Ashe Redhawk was a man used to taking charge, and she had a feeling few people ever challenged his authority. There was a dark, dangerous edge to him, straining against the iron-willed control. Intuition told her he could be a formidable friend—or an equally dangerous enemy.

Casey didn't interfere when Ashe reluctantly crouched by his foster father's body again as if a new thought had suddenly occurred to him. He studied the man's hands, careful not to touch the body in any way. From what she knew about Navajos, that was probably not just due to his police training. Before she took this assignment, Casey had been briefed about the tribe's customs, and remembered learning about their fear of the dead. Navajo religious beliefs held that the good in a man merged with Universal Harmony when he died, but the *chindi*—all that was bad—remained behind to create illness and problems for the living. Even mentioning the names of the dead was considered dangerous, because it was said to summon the *chindi*.

He glanced up at her. "There are fibers of what I think may be wool on his hands, the same color as the ski mask the suspect was wearing. I figure that there was a struggle, and my father managed to unmask the assailant. That cost my parents their lives." His jaw clenched.

There was a broken look in his eyes despite the steadiness of his voice. Casey's heart went out to him. She knew what it was like to face the death of someone dear. She'd lost her mother years back. Yet, despite the sympathy she felt for him, she refrained from offering any words of comfort. Under the circumstances, the last thing he probably wanted to hear were soothing platitudes that as yet had no power to ease his pain. He needed to cling to his professionalism now more than ever, to keep himself together.

"Why don't you look around the house?" she urged again. "You're the only one who can tell me if anything's been stolen or if the killer has left something behind."

Ashe stood slowly, strain and weariness evident in the way he held himself. Then, as if he'd suddenly realized the image he projected, he threw back his shoulders and walked with apparently renewed energy around the room.

"This makes no sense to me," he said. "My foster parents were kind and gentle people. They went out of their way to help others."

Officer Nakai came up to them. "The officer I sent to campus says, so far, nobody has seen Fox since that early class. He'll take another look around, then move on to the local college hangouts."

"It's not like her to change her routine, and even less like her to skip a class," Ashe said. "Take one of the officers from here and check out every coffee shop and store in the area."

"Wait a second," Casey interrupted. "We need these men here to continue processing the crime scene. This is exactly what I was trying to warn you about. You're too close to this case." She paused, then in a gentle voice added, "Go home, or start your own search, if you prefer. Katrina may just be studying, or out with her boyfriend. We have no reason to believe she's in any danger."

Officer Nakai gave Ashe a sympathetic look and glanced back at Casey. "It is our custom to avoid mentioning names, particularly around traditionalists like the detective.''

''I know about your custom of not naming the dead. But I only mentioned their daughter, whom I assume is still fine. I saw her name on some schoolwork inside.''

Ashe exhaled softly and, after thanking Nakai for his consideration, looked at Casey. ''We believe names have power. Repeating them wears them out. If a name is kept in reserve, its owner can use its power in times of danger. That's why I tend to use only her nickname. But I'm a cop, and I don't expect the manner in which we do our job to change or adapt itself to traditional ways. You did not offend me.''

''Thank you for understanding,'' she said. ''And try not to worry too much about that young woman. Just remember that you have no hard evidence to suspect she's in danger.''

''The timing is wrong for any other possibility. I don't believe in coincidence,'' he said. ''The killer arrived here sometime before Fox would normally have come home. If all he'd wanted to do was kill my foster parents, he wouldn't have tied them up first, or beaten them—possibly to gain information.'' He pointed to three cigarette butts ground into the floor. ''My foster parents don't smoke. The perp stayed around after killing them because he was waiting for Fox to arrive. He may have planned to deal with her next. The only thing that drove him off was my arrival. The thing that concerns me most now is that Fox should have been home long before I got here.''

Casey considered the information. This cop might be too close to this case, but he had an orderly, logical mind. Still, there was much he didn't know, facts she could not share with him yet.

Ashe looked down at his foster father's desk and the papers that were scattered everywhere. ''This mess was not my foster father's doing," he said, his voice slow and heavy with sorrow. "He was a stickler for neatness. The perp was searching for something. That's consistent with the beatings, too. He was looking for something he couldn't find, or else he needed information."

"About what? Do you have any ideas?"

"No, and I'd have to go through all his papers before I could even make a guess. But you'll want to have everything on this desk dusted for prints first. In the meantime, I've got to concentrate on finding Fox."

"Is it possible, in any way, that she may have been a part of what happened here? Was Fox getting along with her parents?"

"She is not involved in this, except as a potential victim," Ashe stated flatly, anger evident in his tone. "Fox is a gentle person, and she dearly loved her parents."

"Maybe she drove up, saw or heard part of what was going on, and fled. A female made the call to the station reporting the disturbance here—I heard that much on the radio. Maybe Fox was the one who called. She could be hiding somewhere, afraid to come home now."

"That's one possibility, but she also may have been kidnapped. The most recent set of tracks around the area where Fox parks her car are from this morning. Maybe she was taken close to the highway by a partner of the killer, and her car was taken, too."

His concern was real. But, as much as she wanted to, there was nothing Casey could do to ease his mind. With a heaviness of spirit, she accepted the burden her profession placed on her, as she had many times in the past. To disclose the little she knew would have been to risk compromising the job she'd been sent to do.

A tall, young-looking Anglo man wearing a Western-cut suit and exuding an air of self-importance suddenly came into the house. She didn't know who he was, but her guess was he was some kind of lawyer. From what she could see, the men in the room all seemed intent on looking busy and not catching his eye.

Oblivious to the collective indifference he was receiving, the man came up to her and extended his hand. He was obviously sweating in a suit at this time of year, yet he persisted in wearing a jacket and tie and drenching himself in expensive cologne. "I'm Ben Prescott, the county district attorney. You must be Special Agent Feist. The tribal police captain told me about you."

She nodded and shook his hand briefly. His touch held the practiced false sincerity of a politician.

"We're glad to have the cooperation and expertise of the Bureau on board," Prescott added smoothly. "I'd like to close this case quickly. It's an election year and I'm trying to make my temporary appointment here permanent. Do you have a suspect yet?"

"No names, just a description so far. Our investigation is just beginning," Casey answered.

"I shouldn't have to remind you that, after the first twenty-four hours, the chances of catching the criminal decrease substantially."

Casey now understood why everyone had treated this man like a walking plague from the moment he'd arrived. He was still wet behind the ears, and had just enough knowledge of investigative matters to be irritating. "We learned that at the academy, sir," she retorted. "We're doing our best."

"Good. Keep me informed every step of the way, especially regarding any evidence you uncover. And remember, I want some arrests ASAP."

Prescott drifted over to another unfortunate officer as Casey refocused her attention on what Ashe was doing.

Ashe's gaze was riveted on the contents of a file scattered on the floor near the desk. Having put on rubber gloves, he was sifting through the papers carefully. But it was the pain mirrored on his face that drew her to him. "What's wrong?" she asked.

"These are adoption papers. According to them, Fox was *not* my foster parents' natural daughter. I never knew that. I never thought of my foster parents as people with secrets, but it looks like I was wrong."

She heard the sorrowful disappointment lacing through his words, and every fiber in her body responded to it. She wanted to offer this man some comfort, but knew she could not. Power, grace and strength defined him. For now, his own courage would have to be enough to keep him going. But, as he turned his gaze on her, she felt herself drawn to him on a level she'd never experienced before.

It was all she could do to force herself not to reach out to him, and to look away. "Do you think the adoption is somehow connected to the murders?"

"I don't know, but I'm certain this was something Fox was never told. She wouldn't have kept it from me or my brother."

Casey heard an uncharacteristic hint of uncertainty in his voice.

"Too many secrets," he added in a whisper-soft voice.

Emotions she couldn't quite define flickered on his face and then, in a heartbeat, were gone.

Casey watched him move through the room. As he passed through the different shades of lighting, his face became a fascinating blend of clearly defined angles and planes. He was the most striking man she'd ever met. Yet it was his composure in the face of chaos—that ultimate proof of his courage—that drew her the most.

Instinct warned her that danger lay ahead for her in this case, but her course was set. She'd been sent to find answers, and she would start by learning more about this enigmatic, compelling man.

Chapter Two

After a fruitless two-hour search for Fox, and a futile attempt to reach his brother, frustration gnawed at Ashe.

He'd hoped at least to talk to Travis and share the burden of sorrow with him. Instead, he'd been forced to leave a message asking that his brother call home as soon as possible. Travis's Army Ranger unit was on maneuvers, their location classified, and there was no telling how long it would be before Ashe heard from him.

He'd almost been relieved when Casey had called, asking that he return to his foster parents' home. She needed his help now that the crime team had almost finished processing the scene.

Ashe now sat at Katrina's desk, an old oak teacher's desk from the forties that Nick Johnson had restored. He ran his hand over the smooth, hand-rubbed, light oak finish. Nick had given Katrina this desk on her birthday, soon after she'd started middle school. Ashe remembered Travis and he had helped Nick Johnson carry it out from its hiding place in the garage.

As if that one memory had unlocked a door, others rushed to fill his mind. He remembered their school vacations with special fondness. There were summer trips fishing along the Dolores River in southern Colorado, visits to the State Fair in Albuquerque in the fall, rodeos near the high school and Babe Ruth baseball.

"Is there anything missing from her desk?" Casey asked, interrupting his thoughts.

"Not that I've seen so far." He could sense her frustration over the lack of damning physical evidence. Except for two nine-millimeter shell casings recovered above the arroyo, there wasn't much to go on except the plaster impressions. None of those would be any use until they had a suspect, a pistol and a motorcycle.

Casey would need his help on the case—probably far more than she realized just yet. But first he intended to learn the real reason she'd come to the Johnsons' home when she did. What she'd told him and wanted him to believe might have had elements of truth, but it wasn't the whole story. His gut feelings were seldom wrong. Her presence here, so soon after the call, had been more than coincidence. He didn't believe she'd had anything to do with the crime—he *had* gathered enough facts to discount that— but he still had some serious questions about her that needed answers. If he couldn't get them from her directly, he'd have to find another way.

He picked up Fox's address book and leafed through it. "A few pages have been torn out of here."

Casey pursed her lips and nodded slowly. "Fox might have taken those herself. If my theory is right, she may have decided to hide out at a friend's house. As I figure it, the only way we can protect her now is to find the killer."

Ashe studied Casey's expression, trying to figure her out. For whatever the reason, she was only intent on finding the perp, not Fox, who could clearly be the next victim. "It's time to try a different tack."

"Like what? And, for the record, there's no 'we.' This is *my* case."

He met her gaze for a moment, then shrugged and headed for the door. "Okay. Good luck on *your* case."

She had to jog to match the speed of his long, powerful stride. "If you withhold any information relevant to this investigation, I'll have you up on charges so fast you won't know what hit you. I'm sure you're familiar with the term 'obstruction of justice.'"

Ashe regarded her coolly as she stood dangerously close to him, blocking his way. He had learned a long time ago to lock away his feelings, but Casey still managed to heat his blood to a boil. Few men ever dared to challenge him, yet this woman did so with nothing more than determination and courage to back her up.

"I'm going to the station," he said. "You may leave your car for one of the officers to bring back and come with me, or follow me in your own car, or stay here. As you say, it's your case."

"Wait for me." She hurried back inside and returned a minute later. Casey opened the door on the passenger side of his tribal police carryall as he started the engine. "Tell me about this lead you want to pursue."

He paused, gathering his thoughts, but with characteristic Anglo impatience, she misinterpreted his silence as lack of cooperation.

"The Bureau has access to state-of-the-art equipment, and our agents have the best training in the nation," she added. "All of that can be brought to bear in this case. If you try to handle the investigation on your own, you're going to give the criminals a big head start."

"Crimes aren't solved by technology alone, here on the Rez. You have to know your territory and the people you're dealing with. Clearly, you do not."

"Don't underestimate me, Detective. I *always* get the job

done. I have a reputation for making things happen. People who cross me find out real fast my rep is well deserved.''

The challenge was made with the unshakable confidence that came only from experience. It was clear that she was a born warrior—something he both understood and respected.

"I do have one lead," Ashe said. Casey was right about one thing: She would make a good ally. Her resources at the Bureau would give him an edge. Nothing meant more to him than catching the killer and finding Katrina. "There's a file with Fox's name on it at the station. I've seen it." He filled her in, including his captain's refusal to give him access to the file.

"That's your lead?" she asked, surprised. "But you said your captain told you that file had nothing to do with Fox. What makes you so sure you didn't just make a mistake?"

"I know what I saw."

Ashe turned his thoughts inward, seeking harmony, but anger blocked his efforts. The image of his foster parents' bodies would stay with him until the day he, too, died. One way or another, he'd find the killer. An image of Fox flashed before him. She had to be okay. The alternative was too painful to contemplate. He'd become a cop to protect others. The knowledge that he'd failed to protect his foster family gnawed at him, threatening to undermine the work he now had to do.

Ashe led Casey to the squad room of the small-but-modern tribal police station a short time later. A tense silence filled the room as he stepped inside. He was used to people looking to him for answers but, now, when it mattered the most, he could offer them none.

Captain Todacheene came out of his office and gave Ashe a nod of acknowledgment. "I'm sorry to hear about your family. If you need any time off, the paperwork is ready. All you have to do is say the word.''

''Thank you, Captain,'' Ashe replied. ''May I speak to you in private?''

''Of course.''

Ashe glanced back at Casey. ''Excuse me for a minute.'' Ashe could see she wasn't happy about being excluded, but surprisingly enough, she didn't protest.

He didn't have time to consider it further, however, as Captain Todacheene led the way into his office and closed the door behind them.

''Okay. What's on your mind?'' the captain asked, walking to his desk.

''You know about Agent Feist?''

He nodded. ''We've met. She's in charge of this case now, if that's your question. You know the law.''

''We don't have a motive for the killings yet, but I believe Fox may have been kidnapped. I'd like to work on that aspect of the case. Earlier today, while going through the victims' papers, I discovered my foster sister was adopted. I'd like to subpoena any records—''

''You're not going to sneak anything by me with double-talk. I said this is not your case. The Bureau is in charge.''

''Agent Feist has requested my help. That's what I'm trying to do, without interfering with the homicide investigation she's taken over.'' He was stretching the truth, but not very far. ''Normally I'd need a court order for agency adoption records, but there is one place I could search for answers immediately. I'd like to search through her file— the one I saw here on your desk.''

''I don't have any file on Fox. I told you that.''

Ashe's hands clenched around the arms of the chair, but he kept his body perfectly still. ''I saw the file.''

Todacheene's eyes narrowed. "You saw *a* file, Detective."

Seconds passed by slowly. The silence was so thick it became a tangible presence between them.

Todacheene finally stood, shaking his head and adjusting the belt that circled his ample girth. The massive turquoise-and-silver belt buckle he wore caught a beam of sunlight that came through the window, and cast a strange bright reflection on the wall.

"You're out of line, Detective. Way out of line. If the file you saw contained anything that would give you a lead on the killer, I would show it to you in an instant. There shouldn't be the slightest question about that in your mind. You've had a shock, so maybe your instincts aren't working right. I'm willing to cut you some slack because of the circumstances, but don't push me. That would be a serious mistake."

Todacheene held the door open. "Now, send Special Agent Feist in here. She and I need to get a few ground rules worked out."

Ashe walked out and gestured for Casey to go in. As her gaze met his, he felt a tug on his senses, like the vibrations from a lightning strike nearby.

He let his breath out in a hiss. The agent was, like most women, a distraction—nature's way of bringing another imbalance into his life. He shut her out of his thoughts.

Yet, as he sat down at his desk, she stayed at the edges of his mind, offering him some respite from the pain that weighed on his spirit.

CASEY FELT ASHE watching her as she walked into the captain's office. Even after she closed the door she remembered those eyes—they made her heart forget to beat and her skin tingle in places it had no right to. But she had no time for this. Bringing her attention back to business, she sat down and urged the captain to begin.

"The detective will not be easily dissuaded," Todacheene warned.

"You know him better than I do. Will he at least follow orders and stay out of my way?"

"His foster parents have just been brutally murdered. On duty or off, Redhawk's involved, regardless of what either of us may wish."

Casey nodded thoughtfully. "To what extent can he be trusted?"

Todacheene leaned back and regarded her. "If you're asking me whether he'll follow orders mindlessly, the answer is almost certainly no. But if you're asking me if I believe him to be totally honest, the answer is yes. You should keep one thing in mind, though. He's a man who acts on his principles, regardless of how dangerous it gets."

Casey exhaled softly. "A wild card, then."

The captain shrugged. "If you choose to see it that way."

"What other way is there?"

"You might find his insight and his contacts useful. He could be the best of all possible allies for you, especially here on the Reservation where he is known and respected."

Todacheene's statement had been matter-of-fact, but the message was clear. She'd been warned by her superiors that an Anglo would not receive the tribe's unconditional cooperation. It was obviously a battle she'd have to fight, and it would be up to her to figure out what, if any, concessions to make.

"I will tell you, right now, that nothing short of locking him up will prevent Detective Redhawk from searching for the Johnsons' daughter," the captain continued. "And when his brother hears about what happened today, we'll have to deal with him, too. Ashe and Travis are very different, but in times of trouble, the Redhawk brothers are a formidable team.''

Hearing a knock, the captain stood and opened the door. When Prescott, the D.A., came into the office, Ashe followed him.

''I thought it was time for a meeting,'' Prescott said, standing in front of Todacheene's desk. ''I had to give the newspapers a statement. Admittedly I was extremely vague, but I don't think they're going to let this just drop. Have you got any leads yet?'' Prescott looked at Casey.

''Except for continuing the search for the gunman who ran away, and who remains unidentified, we don't have much,'' she replied. ''We have footprints, a few nine-millimeter shell casings, three squashed cigarette butts and tread marks from the motorcycle seen at the crime scene. The room was vacuumed for hair and fibers, which will be examined to see if they may have come from the assailant. That's it. But keep in mind that the murders were discovered only a few hours ago, and an analysis of the physical evidence takes time.''

Prescott turned to look at Ashe. ''What about you, Detective? Have you got a lead yet on the location of Katrina Johnson?''

Ashe shook his head. ''I'm still working on that.''

''I've been making some calls on my own,'' Prescott said. ''The Johnsons had no known enemies—none that I've managed to uncover.''

''I don't know of any, either,'' Ashe admitted. ''But this situation proves that they did. This was no random killing, or botched robbery. The timing, and the way the murders were carried out, suggests organization and premeditation.'' He paused, then added, ''Another unanswered question is how Agent Feist managed to get to the scene so quickly.

This is the first time I've ever heard of an FBI agent cruising the area, listening to our police frequencies.''

Casey met Ashe's gaze, forcing herself not to react. Despite his dislike for the D.A., he was purposely using the man's questions as an excuse to bait her. She had no intention of rising to it. ''The Four Corners area is new to me. I was trying, and still am, to get to know the Reservation.'' She focused on the D.A., giving him a cold stare. ''And, Mr. Prescott, in the future, please refrain from giving statements or questioning witnesses regarding this ongoing investigation. If you feel you must, please consult with me first. I am in charge of this case.''

Prescott said nothing, but his eyes told Casey he wasn't happy with her reprimand.

''I think we'd be better off dividing the case,'' Ashe said, looking at Casey. ''How about if you concentrate on the murders, while I search for Fox?''

Casey considered his offer carefully. It might serve to keep him out of her hair and let her do the work that she was here to see through. The key to everything lay in finding the killer, and that had to be her top priority. ''Okay, but if you turn up a lead I can use in the murder case, I want you to turn it over to me immediately. Deal?''

Ashe shot a glance at the captain, who shrugged. He then turned back to Casey and nodded. ''If you find anything that will help me find Fox, please do the same for me.''

As he held her gaze, another delicious shiver touched her spine. Casey suppressed it quickly, but not fast enough to mask it from his eyes. She looked away, angry at herself. Instinctively she moved a few steps farther away from Ashe and looked at Captain Todacheene. ''I know we just got them, but have we learned anything about the shoe imprints left by the suspect near the murder scene? Also, was there anything useful or distinctive about the motorcycle tread marks?''

Todacheene looked down at some papers on his desk. ''We know that the motorcycle was a dirt bike. The tires are particularly knobby and easy to recognize. But the make and model are still unknown. The footprints came from a size-ten boot. That's not that unusual, but the brand was. The tracks were identical to a model made by a big-name outdoor-wear company that does a lot of mail-order business. Few around here can afford to spend the kind of money this company gets for their footwear.''

''I'll want to check out any local stores that might carry that brand,'' Casey said.

''There aren't any on the Rez, but there are one, maybe two places in Farmington. The crime team can get you the information you need by tomorrow morning, at the latest.''

Casey glanced at Prescott, who was taking notes, then at Ashe. ''If Fox's disappearance is, as you suspect, directly connected to the murders, then our cases will overlap. I suggest you start by checking into the possibility of a stalker or a jealous boyfriend. You know Fox and who her friends are. Ask around. We don't have any evidence at this stage to support that explanation, but it's an avenue worth pursuing. I saw her photo back at her home. She's very attractive.''

''Yes, she is,'' Ashe answered softly. ''I'll look into that angle.''

She saw the raw pain and worry mirrored in his eyes and her heart ached in sympathy. ''I know you suspect that this whole case has something to do with Fox's past,'' Casey said gently. ''But if her disappearance and the murders are related at all, I think it's more likely to have something to do with her present. On the other hand, it may be awkward for you to look into her personal life. If at any time you want to turn the investigation over to another officer, I'll understand.'' She saw the flash of anger in his eyes and knew his determination was unshakable.

''My priority is finding Fox. I'll do whatever's necessary to accomplish that.''

His words chilled her. They'd been a warning, or maybe even a threat. Though judging people was usually one of her strengths, Casey was having an unexpectedly tough time reading Det. Ashe Redhawk. ''Okay. So we're set,'' she said, looking over at the captain, whose face was impassive. ''Detective Redhawk will concentrate on Fox. He knows more about her and her habits than I do. I'll work on the murders.''

For a brief moment her mind flashed back to the Johnson home and the woman who'd died there in her arms. Alice Johnson's sorrow as she'd begged Casey to relay a final goodbye to her children had touched Casey deeply. She would catch the killer—for that woman's sake and for her own. Only then would she be able to put that memory aside and go on.

As she looked at Ashe's face, Casey wondered how she would have coped if someone close to her had been murdered. Her own mother's death from cancer had been devastating enough. Casey had only learned of her illness at the end. She'd returned home immediately but, by then, it had been too late to do anything except say goodbye. And yet, memories of their final moments together had helped Casey cope in the aftermath. Ashe had been robbed of even that small comfort.

As an awkward silence settled over the room, Ashe walked to the door. ''It's late. I'd better see what can be done tonight and then arrange to get an early start tomorrow.'' While he stepped around Prescott and strode out of the room, Casey's gaze remained on him. Ashe was a remarkable man by anyone's standards. Everything about him spoke of purpose and power.

"Detective Redhawk has a good idea," she said. "I think we'd all better call it a night and plan on an early start tomorrow."

IT WAS A LITTLE PAST 9:00 a.m. when Casey met Captain Todacheene in his office. Prescott walked in right behind her. The man seemed destined to continue popping up everywhere on this case. Casey had learned that Prescott had been appointed to replace a D.A. who had resigned, and was now working overtime to prove he should keep the district attorney's job. He obviously thought a big-news murder investigation—solved, of course—was going to be his ticket to winning the upcoming election.

"Captain, I don't want to interrupt you this morning," Casey said, "so if you'll just point me to the evidence room, I'll be out of your way."

"I'll take you there," Todacheene offered.

Casey followed him, noting with irritation that Prescott had opted to come along with his little notebook. The captain led the way to a makeshift chicken-wire-and-wood-frame caged area at one end of the station.

Casey looked around. "You don't have a full-time clerk here?"

"It isn't needed. And if you're worried about losing evidence from the crime scene, don't. Nobody here would tamper with anything from a murder scene, even if the area was completely unlocked. What belongs to the dead, or is associated with them, is never at risk here." The captain stepped back and allowed them to enter. "There are many things you don't understand about our people," Todacheene added, then glanced at Prescott. "That goes for most Anglos."

"The same law applies here as it does outside the Rez," Prescott said flatly. "I've lived in the Southwest all my life, and I don't buy into this Hollywood Indian stuff."

"Nor do I," Todacheene replied with a mirthless smile. "But on the Rez, things progress at a different pace and are guided by rules you may not understand." He met Casey's gaze. "Trying to ignore that would be a big mistake."

And a costly one, too, no doubt. She knew she was being warned not to underestimate the disadvantage being an outsider placed on her here.

As she signed in and waited for Captain Todacheene to bring out the physical evidence that had been collected at the Johnsons', Casey's thoughts turned to Ashe. She wished she had met him under different circumstances. She suspected that getting to know him would have been a challenge and a pleasure they both might have enjoyed.

Slowly, the meager evidence was laid out before her, including plaster casts of motorcycle and boot tracks, and shell casings. The cigarette butts, fibers and hair samples had already been mailed to the state crime lab in Santa Fe.

Casey sat down and began the painstaking task of using both intuition and knowledge to study the scanty evidence and listen to the story it had to tell. Prescott soon left and as the hours passed, she used all her training to glean what information she could. As she stared at the address book, the last piece of evidence, a new idea formed in her mind. Only a few pages had been taken. Maybe the Johnsons had told their killer something about the people listed on those missing pages, and he had taken them in hopes of finding Katrina.

Done with her work there, Casey signed out and went to her car. Alone in her vehicle, she picked up her cell phone and dialed the one source she intended to keep secret from everyone involved for as long as it took to find the killer.

Less than fifteen minutes later, she was on her way east, heading toward the long, rocky ridge known as the Hogback. As the early-afternoon sun baked the desert, leaving increasingly longer shadows, she was struck by the starkness of the land that surrounded her. Things were different out here; the captain was right about that. To her, the landscape looked like aerial photos of Mars—red and barren. But human nature was the same everywhere, as were motives for murder. Understanding that was her advantage in this harsh, unfriendly place.

Miles outside the Reservation boundary she found the apartment house she was looking for, in a semirural housing area north of the river. The three-story building, crammed on a small lot, sorely needed a coat of paint and some landscaping improvements. Each apartment, she noticed, at least had a small fenced-in area outside a sliding-glass door. The second and third stories had small balconies.

She glanced around the weed-infested, graveled parking area. Only a few cars were there, though she was uncertain whether that indicated a small number of residents, or if the tenants were mostly single or worked days.

She went inside the building and up the dim stairs. The hallway on the third floor had only an exit sign at each end for illumination.

In one of the apartments, a radio was playing loudly. Mournful lyrics about a jilted truck driver rose above the guitars of a country-western band.

Looking around for a light switch, she found one. She was about to turn it on when a flicker of light through an open door at the end of the dark hall caught her attention.

Her senses warned her of danger, and Casey decided not to risk announcing her presence by turning on the lights. She unclipped the strap that held her weapon secure in its holster, and approached cautiously, verifying the apartment number. As the light from inside flickered again, Casey realized that what she was seeing was the beam of a flashlight crossing the room.

Casey glanced down and saw that the lock on the door had been forced open. Drawing her pistol, she prayed she wasn't about to stumble on another murder scene. Her heart sounded like a kettle drum in her own ears as she eased the door open a bit farther and stepped inside. She'd just cleared the door when a large hand snaked out and covered her mouth. Before she could react, she was pulled backward until both she and her assailant were out in the hallway.

Imprisoned against a rock-hard chest, Casey stepped down hard on the man's instep. She knew it was a painful move, but her assailant didn't even flinch.

"Stay still," an instantly recognizable whisper-soft voice said. "It's me."

She nodded. She was curious as to what had brought him here, but there was no chance to ask now.

Ashe didn't ease his hold. His massive hand also covered her nose, making it nearly impossible for her to breathe. She elbowed him hard in the stomach.

This time, he let go.

She gasped for air. "I couldn't breathe!" she whispered.

"Be quiet," he answered quietly, "or both of us are likely to end up short of breath. The guy in there is armed."

Chapter Three

Ashe continued to press her against him, his arm wrapped around her waist. Her senses, always acute in the presence of danger, now urged her to recognize an awareness of a different kind. His warm breath touched her cheek, and as she felt the hardness between his thighs where their bodies touched, a shiver coursed through her. She knew then, without a doubt, that the attraction she felt for him was not one-sided.

He released her slowly and, she imagined, almost reluctantly. They both knew the danger of allowing any distraction in a hazardous situation, but, despite that, something had sparked to life between them. Denying it wasn't an option; putting it on hold was a necessity.

Ashe stepped around her and nodded toward the apartment door. Working as a team, they entered the small living room slowly, weapons drawn.

As Casey stepped closer to the bedroom door, off to the right, she caught sight of their quarry. She signaled to Ashe. Someone tall—a man possibly—was moving around in the darkened room, wearing yellow rubber gloves and carrying a flashlight in his left hand. She could make out the shape of a pistol he'd shoved in the waistband of his pants. She saw him open a small dresser and search it with the swift precision of an experienced burglar. Just then the country-western ballad playing on the radio ended, and the burglar stopped, looking around and listening. Casey and Ashe froze in place. As the radio station started a commercial, the burglar resumed his search.

Ashe crept forward, merging with the shadows along the walls provided by the heavy drapes. She shifted direction, to be ready to give him backup, and stepped on something soft. A loud screech caused them both to jump, and a terrified cat ran past them, out into the hall.

The intruder bolted upright, and caught sight of Casey and Ashe blocking his exit.

"FBI! Put your hands up!" she yelled.

Instead of complying, the intruder slipped through the drapes and out onto the balcony. Casey tried to get a good look at him, though he was wearing a ski mask, but the curtain blocked the view from inside. She glanced at Ashe, who held up his hand, signaling her to hold her position. They couldn't see the burglar, and an armed, point-blank confrontation on a balcony was too dangerous.

"You're three stories up with no place to go. Put down your pistol and come back inside, slowly, and with your hands up," Ashe ordered. "You're trapped and outgunned." He moved around the bed toward the curtain pull along the wall.

Casey heard wood creaking and, as the curtain moved aside, saw the man step toward the balcony railing. She shot forward to stop him. "Ashe, he's going to jump."

Slipping through the open sliding-glass door, Casey grabbed the perp's jacket with one hand as she shoved her pistol into its holster with the other. The man laughed, then stepped off the edge, yanking her with him as he fell.

Casey managed to grab the wood railing with her free hand, and still maintain her hold on his jacket. They were both dangling, but the perp had the advantage. He was closer to the ground.

Ashe grabbed her wrist, supporting her grip on the railing.

With a chuckle, the burglar lifted his arms straight up and the jacket slipped right off him. Casey had no way to stop him as he dropped down onto a patio table twenty feet below.

Still dangling from the railing, but with no desire to pursue the intruder at the present, Casey tossed the captured jacket up onto the balcony, then tried to swing around to get a two-handed grip on the railing.

Her wrist ached and she couldn't seem to pull herself high enough to get the second handhold she needed. Ashe's iron grip kept her from falling. "I'm still here. You're not going to fall." He shifted his anchoring grip farther down her arm and leaned over to reach for her other hand. "Grab on to me."

"No, it's too dangerous," she managed, her voice breaking. "I could pull you over."

Her legs dangled uselessly as she struggled again to grab the railing, but her fingers slipped as she tried to get hold of the wood.

"I've got you. Reach for my other hand, not the railing." Ashe's voice was filled with authority, and his grip on her was steady. "You've got to trust me. I'm here for you."

His voice flowed over her like a golden river. Yet it was meeting his eyes that finally broke through her fear. What she saw there was the courage and determination of a real flesh-and-blood warrior.

His grip never wavered as she reached up with her other hand to grasp his free hand. All his strength was there for her now. He pulled her up slowly.

When at last she was back on the balcony, he pulled her

into his arms and held her. She pressed her face against his chest, feeling his heart thumping in a wild rhythm that matched her own.

Casey held on to him tightly. His body was strong and solid, a haven against the fear that had imprisoned her seconds before. Fiery emotions flickered to life within her as a raw awareness of the man holding her swept over her. As if sensing the needs he'd awakened in her, Ashe twisted her hair around his fist and pulled her head back, then lowered his mouth to hers.

Fire danced in her veins as she welcomed the kiss, opening herself to it. He was life at its best—intense, unpredictable and wild. His tongue filled her mouth, warming her with a heat that rivaled the desert sun's. As his lips slanted back and forth across hers, taking and giving her pleasure, her thoughts became nothing more than a jumble of sensations.

Casey rubbed her hand over his chest. His flesh was hard, yet smooth. She heard him groan as she caressed him; then, a breath later, he slowly eased his hold.

Ashe stepped back and looked at her. Passion raged in his eyes. "You're too much of a temptation, lady. I would apologize," he said slowly, "but I enjoyed kissing you too much to mean it."

"What makes you think it wasn't my idea to kiss you?" Casey countered with a hesitant smile. She could still feel the warmth of his kiss, and taste him on her lips.

He gave her a lopsided grin that tempted her to step into his arms again. But he was right, it was a complication neither of them could afford.

Casey took a deep, sobering breath and looked down at the collapsed table and otherwise-empty yard below them. The sound of a motorcycle off in the distance told the rest of the story. "He pulled the perfect escape, you know, and got me to help him break his fall. He's not only lucky, he's good."

"And it's gravel down there, so there won't be any tire tracks to compare with the ones we have in evidence," Ashe noted.

"He seemed tall enough. Do you think he could have been the killer?"

Ashe nodded somberly and reached for his two-way radio. He called the local sheriff's department, reported the break-in and gave them the brief description they had on the suspect.

Casey retrieved the denim jacket she'd snagged from the perp from off the floor of the balcony and began looking through the pockets. "No papers, ID or anything. But I suppose it's to be expected. A man would have his license and such in his wallet. It's too bad. I was hoping for a break. This jacket seems ordinary, too, so I doubt it'll give us anything definite, even if we manage to track down the store that sold it. But it does have a tobacco smell to it. That is a possible link to the killer. And maybe there will be some fibers on it from the ski mask."

"Our best bet is still to track down his boots, and hope they weren't purchased mail-order instead of locally," Ashe said. "Did they give you a list of stores around here that carry that brand yet?"

"No, but I was assured I'd get one this morning."

"I'll prod them, if you'd like."

"Sure, go ahead."

Casey sighed as she stared at the balcony thoughtfully. "They're never going to let me hear the end of this back at my office when I file my report. I'm lucky I didn't drop my weapon, hanging over like I was."

"That's your pride talking. You literally went overboard trying to apprehend a possible killer."

"Having this guy get the best of me still stings."

"It's only one battle. We'll go talk to the neighbors, once the deputies get here to process the scene."

"We also need to find and talk to the woman who lives here," Casey said, reaching for her notepad. "Mrs. Garwood." She looked up at Ashe. "Which brings me to an interesting question. How did you end up coming here? Do you know Mrs. Garwood?"

He nodded. "Mrs. Garwood is a Navajo friend of my foster parents. She married an Anglo and lived here off the Rez, but she was like an aunt to all of us. I wanted to ask her if she'd heard from Fox." He paused, then asked, "How did *you* know about her?"

"I saw the *G* page was missing from Fox's address book. I couldn't ignore the possibility that the killer might have taken it, so I asked around until I got the name of someone Fox might have listed there."

Casey was about to say something more when she heard a muted cry behind her. She spun around and saw a middle-aged Navajo woman standing just outside the door to the hall. Shock was evident on her face.

Ashe moved toward her. "It's okay. There's no one here now but us," Ashe told her.

Casey approached and identified herself. "Mrs. Garwood?"

The woman nodded, a bewildered look on her face as she turned on all the lights and saw the state the apartment was in. "What happened?"

"I was hoping you could tell us," Casey said. "The man who broke in here was searching for something. Do you have any idea what that may have been?"

She shook her head. "I have nothing of value to a thief, except that old TV." She pointed toward a small portable on a wheeled cart.

"Have you heard about the murders on the Reservation?" Casey asked.

Mrs. Garwood nodded, tears forming in her eyes. "And I know Fox is missing," she said, looking at Ashe. "Does this have something to do with her?"

"It's a possibility," Ashe replied. "Has she contacted you?"

"No, I would have called you if she had." Mrs. Garwood turned back to Casey and gave her a wary look.

Casey knew she had to gain the woman's confidence somehow, but she had no idea how to go about it. "You knew the Johnson family. Can you help us? Do you have any idea who might have wanted them dead?" Casey realized she'd made a critical mistake when she saw the expression on Mrs. Garwood's face change. Casey had been warned about mentioning the names of the dead, but the habit wasn't an easy one to break.

Mrs. Garwood's eyes narrowed. "I will not talk to you. You're a stranger to me and I've had enough of strangers," she said, waving her hand around the room. "This is what I get for living off the Reservation."

As the deputies arrived, Casey reluctantly left Mrs. Garwood for Ashe to interview. He'd have a better chance of getting answers without her there.

Casey identified herself to the officers and turned the jacket over to them for processing, warning them of the possible connection to the double murder. She also requested they send any fiber evidence to the state lab for comparison with the samples from the murder scene. As the team began to search the apartment for other physical evidence, Casey stayed close by, monitoring their progress and helping them search.

Although she'd hated turning over the duty of questioning Mrs. Garwood to Ashe, she had to admit it had been the right thing to do. A glance showed her that Mrs. Garwood was in the midst of an animated discussion with the Navajo detective.

Casey started examining the floor for anything the suspect might have dropped. As she did, she moved closer to Ashe, hoping to overhear at least some of the conversation.

"Don't you worry about Fox," Mrs. Garwood said. "She's got a very good head on her shoulders. She'll be okay."

"I'm worried that she may be way out of her league. We're dealing with a vicious killer."

"I've been thinking about that and Fox's disappearance ever since I heard the news on the radio. Maybe their deaths had something to do with the man who has been bothering her."

"Who's been bothering her?" Ashe's voice grew sharp. "I didn't know anything about that."

"I don't know his name, but I understand he's older than she is, and wouldn't leave her alone. She told me that he'd wait for her after classes, and then follow her around, trying to get her to talk to him."

"Why didn't Fox come to me?"

"She was afraid it would be awkward for you, and you might do something to get yourself in trouble. The man is a police officer from Farmington."

"Did she tell you anything else about him?"

"No, and now I wish I'd asked."

Seeing Mrs. Garwood glance in her direction, Casey shifted to join a pair of officers who were questioning a neighbor. The tenant with the radio that had now, thankfully, been turned off, seemed to have a lot of questions, but no answers to offer.

When Ashe came up a moment later, the tenant's attention shifted to him. Casey didn't blame the woman; Ashe stood quietly now, a lock of black hair over his brow, but the force of his presence made her own skin prickle with excitement.

Ashe drew Casey off to one side, letting the officers continue their questioning undisturbed. "I got a call on my cell phone. Prescott wants us to meet him in Farmington once we're done here. He's asking for a full report."

"Okay. Did the officers inside the apartment find anything?"

"No. There was a screwdriver on the counter, but it was Mrs. Garwood's."

"Has she discovered anything missing?"

Before he could answer, Mrs. Garwood came rushing up to Ashe. "I just remembered something else. The man I told you about rode a motorcycle, but I don't know what kind. All Fox said was that it was big and expensive looking."

As Mrs. Garwood moved away, Ashe filled in the gaps in what Casey knew. She was amazed at how well they worked as a team. It was as if they'd been partners for years, instead of only having met the day before. What Ashe had found out, however, made Casey suspect that the murders were not connected to the business that had brought her to the Rez.

"We seem to have two bikes involved," Casey said. "We know about the dirt bike, and now we're talking about an expensive touring model."

"Bikers often have more than one motorcycle. Of course it's also possible the cycles could belong to two different people."

Casey walked back to her vehicle, Ashe by her side. "We need to question every male friend Fox had," she said. "Stalkers have been known to attack family members they feel are interfering with the relationship they're trying to establish. They thrive on control."

"Looking into the possibility of a stalker was a good hunch on your part." Ashe took a deep breath. "Fox is clearly at the heart of what's happened. But I don't think we should fix exclusively on that aspect of it. I'd like you to do me a favor. Use your Bureau sources to get me everything you can on Fox. Where did she come from before my foster parents adopted her? Was the adoption legal? Who were her biological parents?"

Casey owed him one for his rescue on the balcony, and they both knew it, but there was a matter of duty and professional responsibility that she had to honor first. Some loyalties went above and beyond the personal, although this time, she truly regretted that. There was still one very important question about Ashe she needed answered before she would risk giving him her trust: Had Ashe's curiosity about his foster sister's past compromised Katrina in some way, and led to the Johnsons' death? He'd admitted to having seen the file the captain had in his office.

"Getting that information could take some time," she hedged. "In the meantime, why don't you concentrate on Fox's current friends? If a stalker *is* connected to the murders, we need hard evidence and a suspect, and that's not something that's going to be linked to her distant past."

His gaze hardened. "The present does concern me, probably more than you realize. You should know that I called a friend of mine at the Bureau and it seems that they don't have any files on you."

"Your source is obviously out of the loop. Do you think your captain would have given me access to his department's records, backed me up or allowed me to work with his people if my credentials were bogus?" Casey had to convince him. It was imperative that Ashe not doubt she was on the side of the law. "I *am* a federal agent," she said, looking him right in the eye, and speaking with the confidence she could only muster for the truth.

"I believe you," he said after a long, thoughtful pause.

As Ashe walked off, she realized that he'd obtained more information from her evasions than she'd ever dreamed he could. As he drove away, Casey slipped behind the wheel of her own sedan, her thoughts still on him. Ashe had a way of cutting through her pretenses and making her feel as if he could see clearly into her soul. It was bewildering— and as intoxicating as an entire bottle of brandy. He was, without a doubt, the most dangerous and exciting man she'd ever met.

ASHE FOLLOWED HER across town. Hearing his cell phone ring, he scooped it up and flicked it open with one hand. His brother Travis's voice sounded very far away.

"Hey, little brother. I got a call from my C.O. notifying me that you'd left a message. Something about an emergency back on the Rez? What's up? Did someone punch your lights out, and now you want me to come to the rescue?"

Ashe hated to break the bad news to his brother over the phone—it seemed too impersonal—but he had no other choice. As he recounted what had happened, the full weight of their loss hit Ashe hard. "They're dead. I can't change that," he said, struggling to keep his voice calm and steady. "But one way or another, I'm bringing in whoever is responsible. The killer will answer for what he did."

The silence on the other end was long. "When's the funeral?" Travis said at last.

"The bodies won't be released for a while. There's got to be an autopsy first. It's a legal formality in this case, but a necessary one. After that, we'll be free to set up whatever arrangements we want. But I'm not convinced a funeral would be right for them."

"They weren't Navajo," Travis reminded sternly. "It's their customs we need to honor now."

"I'll search for their will and see what they wanted done. I remember they spoke of being buried in their church's cemetery."

Another long silence followed before Travis spoke. "I'll be home as soon as possible, but I can't get emergency leave for a few more days. I'm on a special assignment I can't discuss. Can you handle things there without me?"

"I'm a cop, not just your kid brother," Ashe snapped. Travis had a way of putting him on the defensive. It had always been that way. But this was no time for competition between them. "There's more," Ashe said, wishing he didn't have to deliver this bit of news, too. Travis was not likely to take it well. "Fox is gone."

There was utter silence on the line for a moment. "What do you mean, 'Gone'?" Travis's voice suddenly became cold and deadly.

"Calm down. I don't have any concrete reason to believe she's not okay," Ashe told him, then quickly explained.

"I'll get there as soon as I can. If you haven't found Little Fox by then," Travis said, using his own pet name for her, "we'll turn the Rez upside down and shake it, if that's what it takes."

"No. I've got things under—" The connection was abruptly severed. Ashe cursed. He loved his brother, but Travis's ways of getting things done were not compatible with a systematic investigation that would hold up in court. On the other hand, he couldn't have asked for stronger support. Nothing had ever stood in their way when Travis and he joined forces. And perhaps that was what Fox needed now—a damn-the-rules mentality that would anni-hilate anything in their way.

As he pulled into the Farmington police station behind Casey, Ashe's thoughts shifted to her. For the first time in his life he understood his brother's feelings for the woman he'd always called Little Fox. A woman could disrupt everything in a man's life and still find a way to touch his heart.

FOR CASEY, THE MEETING with Prescott at the Farmington police station was more frustrating than informative. The D.A. got everything they had, and gave little in return.

An hour later, Casey drove back to the Reservation alone. Ashe had opted to stay behind—a move she was certain would pay off for him. If a Farmington cop had been harassing Katrina, she had no doubt that Ashe would discover the officer's identity. As a man, he'd be able to tap into the good-old-boy network there far more easily than she ever could.

She arrived at the tribal police station a short while later, and went directly to Captain Todacheene's office. Though she hadn't called in ahead of time, he seemed to be expecting her.

He waved her to a chair, then closed the door behind them. "I heard about the incident at the apartment house. I also know Redhawk was there. How did you cover your trail?"

"I gave him as few details as possible. He still doesn't know the real reason I was sent here."

"Sooner or later he's going to see right through your cover. You can only push this FBI thing so far. He's too sharp a cop."

"Yes, I realize that. Tell me something. Is there any way he could have read the file on Katrina that you have here?"

He hesitated. "Not the file he saw on my desk. I got it out of reach too quickly."

"There's a but in there somewhere. I can hear it in your voice."

"There's a computer file on Katrina Johnson, as well." The captain expelled his breath in a hiss. "Ashe Redhawk was heavily involved in setting up our computer system here. He may have left himself a back door—though, frankly, I doubt it. He's not that type of person. And if he does know what's in the file, he certainly isn't acting on it."

"So what we have here is a highly motivated, honest cop with a sharp mind and a lot of questions. That means we'll have a very big problem keeping secrets from him."

"Maybe. But if the person who killed the Johnsons *is* a rejected suitor, or someone with a grievance against the family, that file doesn't figure in at all with their murders, anyway."

"True, but until we know for sure, we've got to move with caution."

Casey left the office certain of only one thing: She had to get a better handle on what kind of man Ashe Redhawk really was.

Outside, in her car, Casey looked at the list of names her source had given her. She had to move fast. Ashe was bound to remain in her way.

As she tried to interpret the travel directions her contact had given her, Casey's mind kept shifting to the next step of her investigation. The Navajo woman she needed to speak to lived in an isolated section of the Reservation. If this woman's response was anything like Mrs. Garwood's, Casey wouldn't have much to show for the long drive after she was done, either. It would all be a waste of time. Casey muttered a curse. She'd come to the Rez with every expectation of making swift progress—something she was known for—but *nothing* on this case had worked out as planned.

As she pondered the situation, a plan formed in her mind. There was one way of making sure Ashe didn't create a problem for her. If she could keep an eye on him, and monitor what he did, she could make sure he didn't inadvertently jeopardize the work she was here to do.

Unfortunately, there was only one way Casey could think of to actually keep close tabs on him, and that had its own dangers. But it was her only option. She had made up her mind to radio the captain and ask that Ashe be assigned to work with her, when her call sign came over the radio.

Casey responded immediately. "This is Special Unit 144." The call was coming in on the local tribal police frequency.

"Switch to channel eight," the voice advised.

Despite the static, she knew that the speaker was Ashe. Her pulse quickened in an instinctive response to his smoky, masculine voice.

"I'm being tailed by someone on a motorcycle," Ashe said. "Dispatch told me they can't find another unit close enough to back me up because of a traffic accident between here and Gallup. Can you respond?"

Casey got his location and quickly checked her map. "Affirmative," she said, giving him her own position in return. Maybe this would even things out a bit. She still owed him one. "Are you in any immediate danger?"

"No. He's keeping his distance. I think he only wants to keep an eye on me. He's good at surveillance, too. It's only luck that I spotted him at all. My guess is that he's the cop I was trying to find today."

"How do you want to handle this?" Casey asked.

"I'm going to head west until I reach the canyon up

ahead. If you'll go about a half-mile farther on the road you're on now, then turn left onto the dirt road past the boulders, we might be able to trap him between us,'' Ashe replied.

''Ten-four.''

As she sped down the highway toward the rendezvous, Casey pictured Ashe growing up here in this land of mesas, sand and sagebrush. It was only then that she began to understand him. Ashe was a man who had chosen to embrace the secrets of his tribe and the desert that surrounded them. In that lay his strength. To him, the past was an integral part of who and what he was. It was little wonder that he was driven to learn about Katrina's background, as well.

''He's still following me,'' Ashe said. ''It's up to us now.''

Casey picked up her mike. ''He's got the best on his tail. He's ours.''

She heard his low chuckle and smiled. Was it the thrill of the chase that was making her heart race, or was it something else? Ashe was danger itself but, heaven help her, she couldn't back away from him. Fate had conspired against her, placing her on a case he was an integral part of, and one she was bound to see through.

''Just be prepared for anything.'' With that single statement, he signed off.

Chapter Four

Ashe needed only one glance in his rearview mirror to know that the man was still following him right into the trap. Ashe knew this area like the back of his hand, but he wondered about Casey and how she was handling it. The terrain here was rough and, if he had her pegged right, she was a city girl through and through.

Unfortunately, during the past few hours, a thunderstorm had been building. The sky overhead was filled with towering black clouds, and just to the southwest the sky was streaked with rain. Already, a few drops were striking his windshield. Unless he missed his guess, they were in for one major gully-washer.

Less than a minute later, the wind struck his vehicle like a rampaging stampede, and rain hurtled from the sky in swirling waves that all but obscured the road ahead. Before he'd even reached the canyon, the track beneath his utility vehicle's tires became a muddy stream. He slowed down, careful to keep the vehicle on harder ground, and switched over to four-wheel drive. One wide turn and he could become bogged down in the softer ground beside the road.

As he reached the canyon opening, his rearview mirror caught a flash of chrome from the motorcycle behind him.

The helmeted driver, though drenched, maneuvered the cycle with the skill of an expert, despite the wind and rain.

Ashe knew then, that, like him, his adversary was used to the swiftly changing weather conditions of the Southwest. His thoughts turned to Casey. The route she was following would take her across two small arroyos that would fill up quickly with runoff in this downpour.

Worried, Ashe radioed her.

"I've had to slow down," she told him, frustration evident in her tone, "but I made it through the washes already. It was like fording a stream. But don't worry. I'll be there to back you up. Count on it," she said.

He was surprised at how easily he pictured the way she would look as she said that. Her eyes would be slightly narrowed and her lips pursed with determination. Though they hadn't known each other for long, instinct told him that she wouldn't let him down. One way or another, she'd keep her word.

CASEY DROVE CAREFULLY up a rock-strewn hillside, a shortcut she'd decided on at the last minute. She'd lost time because of the rain, but if she could make it over this small hill, she'd still be able to cut off the motorcyclist's escape. Of course, if the biker had possessed even two healthy brain cells, he would have turned back by now. Sheets of pouring rain made visibility practically nil, and the ground was like a shallow river beneath the tires of her car.

Halfway down the other side she struck muddy soil, and her vehicle started to wallow. Before she could turn aside, her vehicle sank down to the axles, then stopped all forward motion. Not even all-wheel drive could have helped her now. The mud here was silt, not sand, and it buried her tires, taking away all hope of traction. She was going nowhere.

Reluctantly she threw her door open, grabbed the hand-held, and proceeded on foot through the mush toward the mouth of the canyon. She'd probably make better time walking, anyway. Ignoring the cold, stinging rain, she picked her way through the soggy earth that threatened to suck her shoes right off her feet. Finally, she hit sandy ground and was able to jog to the dirt road. One way or another, she'd be there to back up Ashe.

Casey had just arrived at the mouth of the canyon when the radio at her belt came alive with a burst of static.

"He turned back and made it out of the canyon along a shallow tributary. He's long gone now," she heard Ashe say. "He found a trail with the motorcycle that was too narrow for any vehicle. There was no way either one of us could have followed him."

Casey stifled a groan. "Too bad he didn't do it five minutes ago."

"Why? Where are you?"

"At my end of the canyon where you told me to wait. But my vehicle's stuck about two hundred yards from here, at the base of a small hill."

There was a moment of silence. "You mean you're out in the rain and mud?"

"Brilliant deduction, Detective."

She started the trek back toward her car, cursing the desert, cursing Ashe and cursing the case that had brought her here in the first place. This time she took her time. There was no need to hurry back, and the slog through the mud was tiring.

When she didn't get another transmission from Ashe, she began to worry. Maybe she'd been too curt. She'd need help getting her sedan out. Though she hated asking anyone for a hand, she'd hate hiking all the way back to the highway in the rain even more.

Crossing the muddy terrain was like wading through a giant vat of peanut butter. To her surprise, when she finally arrived, Ashe was already there, and he had attached a tow-rope to her car. Five minutes later, the vehicle was free.

"You're unstuck," he said simply, joining her beside her car.

Ashe stood before her, neither touching her nor moving back. His gaze searched hers as if he wanted to read the secrets of her soul.

Casey's pulse raced. Ashe's wet shirt clung to him, accentuating his powerful shoulders and the planes of his muscular chest. Rain dripped down into his open collar, making his copper skin glisten.

The cold rain did little to cool the fires spreading through her. She yearned for his touch, though her more cautious intellect urged her to move away.

Ashe gave her a gentle smile, then caressed her cheek with the palm of his hand. "You came through for me today. You pulled out all the stops to do it, too. I won't forget that."

As he turned and walked back to his vehicle, the memory of his touch and the enticing warmth it had evoked stayed with her. Desire sang to her of forbidden pleasures. She wanted to call out to him, but did not. They both had other responsibilities and, after those were completed, she'd be leaving here for good. Pursuing the attraction between them would lead only to pain, and they'd both had enough of that in their lives.

Feeling more alone than ever, Casey climbed into her sedan and followed Ashe's taillights back to the highway.

THE NEXT MORNING, CASEY returned to the Reservation. She still needed to question Alice Johnson's best friend, but the woman's address mystified her. "Turn at the rock with the petroglyphs,'' she'd been told. Cripes, couldn't they have nice little street signs, like Tumbleweed Lane or Canyon Road?

Knowing Ashe could help orient her, she once again considered asking that he be assigned to her immediately. After mulling it over, however, she opted against it. She wasn't sure if her desire to seek him out was an excuse—a product of feminine longing—or a genuine investigative necessity. Pushing away the disturbing questions, she focused on finding her way.

After forty minutes of wrong turns and time-consuming corrections, she arrived at her destination. Casey pulled up to a gray stuccoed wood-frame house with a log hogan at the back. The absence of other houses, telephone lines or even roads disturbed her. With her back to the house, Casey could look around in any direction and find no traces of civilization anywhere. She suppressed a shudder. How could anyone stand being so isolated?

Casey parked and went to the door of Diana Begay's house. She needed to find out if anyone had come here recently, asking questions about the Johnsons or Katrina.

As she approached the door, a woman about Katrina's age came out. Casey saw open suspicion on her face, and tried to overcome that with a smile.

She pulled out her badge and ID. ''I'm Special Agent Casey Feist,'' she said, keeping her voice soft and nonconfrontational. ''I need to talk to Diana Begay about the family that was killed,'' she said, remembering this time not to use names.

The young woman did not relax. ''My mother won't talk to you. My parents are traditionalists. You aren't welcome here until you learn our ways. You've already insulted them.''

''I don't understand. What did I do that was rude?''

"You didn't wait to be invited. You left your car and came right up to the door, like some tourist."

Casey took a deep breath. Had there been time, she would have studied the culture more thoroughly before coming to the Reservation. But time was something that was working against everyone involved—except the killer.

"I'm sorry. I really didn't mean to offend. I'm trying hard to catch a very dangerous person before he can harm anyone else," Casey said.

For the first time, she saw the young woman relax a bit. Her shoulders lost some of their rigidity, and the tightness around her eyes disappeared.

"I know. That's why I came out to talk with you. Whoever you're looking for killed our friends. He needs to be found and put in jail for a long time." She led the way to a bench beneath a nearby cottonwood tree. "I'm Ilene Begay. I'm not a traditionalist like my parents, so you can relax."

"Could you tell me if anyone around here has ever had any arguments or trouble with the people who were killed? Maybe a neighbor, businessperson or the parents of one of their students?" Casey wanted to cover as many possibilities as she could think of.

"There was that fight over the land where the school was built, but that was years and years ago," Ilene said.

"Tell me about it. Did somebody attack the John—I mean, the people who were killed?"

Ilene smiled at her predicament. "There wasn't a real fight, like with fists. One family claimed that the land where the school was built was theirs and that the council shouldn't have allowed anyone to build there. But land here isn't really owned by individuals or families. The tribe allocates it. That family didn't have a shrine or anything there, so the tribal council ruled against them. The family argued against that decision for a long time. Now that the school is probably going to shut down, I expect they'll try again to get the land back.''

''Could I ask the name of the family who claims that land?''

''I guess it won't hurt to tell you. It's the Nakais. Officer Nakai, the eldest son, is a cop and a friend of Detective Redhawk's.''

Casey tried to conceal her surprise by continuing with her questions, this time about Katrina.

''Can you tell me if anyone has been around recently, here or at the college, asking questions about Katrina or her parents?''

''Nobody's come here. As for at the college—'' she shrugged ''—I just don't know. I stick pretty close to my studies. I talk to Katrina when I see her on campus, but I don't usually have time to socialize.'' She paused. ''You might want to talk to Elsie Benally.''

''Is she a friend of Katrina's, or a friend of her parents?'' Casey asked.

''Neither, really, though my foster mother and she spoke frequently. I thought of her because she usually knows more about what's happening on the Reservation than anyone else. If there have been people asking around about the Johnsons or Fox, she might be able to tell you.''

''Where can I find her?''

Before she could answer, a woman called out. Ilene looked back at the house. ''They don't want me to talk to you. I've got to go back inside.''

''Directions, please?'' Casey pressed.

''It's north of Big Gap, not far from the road to Redrock. But your biggest problem won't be finding the place. I just don't know how you'll get her to talk to you. Whatever you do, don't go there by yourself. She'll run you off with a shotgun and you could get hurt. She really distrusts out-siders. A lot of families here do.''

Ilene was called again. ''I've got to go.''

Casey returned to her vehicle. Much as she was eager for any excuse to spend more time with Ashe, the thought that she wouldn't be able to do her job without someone else paving the way bothered her. It went against every-thing she liked to believe about herself.

Yet, out here, her training didn't seem to count for much. Clearly, no matter how skilled or well-intentioned she was, circumstances would not allow her to complete this job alone. The admission went against everything in her, but she had to accept it. She pushed back her frustration, know-ing it would do no good, and got under way.

At least she'd learned something useful from Ilene. She'd met Officer Nakai before, at the crime scene, and he'd seemed very cool and professional, except when he'd been around the bodies. He'd avoided staying inside the house, Casey recalled. Had that uneasiness been the product of the Navajo beliefs about the dead, or a criminal's aversion to being at the scene of the crime?

She'd have to ask Ashe about Nakai, and get his opinion on Nakai's shoe size, too. Judging by his height, Casey suspected he'd be wearing less than a size ten, though.

Almost an hour later she drove through the small town of Shiprock en route to the station. As she passed a farming area parallel to the river, she spotted Ashe's tribal police carryall, the unit number emblazoned above the back fender. It was parked beside a one-room house resting on the high ground in the center of an old, reclaimed arroyo. A single cottonwood stood beside the house. Seeing Ashe's cruiser sparked her curiosity. Maybe the investigation had brought him here and, if it had, he was certainly pursuing a lead she didn't know about.

Casey pulled onto the shoulder, turned around, and drove back to the point where she could see his vehicle clearly. A half-dozen goats and sheep in a small pen confirmed that somebody lived in the tar-paper-covered house, which was little more than a shack. A metal pipe sticking out of the shed-type roof gave off faint gray smoke, and the door was open, probably to help dissipate heat from the woodstove.

After a few minutes went by, Casey decided to move in closer. She'd wanted to know more about Ashe, and observing him unnoticed now might give her a few answers. Maybe she could learn something useful, too, from the way he dealt with other members of his tribe.

Casey stepped softly across the sandy soil, getting as close as she could without giving herself away. She stopped behind the cover of the cottonwood tree and listened. From the voices, Casey knew Ashe and an elderly person were inside the shack. Although she could hear the words, she couldn't understand their language.

Suddenly she saw Ashe appear at the open doorway, and look just to the right of where she was. As he stepped outside, Casey ducked back out of sight. Ashe walked down the shallow arroyo, disappearing quickly into a side canyon. She waited, wondering what he was doing, but he didn't return, though his carryall remained beside the house.

Something wasn't right. Casey wasn't sure what he was up to, or what was going on, but her instinct for danger was working overtime now. She followed, creeping along the edge of the arroyo and staying in the shadows.

When she reached the end of the small side canyon, Casey climbed out, as she could see from his footprints Ashe had done. She looked around and spotted him a hundred yards ahead, making his way around an old apple orchard. Beyond it, a wide irrigation ditch ran parallel to the river.

Whatever Ashe was looking for wasn't obvious, but he was definitely searching for something. She decided to stay behind cover and follow, ready to offer her help.

A few minutes later, she realized what he was doing. An olive-green sports van was parked in a low spot overlooking the arroyo. Seeing it now, she knew Ashe must have been trying to approach without being discovered.

At that instant, the van's motor suddenly roared to life and the vehicle fishtailed out of the depression, heading directly toward Ashe.

"Look out!" Casey shouted, forced to reveal herself. Ashe turned in surprise as she ran into the open, hoping to lure the van away from him and toward her. The ploy worked.

Ashe was at her side in a flash and, grabbing her hand, led her through a thicket of willows at breakneck speed. The van was close behind. "We really have to stop meeting like this."

"I hate to ask, but do you have a plan, other than turning us both into instant track stars?" she retorted, gasping as they crashed through the brush. The loudness of the pursuing vehicle told her they were losing ground.

"Not track, but you'd better be a great broad jumper—or else swim like a fish." He swerved abruptly, heading straight toward the irrigation ditch fifty feet ahead. It was almost full of muddy, turbulent water. "We can't outrun the van. That's our only chance," he said, pointing to the water.

"Wait a second—" Before she could get another word out, he tightened his hold on her hand and jumped toward the opposite bank, pulling her with him.

For a second Casey thought that they'd make it, but they hit the water at least four feet short of the opposite side. The current here was powerful, and they were swept along instantly. Although she knew how to swim, no matter how hard she tried, she couldn't seem to get any closer to the bank. As the water carried them forward, Ashe kept one hand wrapped tightly around her wrist. They bobbed like corks, hurtled away from the sides and into the faster-flowing center.

"There's a spillway ahead!" he shouted over the rushing sound. "We have to grab on to something and pull ourselves out!"

The current pounded against them, sapping their strength. Seeing her chance just ahead, Casey lunged and grabbed a willow branch that jutted out overhead, then held it in a death grip. The rushing water hurled them toward the bank.

Three minutes later they lay on solid ground, exhausted and shivering. The swirling water at their feet looked like melted brown crayons because of the silt it carried down from the mountains.

Slowly, they climbed and clawed their way to the top of the berm, which also served as a flood-control levee. A road ran along it. From there, Casey could see the concrete-lined spillway less than thirty feet farther along the ditch. It dropped at a steep angle into a bubbling pool fifty feet below.

"You could have killed us!" she yelled at him over the roar of the waterfall. "What kind of escape plan was that?"

Ashe looked down, then shrugged. "What choice did we have? Would you have preferred getting run over instead?"

"I ran with you because I thought you had a plan. You could have at least tried to think of something else."

He stood. "That's the thanks I get? You walked into this mess by yourself, you know. What were you doing trying to eavesdrop on me, anyway?"

"What makes you think I was doing that?" she hedged. He gave her an incredulous look, then, with a wave of his hand that encompassed the entire river valley, added, "I suppose you just happened to drop by because of your interest in agriculture?"

She considered continuing to deny it, then decided on another tack. "Stuff it. I'm in charge of this investigation. I don't have to answer your questions." Casey headed down the levee road.

He fell into step beside her. "Face it. We can't work this case separately," he said. "We each need something the other has. I know the area and the people, and you have access to resources I need."

She suppressed a sigh of relief. At least she wouldn't have to come right out and ask for his help. Her pride had taken enough of a bruising already. "Okay. You want to work together? While we're looking for a good set of van tracks, you can start by telling me what you were doing here."

"I'm making it a point to find and talk to people who have connections," he answered.

Casey looked around. "What connections? That woman's closest neighbors are bullfrogs and apple trees."

"Your eyes will never tell you the whole story—not out here. Always remember that. The woman at the house back there is a hand trembler. She diagnoses illnesses so that our medicine men can cure them. She's held in high respect and knows just about everyone along this valley. Even the modernists come to talk to her. Almost all of us have traditionalists in our clan who need help sooner or later." Ashe pointed toward what looked like vehicle tracks ahead.

"She does sound like a good source," Casey conceded, glancing at him. A delicious shiver danced through her as she saw the way his wet shirt clung to his muscular shoulders. His smile broadened slightly and she knew he'd noticed her reaction. She looked away. "Was she able to help?"

He shook his head. "She knew nothing that could help us, but she'll keep her ears open."

Casey bent down to examine the tire tracks they'd found. "Are you willing to work with me, on my terms? I'd like you to be my liaison. But it's a limited partnership. I'll be calling all the shots."

His wry smile never touched his eyes. "What you're really saying is that you want to keep an eye on me. But why?"

Ashe was too sharp. He seemed to read her with an ease that she found incredibly irritating. "I've got news for you. You're not my primary concern—this case is," she said in a tone she hoped was convincing. "Besides, wasn't it you who just pointed out we can find answers faster if we join forces?"

Ashe said nothing for several long moments, but Casey was aware of everything about the man. He held his powerful shoulders and back erect. His strong hands flexed and unflexed as he thought things through. He obviously didn't like her terms, but he was considering accepting them. His quiet presence had the impact of a lion's roar as he allowed the silence to stretch.

"If we keep tripping over each other, we'll lose time we just don't have," Casey pressed. "I don't usually like working with a partner, but I can make the sacrifice for the sake of the case."

Ashe took a deep breath. "Our ways are different. But if we both try, I believe we can make things work."

"Just remember I'm in charge, and we'll get along great." She'd said it not as a challenge, but as a reminder to herself. They were agreeing to work together—nothing more. The crazy attraction she felt for this man had to be put on permanent hold. "Will you take a plaster cast of the tracks? We may need that later on for comparison."

Casey walked away, following the van tracks toward the highway. She didn't want to look into Ashe's eyes. Too often what she'd seen there had filled her with a longing she couldn't understand. In those twin dark pools, there was the promise of passion as wild as a summer storm, and as intense as lightning flashing across a dusky sky.

Chapter Five

Casey was just getting out of the shower later that afternoon, when she heard someone knocking at her motel-room door. "Who is it?"

"Ashe."

His voice set off sparks all through her. "I'll be there in a minute." Casey yanked the towel from her hair, pulled on her clothes, than answered the door, finger-combing her hair. "What brings you here? Did the captain tell you where I was staying because there's been a break in the case?"

"*Everyone* knows where you're staying. You'll soon learn that there are few secrets on or around the Rez," he said, stepping inside. "And, no, there are no new leads, except that the van that chased us fits the description of one stolen earlier today from a Farmington-mall parking lot. That's why I figured we both needed to keep digging. I suppose Bureau agents aren't religious about punching the time clock at any particular hour, right?"

He was teasing—treating her like a fellow cop—not an enemy. It felt good. Seeing a grin on his face, Casey smiled back. "No more than cops do."

Ashe sat down in the armchair by the window. "This

case... Well, let's just say it stays on my mind even when I should be off duty.''

Her heart went out to him. She understood only too well. She remembered the pain that had stayed with her like a shadow, after her mother's death. Her mom had been the only family Casey had ever known. Her father had abandoned her mom and Casey as well, breaking her mother's heart. Mom just hadn't been the same after that, and when she passed on, the gnawing emptiness inside her had remained for nearly a year, even though she'd tried to bury it under piles of work. For Ashe it had to be even worse. Right now, his work *was* a reminder. And until he found his sister, nothing could have closure.

''Do you have any idea what our next move should be?'' she asked. His gaze was mesmerizing. Restless, she paced around the room. ''Obviously, we can't just sit tight and hope that van turns up.''

Having Ashe alone with her in this place that was nothing more than a glorified bedroom, made Casey vividly aware of a part of life she'd missed. After seeing how her mother had been destroyed by love, Casey had avoided relationships that might do the same to her. Consequently, she'd never experienced grand passion, never felt that crazy kaleidoscope of feelings that love was supposed to be. The thing was, she'd never thought about it much—until now. Casey found she was still afraid of what those strong feelings would do to her. Needing to stay busy, she readjusted the pancake holster on her belt.

''Why don't we get something for dinner while we work on a plan of action? There's a place near here that's reasonable.''

''That's a good idea. I'm starving.''

As they walked to the parking area, Ashe pointed toward his police-issue four-wheel-drive carryall. ''Let's take my unit. It can get through anything. I'm not certain your sedan is going to make it down some of our back roads right now. The rain's been pretty heavy the past hour or so, and has become widespread.''

''No problem.''

They hadn't gone very far when Casey decided it was time to question Ashe about what Ilene Begay had said.

''I heard today that your foster parents had a problem acquiring the land that their school is on. Did you know about that?''

''I remember hearing about it. But they'd moved here with Fox and petitioned the tribe for the land long before my brother and I ever knew them,'' Ashe said, then fell silent.

Casey knew there was more, so she tried to be patiently quiet as they rode along.

''The dispute was with the Nakais,'' Ashe said at last. ''I remember having a fistfight with John one day at school when he called my foster parents thieves. I guess it was something he'd picked up at home. Eventually he and I became friends, and now we're both cops. You don't seriously think that old land dispute could be a motive for killing them, do you?''

''I don't know. Wars have been fought over land for centuries. What do you think Officer Nakai would do if I brought up the subject?''

''I think he'd just walk away, and you'd lose the cooperation of a good cop. Drop it. It's ancient history now.''

''I'll accept your opinion on that, for now. But if we start hearing that the Nakai family is petitioning for the land back, we should take a closer look.''

''Fair enough.''

They arrived a short time later at a place that could fairly be described as a dive. Police vehicles were parked all around, and it wasn't clear to Casey at first if the cops were there on official business or in search of a meal.

"Welcome to Pig Alley," he said.

"A cop hangout?"

"Yes. Cops usually know where the best food can be found. No laminated menus here."

They went inside and Ashe led the way to a table in the far corner. It was hard to note the decor, if there was any, because the four lights she could see were deeply recessed in the ceiling, and they were dim at best.

"It'll get crowded later, but this is just the start of the dinner hour," he said. "Most of the off-duty Farmington cops will drop by here sooner or later."

Casey smiled slowly, understanding what Ashe had in mind. This glorified bar had not been as random a selection as he would have had her believe. If her hunch was right, he was still searching for the cop who'd harassed Fox.

"Smooth," she commented in a dry tone. "It's easier to pick up gossip about an officer if you give the impression that you're off duty and on a date rather than working a case."

Ashe's gaze was steady. "Fox is still my priority. You understood that all along. But the steak sandwiches here *are* good. And you did say you were hungry."

"I wish you'd played it straight with me."

"Like you're doing with me?"

She studied his expression. There was no anger there. He was simply stating facts. "We both know something about higher loyalties," Casey said slowly. "If there are things I can't tell you, then, as a cop, you should understand that. I'm sure that there have been times you've been forced to withhold information from people you'd rather have trusted."

She regarded him thoughtfully, trying to appear cool,

though the pull he exerted over her senses was absolutely devastating. Ashe looked even more wonderful than usual tonight in a chambray shirt, jeans and brown leather vest. His lean strength and his warrior spirit packed a sensual wallop that made her tingle all over.

Determined to avoid looking into his eyes, Casey glanced around and caught sight of a man approaching their table. She sensed trouble even before he reached them. There was something about the way he carried himself that issued a challenge. He wasn't in uniform, so she couldn't really define how she knew, but she was one-hundred-percent certain he was a local cop. What worried her was seeing how the other uniformed police officers gave ground around the bar as he went past.

"Hello, beautiful." He leaned down toward her, placing one hand on the back of her chair, by her shoulder.

Casey coughed, and moved away slightly. He smelled of tobacco, and his breath was heavy with alcohol, but his eyes were clear. He wasn't drunk, though perhaps he wanted to make it appear that he was. "Sorry, guy. Call it intuition or fate, but I just know there will never be room in my life for you. Why don't you go back to your beer?"

"Aw, now, come on, honey. Have a drink with me," he said, helping himself to a chair. "Good old Ashe always has great ladies with him. Never the same one twice, I've noticed."

"Take no for an answer, Walker, and go back to the bar. The lady is out of your league," Ashe replied, his voice calm but with an edge that was impossible to miss.

The officer sat back and regarded Ashe coolly. "You're really great at making rules for other people, aren't you? You did that with Katrina, and nearly ruined her life. But maybe this lady just needs a comparison test." He looked at Casey and winked. "What do you say? Shall we have a drink at my table?"

Casey considered it. In her book, his "No means Yes" attitude, coupled with the fact that he knew Katrina, made him a possible suspect. They had come looking for information and this guy seemed an ideal source. Before she could answer, the man reached for her hand.

In a heartbeat Ashe intercepted him, pinning Walker's wrist to the table. "Don't touch the lady unless she's made it clear she'll welcome it," he said quietly. He waited for a moment, then released the other man.

Venom shone in Walker's eyes. "Don't even think of trying to lean on me," Walker growled. "The cops in here will back me up. You and your brother may have hassled me when I was a kid, but those days are over now. We're off the Reservation, and you're on *my* turf, here."

As Walker pushed his chair back and stood, ready to square off with Ashe, Casey grabbed Walker's forearm gently. "Instead of a drink, why don't we go for a walk instead? It's such a nice evening."

"Sounds like a plan." Walker put his arm around Casey's shoulders.

Casey saw the way Ashe tensed, but she shot him an icy look that warned him to let her play this out.

As they walked outside into the parking lot, Casey slipped out of Walker's grasp. "You're a friend of Katrina's?"

"Not really. I asked her out a few times, that's all. But let's not talk about her now. I'm with you, beautiful."

Casey sidestepped as he reached for her. "Let's get to know each other first."

"Later." He grabbed her arm and pulled her close, hurting her with his tight grip. "You like cops, do you, baby?"

Casey brought her boot heel down hard on his instep,

then broke free as he jumped back with a yelp. "Put on the brakes, will you? I don't like to rush things," she said softly.

"Well, I do, and I'm through playing." He pushed her against the wall and snaked a hand between the buttons of her blouse, fumbling for her breast.

Casey kicked him sharply in the groin, then, as he bent over, brought the edges of her hands down hard on both sides of his neck in a karate blow that stunned him. Walker sagged to the ground.

"I'm an FBI agent, you moron," she said. "Keep your hands to yourself or you're going to have a truckload of garbage raining down on you. I won't mess around with sexual-harassment charges. I can go all the way to attempted assault. You could be suspended in thirty minutes. Got that?"

Walker stood, brushed off the seat of his pants, then reached for a pack of cigarettes in his shirt pocket. "Well, at least you have more guts than Redhawk's stuck-up little—"

Casey had seen Ashe approach, but she couldn't react in time to stop what came next. In the second it took her to draw in a breath, Ashe spun Walker around, smashing his fist against the other cop's jaw. Walker went down as if his legs had been suddenly removed, and his cigarettes went flying.

Casey saw three other men coming out the tavern door. If this turned into a brawl, she was going to have to explain it all the way to Washington. She turned and faced the men, her badge in hand. "Your friend is trying to get charges filed against him, boys. Is that what you want, too?"

She saw the anger that flashed in their eyes as they glared first at her, then at Ashe.

"You're out of your jurisdiction, Indian," the one built like a refrigerator growled.

"I'm not here to make an arrest," Ashe answered smoothly. "And the lady, here, is a federal officer. We were still in the U.S. of A. last time I checked."

Ashe took a step toward the men, stopping just a few inches in front of Casey. She wasn't sure whether to thank him for it, or to hit him herself for interfering. He should have warned her before he dropped them in the middle of this situation. Whatever was going on here transcended the current difference of opinion. There was obviously some history between Ashe and these men—or at least, with Walker.

Just as she was certain that a fight they couldn't win was about to erupt, two barrel-chested Navajo men stepped out of a newly arrived pickup and waved. Ashe smiled at them, then looked back at the locals. "Things just don't seem to be going your way tonight, fellows."

"Cool the testosterone, guys. We're all law-enforcement officers here," Casey said, looking from man to man. "If we don't walk away now, some of us are going to be facing suspensions and worse, especially once news of this hits the papers. Let's see if we can save a job or two by backing off while we still can." Seeing Walker struggle to stand, Casey offered him a hand up. "Get this officer an ice pack from behind the bar before he *really* gets ugly looking."

She breathed a silent sigh of relief when two of their antagonists actually smiled at her weak joke. They glanced at the Navajo men, then took Walker by the arms and half carried him back inside Pig Alley.

Casey nodded to the two Navajos. "Thank you, guys."

"These are my cousins," Ashe introduced. "Arthur and Eugene Begay."

Casey nodded and, with a smile, extended her hand.

"I'm Agent Casey Feist. What brought you two here tonight?"

"Good timing, it looks like," Arthur replied, shaking her hand after a split-second hesitation.

Casey noted the way the men had exchanged quick glances before the handshake, and realized that shaking hands was probably something else The People didn't do.

"We were on the way home when we saw Ashe's unit parked here. We figured that he might need some backup," Eugene told her. "This isn't friendly territory for any of us."

"I don't understand. What's the problem?"

The men looked at each other and then at the ground or at the cars. Eugene finally answered her. "Turf, rivalry, prejudice—all that. It's never far away, not even here. Navajo cops aren't exactly welcomed with open arms off the Rez unless somebody needs help in a hurry."

Casey glared at Ashe. "You could have mentioned this to me beforehand."

"I wouldn't have let you get hurt. I can take care of myself—and you—in a fight."

Casey believed him, but she wasn't going to let him off the hook. "I can look after myself, thank you. But you're missing my point."

Eugene and Arthur glanced at each other, then muttered quick goodbyes.

As his cousins left, Ashe started walking back with her to his carryall. Casey could feel the warmth of his body as he remained close by her side. It touched her intimately, winding its way around her imagination and sparking sensations she couldn't brush aside. Ashe was strong physically and spiritually, and that was a combination she rarely saw nowadays. She was drawn to him on such a profound level that it scared her.

Annoyed by the direction her thoughts had suddenly taken, she kicked a rock in her path and quickened her pace. "What the heck happened back there with that guy?" she demanded. "You owe me a full explanation. You're one of those cops who never loses his cool on the job, yet Walker pushed your buttons like a pro. What's the history between you and him? Is he the one you think might have something to do with Fox's disappearance?"

Ashe nodded. "But, honestly, I didn't know he'd be in there tonight—not this early, anyway. I came hoping to get word about him, not push a confrontation."

"That's still not enough of an explanation," she said.

Ashe took a deep breath, then let it out slowly. "Jerry Walker has been a thorn in my brother's and my side for years. He had a thing for Fox when we were in high school and she was in junior high."

Casey glanced around and saw several Anglo cowboy-looking types drive up in a big oil-company pickup. They climbed out, most holding beer bottles, and one of them gestured in their direction. "I think we should leave now."

Ashe looked at the men. That was all. He simply looked at them with those lethal obsidian eyes.

The men exchanged shrugs, then turned toward the tavern. Casey blinked, then peered up at Ashe. She'd never met anyone who could command respect with just one glance. It was like something out of a John Wayne movie.

As if sensing her reaction, Ashe captured her gaze, held it, and slowly smiled. "Nothing's going to happen that you and I can't handle."

As she slipped into the passenger seat, her heart hammering wildly, Casey couldn't quite get over the feeling that there was more than one meaning woven into his words. The attraction between them was getting stronger with each passing moment. Just being with him made her feel wonderfully alive, enticingly feminine and ready for anything.

Certain that she was losing her mind, she stared out the window and lapsed into silence.

ASHE PRESSED DOWN HARD on the accelerator. Right now, he felt the need to have the wind rushing past his face. He needed some outlet for all the crazy feelings crashing around inside him. Though he hadn't looked at Casey since they'd started back to the Rez, he was aware of everything about her. Maybe that was the problem. He reacted to her presence on a level he couldn't explain. Things that defied order and logic—like the heat of desire that flashed through him whenever he was close to her—brought confusion and trouble. Right now he needed focus if he was to find his foster parents' killer, and get Fox out of whatever trouble she was in.

"I should point out that I'm being a paragon of patience out of deference to your culture," Casey said, cutting into his musings. "But I still haven't heard a good explanation why there's bad blood between you and Walker. There's got to be more to it than his having had a thing for Fox."

"There's a café up ahead. It's on the Reservation, and there won't be any problems there for us. Why don't you let me make amends for what happened earlier by treating you to dinner? I'll explain everything while we eat."

"Deal."

They were seated at the small family-style café less than ten minutes later. From the way the waitresses smiled at Ashe, Casey could see that he was a favorite here. Of course, few women would have been impervious to the sexy half smile that played on his lips. It even made her own heart skip a beat—though she intended to fight those annoying feelings every step of the way.

She ordered a Navajo taco at his suggestion, and didn't regret it when the food came. The spicy dish—made with cheese, chile, meat and beans all piled on fresh fry bread and topped with lettuce and tomatoes—was simply delicious. She ate greedily but then, noting his silence, stopped and glanced up.

"You're still stalling, and I haven't got all year," she said, reaching for a glass of iced tea.

Ashe nodded and gave her his quirky half smile. "It's really a simple story. Walker is one of those men who thinks that being an Anglo somehow elevates his character. His dad worked on the Rez many years back, and that's when he, my brother and I attended the same high school. Fox was in junior high then. When we heard that he was constantly giving her a hard time after school, we saw he got the same on her behalf. He's never forgotten it, and neither have I."

The waitress, who was setting a nearby table, let out a hoot. "You left out the good part, Ashe."

Casey glared at Ashe.

"Okay, okay." Ashe shrugged. "Travis and I kind of threw him through the library window. He wasn't really hurt, just skinned up a bit. The window was open at the time." He paused, then added with a shrug. "We all got suspended."

Casey laughed. "If he was half the creep back then that he is now, I'm sure he deserved it."

Ashe shrugged, a hint of a smile playing on his lips. "He has gotten smarter over the years. Lately, he's been trying to goad me into a fight when his buddies are around. The cops in Farmington back each other up, just like we do at our PD. He won't take me on one-on-one because we both know I'd wipe the floor with him."

With any other man, she might have suspected such a

statement to be half bravado and half optimism. But she was getting to know Ashe well enough to understand that he seldom, if ever, bluffed.

"Let's go back to the station," she said. "We need more to go on than a size-ten-shoe cigarette smoker as a lead. Maybe somebody found that van, or we can discover something we overlooked if we go over the evidence once more together." Casey knew she'd be better off in more formal surroundings. Her mind would then be more likely to focus on the disciplines of her job, not on the myriad crazy longings that played no part in what she had to do.

As THEY LEFT THE restaurant, Casey's thoughtful silence intrigued Ashe. She certainly wasn't putting all her cards on the table. His gaze strayed from her stern expression to her hair, and suddenly he found himself wondering what it would feel like in his hands. It looked soft, shining with a reddish gold luster that invited his touch.

He studied her hands. They were small and feminine, yet strong enough to wield a weapon or be used with skill in a fight. That duality defined everything about her and it was perhaps what drew him the most. She was part of the law-enforcement world he loved, yet she still retained a special feminine magic that could tempt him with just a look or a smile. Most appealing of all, underneath her extraordinary self-discipline and control, there was something wild about her. He'd felt it when she'd kissed him; everything male in him had responded.

As they drove across the Rez, the blackness that surrounded them was pierced only by their headlights and a maze of stars in the moonless sky.

"I've never been in a place where it's this quiet at night. And lonely, too," she added, her voice barely above a whisper. "Life out here can't be easy."

"It isn't, but it is *our* land. This is the Dinétah, the place that defines us and carries our history. There are times of trouble and times of plenty, but not much in between. Some years the land is parched, and the rains don't come. Then our people and our animals go hungry. Other years, the rains and snows come in the right proportions like they have recently, and there's plenty of corn, melons and alfalfa. I belong here. It's all part of me. I would never live anywhere else."

"Yet your brother Travis chose to leave. Are you two so different?"

He nodded slowly. "Yes. Travis is not much on tradition. He makes his own rules as he goes. My brother is like the wind. He doesn't like anything that holds him back or stands in his way. He and I have our differences, but blood still binds us and, in that way, we are the same. He's out of the country right now—probably half a world away—but I expect he'll arrive on the Rez soon. Nothing will stop him, particularly now that he knows Fox is missing. Neither of us will rest until she is found and the killers are in custody." He paused for a moment. "Speaking of Travis, I have an idea I'd like to follow up on right away. I know a place where we should look for Fox."

"Where?"

"Our family shrine, near Rock Ridge. I know my brother took Fox there a few times. Few people outside our family know how to find it, but it's a place of power and truth."

"I don't understand."

"I can't explain it any better than that," Ashe admitted. "But I'd like to check it out next. You want to come with me?"

"Sure."

Ashe drove quickly down the nearly empty road, then turned up a dirt trail that was barely wide enough for his vehicle. The road was full of ruts from the just-ending rains, but at least it was sandy instead of gooey mud.

It took another twenty minutes of hard driving along what was essentially a horse trail before they reached the base of a tall cliff. The rising moon bathed the sandstone mesa, casting imposing shadows over its rugged surface. "From here, we reach the shrine by climbing," he said. "It's only steep in one place."

"You think Fox came here?" Casey looked around. "But there's no vehicle around."

"She wouldn't have driven here. She would have ridden bareback on one of the horses the Benallys keep in the pasture near the turnoff. If she released her mount, nobody would have known she'd come here since the horses know how to find their way back. Wait for me here, if you'd rather not climb up at night. It'll take me about an hour, there and back."

"What's up there?"

"On the top there's a rock cairn, a shrine to Changing Woman. There's something very special about this particular mesa. Even Fox felt it, though she doesn't share our beliefs. If she was frightened and in trouble, it's possible she might have come here. My brother always said it was to be our stronghold. He hid supplies up there in a cave, and—"

"And what?"

"I just remembered something. My foster father came here once. He said he wanted to leave something he considered important to him—in deference to us, no doubt. It's possible that whatever it is may give us some answers to what happened."

"Then I'm going with you."

"Somehow, I knew you'd say that," he said with a grin.

As they approached the rock face, Ashe stopped. "Wait."

Staring off into the distance, he sang a Navajo prayer, as was the custom before approaching a sacred area.

"Offering a prayer appeases the gods," Ashe explained, answering the question he could see in her eyes. "Otherwise, the site is profaned and the holy beings depart. Many believe that it's the failure of our young people to follow our ways that has brought the tribe a lot of the troubles we face today."

He started walking up a narrow trail and, true to her word, Casey stayed up with him, remaining almost at his side. His hands were tough and callused, but hers were not. The weathered sandstone could abrade skin like a file drawn across the fingertips. Without a word, he dug his leather gloves out of his jacket pocket and offered them to her.

Casey never once complained as they continued to climb, though the higher they went, the more difficult it became. His respect for her grew. He felt he understood her and what drove her. She was like him in a lot of ways. An invisible-yet-impregnable bond seemed to be forming between them. It wasn't the best time for it, but fate often made its own rules. For now, all he knew was that Casey was the only respite his heart knew from the pain that surrounded him.

They were at the most challenging section—a steep, forty-five-degree slope of rock—when Ashe noticed a glimmer of light coming from below and behind her. "We're being watched," he said. "Someone must have followed us."

"Where?"

"Don't worry about it now. Just concentrate on the rock

face,'' he said. ''It's tricky here, and you don't want to slip. Lean into the rock, and grab on to handholds.''

A second later, a shot rang out. The weathered stone beneath her fingers suddenly crumbled, and she began to slip down the rock face.

Ashe slid down after her as quickly as he dared, hugging the rock. A heartbeat later, he reached down and grabbed her arm, then dug his other hand into the first opening he felt in the rock. They came to an abrupt stop.

''Thanks,'' she said, bracing herself quickly to avoid slipping farther downslope.

''Are you hurt?''

''No. My right arm hurts, but the bullet didn't hit me. I just got a little scraped up by the loose rocks. Let's keep going. I'm okay.''

Suddenly fragments of sandstone peppered over them as a second shot rang out, echoing for miles.

''He's got us. We're sitting ducks!'' Casey said. ''We can't reach for our weapons or take cover here.''

''We'll be all right. His aim's off. He's still shooting high, and doesn't know where the bullets are hitting. We can handle this,'' Ashe said quietly, leading her sideways toward a shadow formed by a big crack in the rock face. ''This is a place of power. The scales will tip back our way.''

Chapter Six

Several rounds whined over them, ricocheting off the rock face. Casey tried to match Ashe's quick pace as they moved toward the more shadowy half of the cliff. "Either he's a lousy shot, or a great one. The bullets are missing us, but not by much," she said.

"Our people say that each mountain has a spirit within it. It is that spirit that will help us now."

She envied him his beliefs that gave him such unshakable courage. All she felt at the moment was the incredible urge to find something to hang on to while she returned the fire.

"Don't let anger or fear cloud what you have to do now," he warned.

"How did you—"

"Know what you were thinking?" Ashe finished for her. "It's human nature to want to fight back. And, believe me, we *will* fight back. But right now we've got to stay alive long enough to be able to do that." He reached out for her, steadying her as she moved toward him and onto a level spot that was barely fourteen inches wide.

As they entered the shadows, she realized that their attacker had stopped shooting. "Do you think he's out of ammunition?"

"No, but maybe he's figured out that all he'd be doing now is wasting bullets. The shadows here will shield us effectively, and he'll be shooting blind. We're no longer dark spots against the cliff. Are you okay?" he asked.

"Yes, but how do you manage to keep your balance so well here?"

"Knowing this place gives me an edge." He called in to the station using his handheld radio. "They'll send backup here as soon as they can," he said once he'd finished the transmission. Hearing the distant rumbling of a car engine, he added, "But I expect it'll be long after the sniper is gone. It'll be up to us to gather as much evidence as we can."

They worked their way back down slowly, staying in the shadows. "Were you able to get a fix on the sniper's location?" she asked.

"A general area, yes, but not much more than that."

"I want to search for footprints down there, and anything else we might be able to use to nail this creep." She watched Ashe, trying to emulate his movements down the steep trail.

Although he seldom looked back at her, she knew he was aware of every step she took. What she liked most about him was that he wasn't coddling her. The help he offered seemed rooted in respect for an equal, and that was precisely the way she wanted to be treated.

Ashe led the way toward a pile of massive boulders that had been part of the mesa before weathering and erosion had allowed them to break free. "The muzzle flashes I saw came from this general area."

Following her own instincts, Casey started her search in a place she would have considered ideal, had she been the sniper. She spotted a smaller, solitary boulder about six feet tall and crouched down, studying the ground beside it. Several nine-millimeter shell casings were lying just to the right of a grouping of clear boot prints. "This is where he was at," she said. "He must have braced his weapon on top of this rock. And, from these shells we know it was almost certainly a handgun. At this range, it's surprising that he managed to hit that close to us, even with support. It's a real stretch for any pistol."

"You're right. A rifle would have done the job much better." Ashe joined her, pointing out vehicle tracks about ten feet away. "He didn't use a motorcycle this time, either. Maybe it was the van. It would have been quieter. We'd better start making plaster casts of these vehicle tracks and footprints so we can compare them to what we already have." He crouched down. "These boot prints look smaller to me, and aren't the same brand." He stood. "I'm going back to my carryall. I have what we need there. Then, while the plaster is setting, we can go back up the mesa."

Casey glanced at the steep rock face, dreading a second climb and knowing that it was inevitable. "Do you still think Fox may be up there?"

Ashe checked his vehicle to make sure it hadn't been tampered with. "No. Had she been up there, she would have made her presence known and done her best to help us, even if she'd had to turn herself into a target," he said, concern for his foster sister an ever-present companion for him now. "But the shrine might hold some other answers for us." With Casey's help, he took out the supplies he needed and carried them back.

After the plaster casts were made and left to cure, Ashe and Casey returned to the base of the cliff. Ashe reached into the medicine pouch he carried and placed a pinch of the contents at the base of the rock. Holding the small pouch out to her, he invited her to do the same. "It's an offering made of pollen, white shell and other gifts to appease the spirit that resides within this mountain. It's a sign of respect, and considering what we've been through, I think it might be a good idea. That is, unless you find the gesture offensive.''

''Not at all.'' She followed his lead, placing the offering on the ground.

This time the climb up was easier and they reached the summit without any further incident. Ashe, using a small flashlight, led the way past the cairn of rocks to a narrow opening in the rock face that led downward into a small, dry cave. They searched together, but there was no sign that Fox had been there recently. Finally, Ashe spoke. ''My brother, my foster father and I placed items of special significance to us in this cave. It was a symbol of our unity. My brother hid a duplicate of the medicine bag our real father always carried with him.'' He pulled it out from behind a large rock and showed her a small leather pouch with a turquoise beaded design. ''He had it made as a reminder of our past. It contains soil from our sacred mountains.''

''What did you leave?'' she asked, eager to know more about the powerful man beside her.

He pulled out a small box. Inside was a glistening black rock. ''This was given to me once by a *hataalii,* a medicine man. Flint is said to protect us from evil. It was the only thing I owned that I felt was worthy of this place.''

He paused, then continued. ''I never knew, nor did my brother, what our foster father left.'' He brought out a small metal box. ''It wasn't necessary that we know. We loved him for caring enough to leave an item he considered important here at our stronghold.'' He stared at the box, lost in thought. ''I wish he was here now, and that none of this had happened.''

Her throat constricted as the sorrow he felt touched her.

"He left that box as a symbol of what he treasured," she said. "But what he shared with you three was his real gift. He may be gone, but his legacy will remain with you always. That, to me, is the ultimate proof of a life well lived."

His expression gentled as he gazed at her. "Thank you for saying that. I think he would have agreed with you." Ashe opened the box carefully. With a puzzled expression, he brought out a .45-caliber pistol cartridge that had a curious indentation on its side. "What on earth?"

"May I see it?" She took it from his hand and studied it. "It's a damaged, but unfired round. Looks like it jammed in the chamber. Any idea what this is supposed to mean?"

Ashe pulled a small piece of paper out of the box. "This note has a partial explanation. It says that when the bullet jammed in the chamber of the pistol, his life was spared. That enabled him to go on and eventually become a teacher and the father of three special kids. He believed that his fate was ultimately determined by this one bullet." He placed it back in the box, his expression mirroring his unanswered questions.

"Was your foster father a cop at one time?"

"Not that I knew. I don't know if he ever served in the military, either. But somebody tried to shoot him, and failed." He shook his head. "The more I learn about my foster parents, the more questions I have." He took a deep breath, then let it out slowly. "We should go to the school and look through all his papers as soon as possible. We may find some useful leads there."

She nodded slowly. "I agree." She wished she could have made things easier for him. Yet, she couldn't even help him by sharing the information she did have. She had a job to do and duty made its own demands. The only way she could help him was to find the killer or killers, and that was something she intended to do. With a heavy heart, she descended the cliff with Ashe and returned to his police vehicle.

TWO HOURS LATER, AFTER a meeting with the backup officers who'd arrived at the scene, and signing the collected evidence over to them, Ashe and Casey drove to the Johnsons' school.

It was nearly nine when they pulled up a long gravel driveway leading to three cinder-block buildings, all with Southwestern-style flat-topped roofs. The school looked like any other private school in the area that wasn't particularly well funded.

Ashe strode to the entrance of the main building, and unlocked the door with his foster father's key chain, having taken the keys from his desk earlier.

The tiled hall, lined with metal half-lockers, echoed with the sound of their footsteps. Ashe went to the main office, unlocked that door, then walked inside, hitting the light switch as he passed. The principal's office, which was open, had a plaque bearing Nick Johnson's name attached to the door.

Casey watched Ashe hesitate, then force himself to enter.

"Would you prefer I search his office while you check the files in the outer room?" Casey asked.

He considered it for a moment. "No. This is my responsibility. It's something I have to do. For him, for Fox, and for myself."

"Okay. I'll go find the employee files. We need to check out everyone who worked here."

"Let's get started," he said, opening the file cabinet. "I have a feeling this is going to take a while."

Casey, using the keys Ashe provided, unlocked and searched through the personnel files. Her admiration for

Ashe was growing with each passing minute. Ashe was a strong man—the only kind a woman like her respected. He never backed down, though the case had dealt him one crushing blow after another. She wondered if she would have shown as much courage, had their positions been reversed.

Almost forty-five minutes later, Casey uncovered a lead they could pursue. Just as she was about to call Ashe, she heard him closing the door to Nick Johnson's office.

"Anything?" she asked.

"No. All I found were the school's business records, purchase orders and student-discipline folders. What about you? Anything useful?"

"Yes, I think so." She placed the employee file before him. "These were all locked up, of course. It looks like a man by the name of Patrick Gordon, a former teacher here, was giving your foster parents a hard time. Apparently, he had lied about his qualifications on his employment application. Since he wasn't certified in the areas he was hired to teach, he was subsequently fired."

"I remember hearing about this. Gordon then decided to use this school as part of his references, probably thinking no one would really check. When my foster parents were contacted by another school system that was considering hiring him, they explained why Gordon had been fired, and refused to recommend him. Gordon found out, and threatened to sue them for defamation of character."

"There's more to it than that," Casey said. "He apparently wrote them several threatening letters." She pulled one from the top of the stack of papers the file contained. "I've seen worse and, admittedly, he doesn't directly threaten their lives, but we still should check this guy out as soon as possible."

He studied the file. "I knew Gordon was harassing them,

but my foster father assured me he could handle the guy. He told me Gordon was harmless, though it was obvious that he had some psychological problems.''

''Your foster father may have underestimated the man.''

Ashe dropped down heavily into a chair. ''I should have insisted that he let me take care of the matter. But he was completely convinced that it was nothing to worry about. When his mind was set, there was no arguing with my foster father. He could be incredibly stubborn.''

''I also discovered something else,'' Casey said. ''Your police captain's daughter apparently went to this school. The captain wrote a letter to your father complaining about the teaching and counseling methods used here. A copy was in each of her teachers' files.''

Ashe nodded. ''I know about that. Like the Nakai land issue, there's nothing secret about it. Amanda was one of the top students here. When she graduated, she decided to break with family tradition. She left to attend an Ivy League college back East on a scholarship instead of going to the community college. The captain and his wife were very upset about that.''

''Why would the captain and his family blame your foster parents and the teachers here for their daughter's choices?''

''The captain and his wife both believed that the people at this school encouraged Amanda to follow her own heart, even if it meant bucking tradition. The Todacheenes were right about that, too. My foster parents believed each person deserved a right to choose their own life's path. The staff here mirrored that philosophy.''

Casey saw the lines of weariness that edged Ashe's eyes, and compassion filled her. ''It's late. Let's call it a day. We can start early tomorrow and get a fresh start.''

"You're right. I'm too tired to think straight and that's always a bad sign."

Casey gently placed her hand on his arm. "I know this has been very difficult for you. I just want you to know that it's okay with me if you need to let off some steam now and then. I promise to ignore it if you decide to suddenly punch the wall or something. It's one of those things partners do for each other."

Ashe gave her a tender smile that practically tore her breath away.

"The way we work together has a certain magic all its own, doesn't it?" he murmured.

Her pulsed raced as she surrendered for a few precious seconds to the power he exerted over her senses. Desire ribboned through her. Aware of the danger, she took a step away from him and averted her gaze. She had to be more careful. She would not lose her heart to this man who would never be part of the world outside the Rez, where she belonged.

As they rode to the motel, she forced her mind back to the case. "Tomorrow we'll go over the evidence from the site where the sniper was, and then we'll track down Gordon."

"We'll have to work hard and make our own breaks on this. I have a feeling nothing's going to come easily to us," he said.

"I don't mind fighting for results," Casey admitted softly. "A case is solved through logic, and that's something I can deal with just fine."

"As opposed to feelings? Those aren't as reliable, are they?" Ashe whispered in the darkness of the carryall.

"No, they're not," she managed in a thin voice. "Emo-

tions can't be trusted. Life taught me that a long time ago.''
Even as she said it, she knew that the words she'd lived by
once no longer applied. Life on the Reservation was teaching her a whole new set of rules.

Chapter Seven

Ashe walked Casey to her motel-room door. He wouldn't get much sleep tonight. It was more than the case; it was the way Casey was getting under his skin. There was something special happening between them. Being with her felt right, despite their occasional clashes.

"I'll see you tomorrow," she said, stopping by the door.

A battle raged inside him. He wanted to kiss her, but knew that she would not welcome it. Casey, like him, was struggling to put things in the right perspective. "Yes, tomorrow," he said, but did not move.

He saw his own desires mirrored in her eyes as she gazed at him. She wanted him to stay, probably as much as he wanted to spend the night with her. The thought of her reddish gold hair threaded through his fingers, falling against his chest, her softness against his hardness, made his gut tighten with needs too powerful to suppress.

"I should go," he said, his voice taut.

"I suppose so, yes."

The hesitation he heard in her voice was practically his undoing. He touched her face, caressing it with the palm of his hand. She pressed into it, kitten-like.

"We have duties..." he said.

"Yes." Casey looked up at him.

He had to leave now, while he still could. Looking into her hazel eyes was like being pulled into a pool of enticing warm water that held a myriad of untold dangers beneath the surface.

"Good night," he said, and somehow found the will to walk away. She was not his, but, tonight, images of Casey would fill his heart and help ease the coldness there.

CASEY WALKED INTO THE station a bit after 8:00 a.m. She looked edgy and filled with restless energy. Yet there was a vibrancy about her every movement that made it impossible for Ashe to take his eyes off her as she approached his desk.

She came up beside him and looked down at the computer screen. "I see you're researching your foster father's background. Good move. Did you turn up anything I should know about?"

"All I've managed to learn at this point was that he was never a cop in this state." Frustration and anger over his foster parents' deaths had formed an ever-present shadow clouding everything he did. "Accessing any military records that might exist is going to take some time. I'll have to fill out a dozen requests."

"The military doesn't usually cut corners for anyone," she said with a sigh. "I've dealt with them in the past and it's never easy." She sat down in the chair beside him. "I checked with the sheriff's department. The only usable trace evidence on the jacket from the suspect in Mrs. Garwood's apartment came from the ski mask. It matches the fibers found at the murder scene. What we have to do is follow up on the boot prints the sniper left, and we still need to follow up on the expensive size-ten boots found at the crime scene."

"I followed up on the sniper's tracks, and it looks like

the man who shot at us last night was wearing boots a size smaller than the killer's—a size nine, and a common, inexpensive brand. The tire prints from last night match the van that chased us, however, and the shell casings seem identical, though the experts will have to confirm that. If we'd been able to get that guy last night, we probably would have had the killer's partner.'' Ashe shook his head. ''Now we have to start from scratch to ID a suspect. I'll see about getting that list of stores carrying the expensive brand. We should have gotten that information by now, but with an understaffed department, things tend to take longer than planned.''

Loud voices and the sound of a physical struggle breaking out a few feet away made Casey turn around quickly.

Ashe saw Officer John Nakai lift an unruly suspect off the floor and then push him into a chair. ''Knock it off, Spencer. You're only making things worse.''

''I wasn't trying to get away. I was just going to go pay my old buddy Ashe Redhawk a visit—up close and personal.''

Ashe leaned back in his chair and regarded him coolly. ''I hope you didn't go to all the trouble of getting arrested just to come look me up.''

''The only place I want to see you is in a coffin.''

Ashe didn't move a muscle. He knew Delbert Spencer wanted a confrontation.

''You're a double-dealing cop whose word isn't worth a plug nickel.''

''I'm glad to know I'm appreciated. Tell me, are you trying to get sent back to prison for threatening a cop?''

''I'm just telling the truth, and you know it. You set me up and nearly got me killed,'' Delbert Spencer said, getting to his feet.

Nakai pushed him back down into the chair. ''You move

one more time, and I'm throwing you in jail. Your parole will be revoked and your next stop will be a prison cell. It's your call.''

Spencer remained sitting and glared at Ashe. ''Man, you're still setting me up.''

''You're wrong. You're doing it all by yourself.'' Ashe looked at Nakai. ''So, what's he in for now?''

''He's not being charged—yet. I went out to question him about a recent car theft and he suddenly decided to split. I figured a trip to the station might calm his nerves a bit.''

Ashe looked at Spencer. ''He's cutting you some slack. I hope you appreciate it.''

''Some favor,'' Spencer spat out. ''I was on my way to a job interview. I need to find work so I can stay out of prison. It's a condition of my parole. Now, thanks to this harassment, I can forget about that job.''

''You still have an hour. You'll get there in time if you answer my questions and stop messing around,'' Nakai said.

Spencer shot Ashe a hate-filled look. ''Don't you have better things to do with your time than hang around the station? I understand you don't even have a clue as to who killed your white parents.''

Ashe swallowed back his anger and remained silent, looking thoughtfully at Spencer's shoes instead.

''Or maybe that's the real reason I'm here,'' Spencer continued. ''Not this bogus story about a car-theft ring. You were responsible for spreading that phony story around saying I was a police informant. You nearly got me killed. Maybe you figured I'd even the score by whacking the people you care about.'' He smiled. ''I've got to admit that certainly fits my idea of justice.''

Ashe took a step toward the man. Sensing the darkness

that had descended over him, Casey quickly blocked his way before he could reach Spencer.

"Don't do it," she whispered, and turned to face Spencer. "Murder is a federal crime on the Reservation," Casey said, flashing her badge. "Are you claiming responsibility? I'd like you to sign a confession right now, if you are. Let's hear the details, including your shoe size."

"Confession? Shoe size?" Spencer smiled, shaking his head. "You guys haven't got a clue, and now you want me to make things easy for you? Do your job, and if you *really* have evidence that I did those people, then we'll talk," he said calmly.

Ashe turned away from Spencer and strode back to his desk. "Your feet are too small, and you don't have the brains to commit a crime like this. Stupid criminals like you always get caught."

Spencer bolted to his feet and lunged at Ashe, but Nakai intercepted him and forced him against the wall. "That's it, buddy. You're going down."

A tall, middle-aged, auburn-haired woman walked into the room. "I'm Ruth Austin," she announced. "I'm Delbert Spencer's parole officer. What's going on?"

Spencer, still being pressed to the wall, turned his head and gave her a contrite look. "None of this is my fault, Ms. Austin. They came to my place just as I was getting ready to leave for the job interview you arranged. They hauled me here. I had no choice in the matter."

"That's because he refused to answer my questions," Nakai said. "And just now he compounded his problems by attempting to assault Detective Redhawk."

"I don't know what they're talking about, Ms. Austin. I was going to the coffee machine, that's all."

"What about your confession?" Casey asked. "Are you rescinding that, too?"

"Confession? What confession?" Ruth Austin asked.

"They think I had something to do with the school-teacher murders. I told you that sooner or later they'd try to pin that on me. Apparently they're looking for someone with big feet. Look at my shoes—they're size eights."

"Everybody knows about those murders. About what time did they take place?" Ruth asked, ignoring Spencer.

"Somewhere between 9:00 a.m. and 11:00 a.m. The medical examiner hasn't narrowed it down any more than that so far," Casey stated.

"Then this man's not guilty. Spencer spent that morning in my office. I was trying to teach him how to handle himself during a job interview."

Prescott strode into the room from an adjoining office. "I was in the next room, but I saw Spencer lunge at Detective Redhawk." He looked at Ashe. "It's your call. I'm more than willing to contact the parole board."

Ashe looked at Spencer consideringly, ignoring the venomous look the ex-con gave him. Despite the temptation, he knew it would serve no purpose to throw him in jail now. If he was going to be pivotal in sending Spencer away, Ashe wanted it to be on more substantial charges that would put him away for a long time.

"Look, Delbert is no model citizen," Ruth said, "but I'm his parole officer and I know him better than anyone else here. Give him one more chance. He's close to getting a job and putting his life back in order. If he returns to prison now, nothing good will be accomplished by it."

Prescott just looked at Ashe.

Ashe knew it was up to him. He glanced at Spencer and saw the fear and hatred mirrored there. "Let him go. He's not important enough to worry about."

Prescott nodded once, then looked at Spencer. "You got

off lucky. But if you step out of line again, and I hear about it, it's back to prison, clear?''

Ruth glared at Spencer. ''Answer this officer's questions,'' she told him, gesturing to Nakai, ''and then I'm driving you to the interview myself.''

''I really appreciate that, ma'am,'' Spencer said.

''Save it. I just don't want any more excuses from you. You've cost me too much time already.''

Ashe headed out the door and Casey followed.

''Okay, what's the story there?'' she asked. ''Why did you leak the fact that he was an informant?''

''We have a man undercover, a Navajo cop from another part of the Rez, working a burglary ring. Spencer was about to finger him to the perps. We had to discredit him fast and also give him a reason to come to us with state's evidence.''

''I can see why he hates your guts.''

''He's no killer, though,'' Ashe said. ''He'd have backed down instead of throwing a punch. And, besides that, his shoe—''

''Size *is* too small. Unless he wore oversize boots with two pairs of socks just to throw us off,'' Casey finished. ''I recommend we keep an eye out for Spencer, anyway. He obviously has it in for you. What next? Shall we go look up Patrick Gordon?''

''I'd rather catch him later today, when he's a bit tired. How about if we follow up on the expensive boots?''

''Good idea. Before Spencer interrupted us, I was about to say I did get that list of stores this morning.''

They spent the rest of the morning questioning clerks at the three more expensive shoe stores in the area. The boots were not a popular item because of their price. A few county officials and wealthy ranchers had bought them, but checks on those people clearly indicated they had no apparent connection to the Johnsons. At the third and last store, the clerk, a young Navajo woman, identified Captain Todacheene's wife as a customer.

Casey looked up at Ashe as they left the store. "What do you think of that?"

"I know what you're thinking, but I know my captain. He may wear expensive boots, and size tens as well, but he's not our man." Ashe wouldn't be able to convince her so easily, he knew that, but he was certain.

As they drove away, Casey remained quiet.

"What I really need on this case in order to track down the killers, is a better feel for your family," she said at last. "I need to know the victims in order to identify their enemies."

"I work that way, too," he acknowledged. "I'll try to help you with that. I have some photo albums at home that will give you a better idea of who they were and what part they played in our community."

"Let's go take a look."

As Ashe drove down the highway, his thoughts were on the woman beside him. She didn't know it, but showing her the albums meant opening a part of himself to her, and letting her see a side of him few ever saw. Yet, once she saw his home and his simple way of life, she was sure to back away from him. Few Anglos were able to see beauty and harmony in a life-style like his unless they were raised to appreciate it. The thought saddened him, but it was for the best. Casey had no place in his life.

IT DIDN'T TAKE LONG to reach his old trailer, parked in the middle of an empty field a mile from the main highway. Sunflowers and purple asters brightened the desert floor around it, their colors vibrant in the afternoon sun. A hawk cried out shrilly overhead, sending a jackrabbit scampering into a large clump of brush. Casey had never seen such a peaceful place. Everything around her seemed to belong.

She glanced at Ashe. To her, he was like a man who'd stepped out of the pages of history, his life rooted in a rich past she'd never studied in school. Tradition was a living entity here that breathed with the wind that gently shook the wild grass and flowers.

"It isn't what you're used to, is it?" he asked.

His hollow tone startled her and she looked at him in surprise. "It's different here from the life I've known, but there's something about it that soothes the spirit." She shook her head. "I'm putting it badly, I know."

As she glanced at him, she could see that her answer had disturbed him. Trying to understand him sometimes left her feeling as if she were trying to decipher some unknown code.

As they walked to the door of his home, she saw a brand-new, six-wheel extended-cab pickup truck parked beside the end of the trailer. It had fog lamps, a massive front bumper and a custom double toolbox in the lined bed.

She knew precious little about trucks, except for being able to identify makes and models as part of her job skills. Yet it didn't take any special knowledge to know that this one, loaded with accessories, must have cost him a year's salary. The extravagant purchase surprised her. It seemed out of character with everything she knew about Ashe. But then again, maybe that was the problem. She didn't know him well enough yet to say for sure what *was* in or out of character.

"Nice truck. Had it long?" Casey asked delicately.

"Less than a month now. It still has that new smell." Ashe smiled as he unlocked the front door of his mobile home, then gestured for her to enter. The interior was as simple as she'd expected. There was one well-worn, built-in sofa against the end wall of the small living room, and a single wooden straight-backed chair that looked as if it had been a one-of-a-kind at a yard sale. The Navajo rug that hung on the wall above a small bookcase was exquisite, however. An antique, she had no doubt.

"Have a seat," he said, taking some photo albums from the cinder-block-and-wood-plank bookcase and joining her on the couch.

Ashe hesitated for a moment before opening the photo album. It was then that she knew he was sharing something deeply personal with her by showing her these, here in his home. The knowledge filled her with a warmth that went deeper than any physical attraction ever could. As he turned the pages, his voice resonated with love and pride. There was sorrow there, too, as he acknowledged the death of the two Anglos who'd taken his brother and him in.

Casey pointed to a photo of Nick Johnson standing beside two boys wearing football uniforms, helmets held in their hands. Physically, the two boys looked similar, but their expressions were vastly different. Ashe looked completely miserable, while the other boy wore a contented grin. "That's your brother?"

He nodded. "That was the year he conned me into dropping soccer and going out for football. He razzed me continually about soccer—what he called a 'wimp' sport. So I decided to prove to him that I could do whatever he did, and better, so I tried out and made the varsity team. That year, I scored more touchdowns than any other player, Travis included."

"But you had to play a sport you didn't choose," she observed with a tiny smile. She knew what it was like to feel the need to prove oneself. She'd done that most of her life.

"I only played for that one season—long enough to

make my point. The following year, as a junior, I went out for soccer again. My brother was furious when I refused to sign up for football, and we got into it. He ended up with a split lip. I came out with a broken finger.'' He held up his hand, showing her a crooked index finger. ''It never set right because I couldn't tell anyone about it without getting both of us into trouble.''

She smiled. No matter where one grew up, some things like sibling rivalry never changed. ''Do you still find yourself competing like that with your brother?''

''Naw. My senior year in high school I finally started liking myself,'' he said with a cocky grin. ''I realized that I'm much more personable and better looking.'' He gave Casey a teasing glance that proved the brothers' rivalry was not dead.

''Oh, you are, are you?'' She laughed. ''Don't forget 'modest.' ''

''Of course.''

As he turned the page and saw a photo of his foster mother standing next to a table filled with baked goods, he suddenly stopped speaking.

''She was beautiful,'' Casey observed.

''Yes, and her beauty went deeper than the physical, too. There was a gentleness about her. That photo was taken at a fund-raiser. She'd taken the day off to work at a bake sale for our high school, even though we went to Shiprock High, not the school she ran. My brother and I went to the public school because they had the best sports programs around. But that never mattered to her. She was like that. When our team needed to raise funds, she was there. She never walked away from anyone who needed her.''

''You're the same way,'' Casey said.

He turned his gaze on her, his dark eyes piercing her with a tenderness she hadn't expected. Her heart drummed inside her. She could feel the impact of that one look throughout her body.

"Thank you for saying that. It means more to me than you know." Then he continued, saving her from having to comment or ask further questions. "There's one photo I really want you to see."

He turned the pages. "We were all there—a rare occurrence in our adult lives." He pointed to a photo of a family gathering. "It was a credit to my foster parents that we all managed to make it here for Fox's eighteenth birthday. We knew it meant a lot to them to have us all together that day, so my brother and I pulled out all the stops. Travis managed to trade assignments and con his commander into giving him the leave he needed. I was supposed to attend a law-enforcement seminar, but managed to find someone else to take my place." He gave her a rueful smile. "Later that day, they told us that they never doubted we'd be there. They knew my brother would bulldoze over any obstacle, and I'd find a way to come."

Ashe closed the album. "They weren't our real parents, but they sure took the time to know us. We were accepted and valued for who and what we were. When we got into trouble, which was often, they were always there to put us back on the right track. Yet when they needed us the most, neither of us were there for them. And now their daughter is missing. I don't know how yet, but I *will* find her." He stood, walked to the window, and stared outside. "I failed my foster parents. I won't fail Fox, too."

Casey came up behind Ashe, and placed her hand on his shoulder. "Your foster mother did not see you as a failure, and neither should you. Remember her last words. She loved all of you, and that love was as total as it was unconditional."

He turned around slowly. "Once again, thank you for

reminding me of something I should know—that love's demands are simple and gentle in nature.''

Ashe threaded his fingers through Casey's hair, tilting her head back to meet his descending lips. His kiss was tender and unassuming, as if he were seeking nothing more from her than a bit of warmth to ease the chill in his soul. She couldn't pull away. She didn't want to. Desire swept through her, awakening emotions hidden deep within her.

Only then did Casey realize the danger and reluctantly eased out of his embrace. If she did anything that would interfere with the job she'd been sent to do, she wouldn't be able to live with herself. Her work was everything to her—or, at least, it had been until now.

She moved to the window and stared at the shiny new pickup outside. Questions filled her mind. Instinct told her that Ashe was an honest cop and could be trusted, but experience told her not to discount hard facts. Had Ashe been bribed to sell out Katrina, and was the payment for that treachery parked outside? She couldn't afford to lower her guard around him until she found out.

''Are you okay?'' he asked, his voice quiet.

She looked down at the strong fingers that rested gently on her arm, trying to smother the fires his touch had sparked. His strength could be tempered with exquisite tenderness.

Ashe's phone suddenly rang. Casey sighed softly as he moved across the room, glad to have more distance between them.

Ashe picked up the receiver and listened. ''Wait—'' he said abruptly. A moment later, he hung up the phone and turned to look at her.

His face had grown a shade lighter, but there was an easing of tension around his eyes as well as an urgency she couldn't explain reflected there.

"What happened?" she asked. "Who was that?"

"Fox."

Casey felt her skin prickle. There would be trouble now. Apprehension knifed through her, slicing past her defenses. As she faced him, it felt as if a cold wind were blowing clear into the marrow of her bones.

Chapter Eight

As Ashe looked into Casey's eyes, an instinctive knowledge knifed at his gut. He'd expected Casey to share his excitement at the good news that Fox was alive but, instead, all he could see on her face was apprehension. The incredible relief he'd felt when he'd heard his foster sister's voice gave way to the need to have other pressing questions answered.

He had no doubt now that he'd been right about Casey; she was hiding something and had been all along. He had to learn what that was and soon, but at the moment, there was something much more important for them to do.

"What did Fox say?" Casey asked, her voice taut. "Did she tell you where she was?"

"No. The phone went dead all of a sudden. All she managed to tell me was that she was all right and that I shouldn't worry."

"Well, then, she's obviously hiding out somewhere, and has been staying out of touch, maybe to protect herself. This should set your mind at ease. Now we can concentrate on the murders."

Ashe gave Casey an openly incredulous look. "You're not serious, are you? Her call tells me nothing except that she's alive. For all I know, she could have been forced to make that phone call just to get me to ease up on my search.''

"That's a possibility, I suppose," she conceded. "So, what do you propose to do now?"

"Track her down." He punched the code on his phone that redialed the number of the last caller. "There isn't any answer. I don't have caller ID here, either, so I'm going to have to call a friend of mine at the phone company and get some help."

"You do that. In the meantime, I'll go check with Bureau sources and see if there's a faster way to find where the last call originated." She started toward the door, then stopped. "I'm going to need a ride back to my car."

"Right."

Halfway to the station, Ashe spotted John Nakai's vehicle, and signaled for the officer to pull over. Arranging for Nakai to take Casey the rest of the way, Ashe continued to the phone company alone.

It took him over an hour to locate his friend at the phone company and get the information he needed. Armed with an address, Ashe drove to the Roadrunner Motel in Bloomfield, thirty minutes away. On the way he tried to contact Casey, but his police radio was inoperable in that stretch of countryside, and his cell phone wasn't getting through to Casey's, either.

Ashe parked across the street from the motel and walked to the phone booth that stood at the corner of the building. There was no sign of Fox now. Ashe went directly to the motel, fished out a photo of Katrina from his wallet, and showed it to the clerk. "Have you seen this woman?"

After a moment the clerk, a man in his early sixties with thinning hair, handed it back to Ashe with a shrug. "We've had only one couple check in and out recently, but I never saw the woman up close. My vision isn't that great at distances so all I know is that she was wearing one of those floppy hats. I can't even tell you her hair color. The couple left about twenty minutes ago. The man was an Anglo in his mid-fifties. He had on a Rockies baseball cap and dark glasses, and was clean-shaven. I'd recognize him again, I think. Got any more pictures?''

"No, sorry. I hope to, soon. May I see your records?''

"Sure, but it won't do you any good. All I've got is a signature and an address, and lots of those are phony nowadays. Our guests always pay in advance, and this guy used cash, no credit card. We don't take checks.''

Ashe glanced at the sign-in sheet. All that was written there was an entry for a Mr. and Mrs. Smith. Not exactly original.

"I do remember something else about the guy, come to think of it. He wore a blue windbreaker, and those kind of thin driving gloves. I've never seen those worn by anyone around here except on a golf course.''

"Me, neither.'' It was, however, a great way not to leave prints. "Can I see their room?''

"Oh, sure.'' He threw a room key across to Ashe. "It's room ten. Make sure it's locked when you leave.''

As Ashe walked down the sidewalk, he looked around, unable to shake the feeling that he was being watched. He took in his surroundings with methodical precision, but he couldn't see anyone. The hairs on the back of his neck were standing on end as he unlocked the door to room 10 and went inside.

The place was fairly tidy, considering they'd just checked out. Ashe looked at the unmade bed, then carefully picked two hair strands from the pillow. Both were long and blond like Fox's. He folded them into a piece of paper from his pocket notebook, then placed the paper carefully into his shirt pocket. Searching the room further, he discovered there was no trash—not even a discarded candy wrapper—in the two wastebaskets. Something told him that the male occupant had deliberately taken the trash with him. The only clue he had about the man who'd been here were two short, dark hairs in the bathroom sink.

Ashe considered everything he'd learned, trying to come up with some answers. Fox had sounded rushed on the telephone, but not afraid. He knew her well enough to know the difference. As he stepped back out of the room, the clerk he'd spoken to came jogging up to him, breathing hard.

"The young fellow who works graveyard shift just came in to pick up his check. He's just arranged to go on vacation for the rest of the week. If you want to talk to him, you better do it now. I asked him to wait for you."

Ashe thanked the man and hurried back to the motel's office. A short red-haired man in his early twenties was leaning against the counter, reading a paperback mystery.

Ashe pulled out Katrina's photo and held it up. "Do you recognize this woman?"

The young man glanced at the snapshot distractedly, then shook his head. "Nope. Wish I did, though." He dog-eared a page in his book, then closed it.

"Are you certain you don't recognize her?" Ashe pressed him to take a closer look.

The clerk looked at the photo again, this time more carefully. Finally, he shook his head. "The only woman I've seen around here was older than this one, maybe in her early thirties. She had black hair, the almost-blue shade that you know is dyed. She was good-looking, too, but in a hard kind of way, like she'd been around the block a few times, if you know what I mean. It certainly wasn't the woman in that photo."

"Okay." Ashe placed the snapshot back in his wallet. "I hear you're taking an unexpected vacation."

"Yeah. I'm going rafting for four days. I've worked here for a year and they owe me some time off. I figured I'd better go now while the owner's son is still in town. He's taking my shift later tonight."

It sounded plausible, but the clerk's decision to leave town was sending warning signals to his brain. "Where are you planning to go rafting?"

The red-haired man reluctantly told Ashe the particulars of his trip. "It's no big deal. I'll be on the Animas River above Durango. I'll be fishing a bit, too. If you need me again, I'll be back this weekend. Or you can drive up and look for the raft."

"I may do that," Ashe said, keeping his tone hard as he handed the clerk his card. "Call me at the station if you remember anything about the people in room ten." If something was going on and this guy was part of it, he wanted him to know he'd be on his tail. Seeing the wide-eyed look the young man gave him satisfied Ashe.

As he stepped out into the parking lot, Ashe tried to reach Casey again. This time, the transmission on the cell phone went through. She made a quick apology, explaining that he must have called when she'd turned off the unit to replace the battery.

He filled her in on his progress. "But it looks like this trail's gone cold."

"I'm on my way to meet you right now. Hang tight," she said, then added, "I ran into a bit of a snag myself when I tried to contact my sources for the address and number. My supervisor from the Bureau got all over my case. I haven't been as religious with the daily reports as I should have been, and he made it clear how displeased he was. It took some time to talk my way through that."

Ashe said nothing. He didn't believe her—not for one second. She probably had just turned off her cell phone, knowing he couldn't reach her without it unless she was in her vehicle. Though he believed her when she said she'd been doing her job, he couldn't figure out exactly what that job was. Instinct assured him that they were working against each other on at least some aspects of the case. On the other hand, he was convinced that her determination to find the killer was real.

"I've had our department on the lookout for Fox's car, but I'm ready to put out an APB on her, as well."

"I think that would be a mistake. If no one can find Fox, then she's probably safe from the killer, too. If we start calling attention to her, that could make things a lot worse."

"Point taken," Ashe agreed. "But I'm not having them back off on the search for her car. If it's around, the killer can find it as well as we could, and the best chance she's got is with us."

"Do you really believe Fox lied to you on the phone?"

"'Lied'?" He paused. "That may be too harsh a word. I think she may have been coerced, or conned into calling me."

"Did she sound afraid, or just in a hurry?"

It was as if she'd read his mind. The thought disturbed him. There were too many other feelings between them— feelings best left unacknowledged and unexplored. "She sounded in a hurry," he admitted reluctantly.

"Don't you think you could be borrowing trouble?"

He still hadn't answered her when her car pulled into the parking lot. He watched her step out of her vehicle and walk up to him. She moved gracefully; her hips swayed with a sensuality he knew she wasn't aware of.

Casey smiled at him, then looked around. "I hate to

point this out, but you might not have liked the answers you could have uncovered, had you actually found her. If Fox had been kept against her will in a place this small, the clerks would probably have noticed something wrong,'' she said, waving her hand around. ''It's hard to hide anything in a place this size. It's not as if Fox and a kidnapper could have disappeared in the crowd.''

She had a point, but he'd still bet on his own gut feelings. Fox was in some kind of trouble. He was as sure of that as he was of his own name.

''Let's get back to work on the case.'' She shrugged. ''We need to track down Patrick Gordon. It's a bit earlier than we'd planned, but—''

''I have a better idea. My foster parents had a safe-deposit box. Those take special authorization to open, but I know where they kept their key, so that might expedite matters.''

''I can help you get the clearance you'll need. Let's go back to the station, and I'll make a few phone calls.''

When he looked in the rearview mirror as they drove back, he saw Casey talking on her cell phone. Right now she was all cop, but he knew the other side of her—her softness, her gentleness—which tugged at him, winding itself around him, making him want her despite his conviction that she wasn't all she seemed to be.

He forced those thoughts from his mind. He could share nothing of himself with someone he couldn't trust.

Determined to get some answers, Ashe picked up his cell phone and dialed his old friend at the Bureau. The agent had served in the Reservation area while Ashe had been growing up. Nowadays he was more of a desk jockey in Albuquerque, but that suited Joe Sandoval just fine. He only had a year left before retirement.

Ashe pressed him again about Casey.

"Like I said before, I can't find anything on her," he replied. "But let me ask one more person here. I'll get back to you shortly."

"You've got my number."

Ashe hung up, an uneasy feeling spreading over him. Something told him that the time had come to dissolve his partnership with Casey, and go after the truth on his own.

WHEN THEY ARRIVED AT the station a short while later, Casey immediately commandeered an office and a telephone. He gave her the privacy she seemed to want, but not as a courtesy. He was still waiting to hear from Joe, and he preferred not to be with Casey when the call came.

After fifteen minutes, Casey came to the door of the office and gestured for him to join her. "I've found a judge who'll give us the paperwork we need to get into the safe-deposit box right away."

"That's great."

"Do you have the key with you?"

"It was part of the evidence we collected, so it's here at the station."

"Good. You'd better go sign for it." Hearing the phone ring behind her, she excused herself and went back inside.

As Ashe walked to the evidence room, his cell phone rang. He flipped the unit open.

"It's Joe. Hey, buddy, are you sure you got her name right? According to the senior agent on hand today, we don't have anyone by that name assigned to your area."

"Are you saying that she's an impostor? That there is no Agent Feist working for the Bureau?"

"No, not at all. Her files could be an eyes-only thing. I'm just telling you that I can't find anything on an Agent Casey Feist, and nobody I've asked seems to know her or have heard of her."

"Interesting," he answered, then heard someone approaching.

"Are you ready to roll?" Casey said from behind him.

"Just about." Saying goodbye quickly, he closed up the phone, wondering how much she'd overheard. After signing for the key, he walked out of the evidence room with her.

"Did you mention my name to someone on the phone just a moment ago?"

He met her gaze. "Did I? Maybe I was thinking about you," he said half-teasingly.

"Out loud, to someone on the phone?"

"Hey, it's just guy talk." He gave her a crooked half smile. "Does that bother you?"

"You bet. I don't like having my name tossed around."

He saw the apprehension on her face. She was as wary as a coyote walking on ice.

"You said there is no Casey Feist, or something like that."

He hated lying to her, but there was no choice until he'd figured out what game she was playing. "And there isn't— not in my personal life," he said. "People are constantly trying to pair me up with whoever they see me with. Women, that is. The Reservation is like that when you're not married. They do the same with my brother whenever he's at home."

She smiled. "Oh, *that* I understand. The same thing happens to me. I think people find fixing up a single friend or associate an irresistible temptation."

As they got under way, he could feel the special electricity that sparked the air between them. In the confines of the carryall, every breath he took filled his lungs with the scent of her. Her perfume reminded him of a field of mountain wildflowers.

"How come you haven't married?" he asked.

"It's too hard for me to really lower my guard around anyone for any length of time. As you noted once, I don't trust easily. What about you? Why are you still single?"

"I always figured I'd marry a woman from my tribe, but my work and life-style make it difficult. On a personal level, I have more in common with the traditionalists, but they don't approve of what I do for a living. The modernists think I'm too much of a traditionalist and that I wouldn't have enough in common with them."

"Sounds like you're going to be single for a long time."

"Maybe so, but you never can tell what the future holds." He saw the way she'd glanced at him when he'd said that. Longing and logic were at war in her hazel eyes. He understood that only too well. Even now that they both knew there were secrets between them, that special chemistry they shared continued to tug at them.

As they traveled along the river valley, with desert on both sides, silence descended between them. His thoughts shifted to the safe-deposit box they were about to open. He wondered what lay hidden there and if fate, as it had done so far, would continue to exact a harsh penalty for every secret he uncovered.

CASEY GATHERED HER thoughts as she entered the bank with Ashe beside her. She had to hand it to him. He was a very good cop. But, despite his smooth evasions, she knew that he'd checked her out. She couldn't blame him and, in fact, had expected it. That was why she'd been careful to cover her trail. The Bureau would back her. Ashe's source would get an unpleasant surprise soon enough.

It was nearly closing time, but they were expected. Casey flashed her badge as she met with the bank manager. A moment later they were ushered to the vault. She could feel the tension in Ashe as clearly as she felt her own. They needed a lead to the killer, and the more time that elapsed without one, the worse it was going to get.

"Would you prefer that I remain present?" the bank manager asked.

"That's not necessary," Casey said. "Thank you."

As the manager left, Ashe opened the safe-deposit box, and set it on the table beside them.

Casey was right next to him as Ashe pulled out several envelopes and placed them on the table.

"My foster parents' will is here. And these are Fox's adoption papers, the originals. I don't recognize the last name of her parents, but both are listed as deceased."

"What's in those other envelopes?" Casey asked, reaching around him and taking some official government documents from the box.

Ashe glanced down as she unfolded the letters. "Army discharge papers?" he queried, taking one from her hand while she looked through the others. "Another mystery," he added, shaking his head. "Here's a letter of commendation, signed by an army training officer at the FBI Academy at Quantico, Virginia."

"If he was in the army and trained at Quantico, he must have been in the CID, the Criminal Investigative Division. He would have conducted criminal investigations on bases, or maybe been involved in counterterrorist work. They also work with hostage negotiations, drug investigations and protection duty," Casey explained.

"Any of that could have placed him in danger. That must be where the bullet came from." He exhaled softly. "I can't believe that he never once mentioned his military career to us."

"It wasn't the kind of work that fosters talkative people."

"Good point," he conceded. "But there are years missing. He was married when he joined the military at twenty-two, after college. He spent ten years in the service. But there are six years unaccounted for between his discharge and the time he opened the school on the Rez. I wonder..."

Casey couldn't even begin to imagine what Ashe was going through. The loving family he'd thought he'd known was slowly disintegrating, becoming nothing more than an enigma couched in secrecy and shadows. Her heart ached not only for the loss he'd already faced, but also for what was yet to come.

"You have no idea what happened in those six years?"

"No. Can you get any more information for me on his military background?" Ashe asked. "After a career in the CID, there's no way of telling how many enemies he made. Or if his expertise led him to something else after his discharge that is linked to this case."

"I can try to get something, but the military moves at its own speed. Don't expect any instant answers."

"The Bureau can exert pressure."

His eagle-sharp eyes bored through her. She felt the separate impacts of the warrior and the gentle man she'd kissed as he held her gaze. He was at war with himself, as she was. What made things even worse between them was that her cover as a Bureau agent was wearing very thin. But she couldn't tell him the truth—at least, not yet. "I'll give it my best shot."

"Will you also run a full check on Fox's natural parents?"

She hesitated. "All right, but I honestly think the answer to the murder lies closer to home. What do you say we go pay Patrick Gordon a visit?"

Ashe placed the contents of the box in a large manila envelope, then replaced the box. "Yeah. I think it's time he and I met face-to-face."

The words chilled her. She knew Ashe was walking a thin line. She wasn't sure if he wanted trouble, or was just steeling himself to face whatever came. There was a dangerous edge to him now.

As his phone rang, Ashe opened the receiver and identified himself. Casey led the way out, aware of him behind her, but not looking back.

"Yeah, I'm listening," Ashe spoke, his voice taut. "Wait a minute. You're saying that everything checks out, and you were given bad information before?"

Casey wasn't sure whom he was talking to, but she could make a good guess. The machinery covering her had finally clicked into place and his source in the Bureau had suddenly found himself forced to backpedal at high speed. Yet, she could tell from Ashe's tone that he wasn't buying the cover-up.

As they got under way, Ashe lapsed into a long silence. The documents he'd retrieved from the safe-deposit box and signed out of the bank were on the seat next to him.

"Gordon's home, according to the address we have, isn't far from here," Ashe said. "Maybe this will be the lead that closes the case once and for all."

As he glanced over at her, Casey's breath caught in her throat. A sudden and startling revelation shook her all the way to her bones. The truth was, she didn't want the case to end. She'd found something here with Ashe that she'd never experienced before. The magic that happened whenever they were together, was opening her heart and mind to a world she hadn't known existed; magic that made everything she did mean more. There was beauty in simplicity here that she was only just beginning to see and understand.

For one wild instant, she felt the urge to reach for Ashe's hand. She wanted to be part of him and his world, even if only for a moment.

Aware of the recklessness of such thoughts, she glanced out the window, determined to think about something else. "Nothing in this case has been simple," she warned Ashe. "I wouldn't count on finding any fast answers when we question Gordon, if I were you."

The drive to Waterflow, a small agricultural community just east of Shiprock, didn't take long. Ashe pulled up to a duplex with a run-down yard. Waist-high tumbleweeds occupied the area where a lawn must have been at one time.

As they walked up to the front door, Casey's skin began to prickle, her senses suddenly alert to danger. She glanced at Ashe, and saw his jaw clench and his shoulders grow rigid with tension.

"You feel it, too, don't you? Something's wrong here," she whispered.

"I think Gordon knows who we are, and why we're here."

They both made a point of staying to the sides of Gordon's front door, and they each had one hand on their sidearms. Ashe knocked hard. "Police, Gordon. We need to talk to you."

They heard a sudden loud crash, followed by running footsteps, then total silence.

Chapter Nine

"He's making a run for it," Ashe said, then kicked the door open.

"I'll go around. We can try to cut him off," Casey said.

Ashe raced through the small apartment and, as he reached the kitchen, saw the back door was open. Gordon was across the yard, trying to climb over a neighbor's coyote fencing, but the closely spaced vertical cedar poles posed a difficult obstacle. He jumped for the top, lost his grip, and fell to the ground hard.

Casey reached him before Ashe did. Identifying herself as a federal agent, she rolled him over, facedown, and frisked him.

"Care to tell us why you ran?" she demanded, stepping back and letting him get up after making sure he was unarmed.

"You were chasing me." Gordon was disheveled looking, with black hair uncombed and a stubble of beard on his chin. His clothes smelled of sweat and cigarettes.

"We didn't chase you until you ran," Ashe said, his voice too calm.

Ashe caught the look Casey gave him. She knew him by now, and the concern mirrored in her eyes was evident. She was worried he'd rearrange Gordon's face.

Ashe took a deep breath and gave Gordon a cold, hard stare.

"We're going back to your apartment," Casey said, motioning toward the door. "If you even breathe wrong, I'll arrest you on the spot and take you in."

"I haven't done anything wrong."

"Don't you know it's bad form to run when law-enforcement officers identify themselves and want to question you? What do you expect from us now," Casey added, "the bronze medal in the hundred-meter dash?"

Gordon scowled, brushing back his hair with his hand. "Look, lady, I'll play it straight with you, but I can't afford to let my guard down with your partner," he said, cocking his head toward Ashe.

"What makes you think Detective Redhawk might be a danger to you?" Casey pressed.

"I read the papers. I know his foster parents have been murdered. Through no fault of my own, I'm now probably one of your suspects."

Casey stayed right by his elbow as they entered the apartment. "What makes you think that?"

"Don't play games with me," he snapped. "I'm an educated man. I know how it looks. The Johnsons ruined my chances of getting hired by another school, so I fought them. I had to. And now that they've been murdered, you need a suspect to nail for the crime. So here I am, caught in the middle. Never mind that *I* was *their* victim."

"The martyr angle never works with law-enforcement officers, so save the sob story and keep to the facts," Casey replied.

"You'll want an alibi, but I don't have one. The day of the murders I was here, alone. I was writing letters, working on my résumé, and surfing the Net, trying to find a job."

Ashe studied Gordon with the same detached indifference he would have reserved for a particularly disgusting beetle that had crawled out of the drain. There was something feral about this man. His face was taut and strained, and his eyes darted about like those of a cornered animal. Instinct warned Ashe that Gordon was like a hand grenade with the pin already pulled.

"You're just aching to make a case against me," Gordon whined. He turned to Casey. "That's really why he wanted to get into my home. I'll bet he's going to plant some evidence here." Gordon caught the look on their faces, then crossed his arms and sat down in a chair. "Surely you realize I can't trust him or his buddy cops not to do all they can to pin those murders on me. I'm just too convenient, don't you see?"

"If you don't stop whining, *I'll* be tempted to pin the murders on you just to shut you up," Casey retorted.

Her response, so close to what he'd been thinking, almost made Ashe laugh out loud. "Let's go to the station. We can finish our questions there so Mr. Gordon won't have to worry about entrapment."

"You're arresting me?" Gordon asked, his voice rising an octave.

"Not unless you push it," Ashe told him. "Let's just say you're assisting us in our inquiries and it'll be easier on all of us if we go to the station."

"I want to talk to my lawyer before I answer any questions. That's final," Gordon insisted.

"You can call him or her from the station," Ashe said.

"This is really unfair," he protested, acceding to their request, but continuing his litany of complaints all the way to Ashe's vehicle. "I can't afford any more legal fees. Those court-appointed lawyers won't be any good, either. Why should I suffer just because you need a suspect? I've done nothing wrong."

Casey helped him into the back seat and slammed the door shut, but Gordon never stopped talking. "This is going to be a real long trip," she said to Ashe.

"Yeah. The joys of police work."

As THEY ENTERED THE station, Ashe's cell phone rang again. His brother Travis's voice came through clearly. Excusing himself, Ashe took the will and the contents of the safe-deposit box into an unoccupied office.

"Have you found Little Fox?" Travis asked immediately.

"Not yet," Ashe replied, sensing his brother's mood. "But I did speak to her," he added, and went on to explain.

"Who the hell is this guy holding her?" Travis roared. "If you don't find her by the time I get home, I'll do it for you—my way!"

"Just calm down. When do you expect to arrive?"

"I'm not in the States yet, but I'm lining up some transportation now. I hope to catch a hop out tomorrow, if my paperwork comes through. I won't be long. What about the funeral?"

"They wanted to be buried on church grounds. I don't expect that'll be a problem. But they didn't want a funeral held. I think that's in deference to you and me."

"Any idea when their bodies will be released?"

"It shouldn't be long."

"Good. Maybe we can take care of that as soon as I get there. In the meantime, get me the name of the guy with Little Fox."

"Why? What would that matter?"

"I'd like to know the name of the guy I'm going to break in half."

Ashe heard the jealousy in Travis's voice. Some things

never changed. "This is still a police matter. I don't want to have to throw your sorry butt in jail."

"Little brother, you always did dream big."

Ashe heard a click and then the connection was terminated. He returned to the squad room.

He and Casey interviewed Gordon. After trying to get his lawyer on the phone and failing, the man decided to forgo an attorney. Even though Casey and Ashe both had a great deal of experience questioning suspects, they couldn't get a thing out of Gordon, except rambling excuses and cries of innocence.

Two hours later Ashe could barely contain his aversion for the man. Free to go, Gordon left the interview room quickly.

"He needs a psych evaluation, you know." Ashe shook his head.

Casey nodded in agreement. "He's so paranoid, it's a wonder he didn't try to attack one of us. He thinks the entire world is after him."

A young tribal police officer came over and handed Casey some papers.

Casey glanced down, smiled and headed for the door. "Let's go. We now have a warrant and can search his place for the murder weapon, boots to match the tracks and any papers establishing a link to a dirt bike. If we're lucky, we'll get there before he does."

Casey almost ran into Gordon, who'd remained just outside in the hall, apparently listening. "You're going to search my place? I knew it! You're trying to frame me. I demand to be there! If you don't give me a ride back, I'll find somebody who'll do it for money. There's no way you're searching anything without my being there."

Ashe glanced at Casey and saw the flash of anger in her face. It was masked a second later, but he knew that she hadn't expected this complication. They couldn't stop him from being present, either. The right to search didn't give them the right to ban the owner from the premises unless the suspect had been arrested.

"We'll give you a ride back," Ashe said, and saw the glare Casey gave him. "But if you interfere with our search, we'll place you under arrest for tampering with evidence and interfering with an investigation. Clear?"

They arrived at the apartment a short time later, but as much as they both wanted to find something linking Gordon to the Johnsons, there was no such evidence except ashtrays containing cigarette butts. They weren't the same brand as those found at the murder scene, however. Gordon admitted to being a smoker, and lit up several cigarettes while they were searching.

"Look what you've done to my home!" he complained. "Do you really have to set everything out onto the floor and trash the place?"

"We didn't trash anything," Casey snapped. "But if you really insist, we could stay here for hours going over everything two or three times."

Ashe knew then that the man's constant nagging had tried Casey's patience to the limit. Gordon had kept clear of Ashe, probably out of fear, but the man had misjudged the situation. If anyone was going to slam his face into a wall today, it would be Casey.

"Let's go," Ashe said to her, leaving Gordon to mourn over his disrupted possessions.

Ashe took Casey's arm, urging her out of the apartment. The touch had been casual, yet the stab of desire that followed took him completely by surprise. She leaned into him for a heartbeat, and then, as if suddenly aware of what she'd done, quickly stood straight.

She quickened her pace and walked past him, her hip

accidentally brushing his thigh. The contact nearly destroyed him. He bit back a groan; the woman was killing him.

Ashe watched Casey as they walked toward his carryall. The more time he spent around the woman, the more he wanted her. Navajo teachings held that all secrets were revealed when a man and a woman made love. There was nothing he wanted to do more than to put that ancient belief to the ultimate test.

He muttered an oath under his breath. He had to stop thinking like this. A night of passion with Casey, or even several, would never be enough for him. His feelings went too deep for a casual fling. What he wanted from Casey was the willing surrender of her heart.

"Now what?" Casey mused. "Maybe we should go talk to Elsie Benally," she said, remembering the woman Ilene Begay had told her about. "I was warned that my only chance of getting her cooperation was having someone along she trusted. Someone like you."

He considered it. The need to avenge his foster parents and find Fox drove him relentlessly. And it was precisely because of that he knew he had to be careful how he approached the few possible leads he had. "It's late now. Tomorrow morning we'll talk to her. But before we go there, I think we should speak to Gordon's attorney. He mentioned her name in the threatening letter he wrote my foster father."

"What can you possibly expect to learn from his attorney?"

"Let's find out if Gordon's involved in any other legal cases, whether as a plaintiff or defendant. I'd like to know if he's a killer, or just a crank."

After Ashe dropped her off at her motel, Casey sat alone on the edge of her bed staring at the stark room. A cold emptiness engulfed her. She yearned to be with the only man who had ever made her heart sing, but it was not to be. Ashe would be with her tonight, but only in her dreams.

THE FOLLOWING MORNING they arrived at a Legal Aid office in an old brick building right off Main Street in Farmington. A redheaded woman in her early forties ushered them from the reception area to a cramped office at the end of a long hallway.

"I'm Serena Muldair," the young brunette behind the desk said, rising and extending her hand. "What can I do for you?"

"We need some information," Casey said, flashing her ID and introducing Ashe. "It's about a client of yours, Patrick Gordon."

"I don't know how cooperative I can be on a matter that affects a client. Is there something specific you want to know?"

"Are you handling more than one case for him?"

Serena leaned back in her chair and regarded them thoughtfully, taking off her glasses and setting them on the desktop. Her shoulder-length hair fell in a soft cascade around her shoulders. To Casey's irritation the young attorney seemed more interested in Ashe than in her, though she was the one asking the questions.

"Mr. Gordon has several civil suits he wants us to handle. Why do you ask?"

"He's implicated in a serious felony—a murder."

"I don't handle criminal cases," she said flatly. "Mr. Gordon will have to retain other counsel to represent him on that matter."

Casey's cell phone rang and, as she excused herself and moved away, she saw Ashe quickly establishing a rapport with the woman. Casey listened to her supervisor demand an immediate progress report. Stepping out into the hall-way, she promised a written report by the end of the day.

By the time she returned to the office, Ashe and Ms. Muldair were sipping soft drinks and the mood had light-ened considerably. "Things are always busy here," she was saying. "That's why Patrick Gordon is such an annoyance. He brings in every problem he has with his neighbors and employers, and expects me to sue them naked."

Ashe obviously had a gift for getting along with people, and a special magic that communicated itself to the oppo-site sex. The lawyer was clearly eager to please him. Casey tried to analyze his technique. Maybe it was his eyes and the way he could make a woman feel as if she were the only person in the room. Or maybe it was the way he walked and carried himself. He was certainly the most virile man she'd ever met. She really didn't blame Serena for responding to him.

Realizing that neither Serena nor Ashe seemed particu-larly aware that she was back in the room, Casey cleared her throat. The young attorney's attitude changed in a flash.

"I'd better get back to work," she said crisply. "I'll tell you both one thing. I've already informed my director that I won't handle any more of Gordon's legal matters. I've had it with that man. Gordon is his own worst enemy."

"Off the record," Casey asked, "do you think he's the kind of person who might be prone to violence?"

Serena considered it, then shook her head. "I'm no psy-chologist, but my impression is that he's harmless. I do think he'd love to be thought of as dangerous or, at the very least, a force to be reckoned with. That's why I think he's always wanting to sue someone."

As Casey and Ashe walked to the door, Serena stepped around her desk and handed Ashe her card. "Give me a call if at any time you need a legal question answered. I'll be glad to help.''

Casey tried hard not to let the fact that Serena was hot for Ashe bother her, but it did. Logic didn't help much, either. She knew she had no claim on Ashe. There was nothing between them. After the case was closed, he'd go on with his life, and she would move on to another assignment.

That thought suddenly left her feeling hopelessly depressed.

"You're certainly quiet," Ashe said.

She masked her thoughts quickly and gave him a playful smile. "I was just trying to figure out how a guy who's a magnet for women handles the pressure."

Ashe chuckled. "Did you just call me a maggot?"

"Magnet. Trust me, I can read the evidence on this better than you can."

"Naw, you're just jealous."

Casey choked. "You're hallucinating. I have no interest in you except as my partner."

"Yes, but as what kind of partner?"

The words caused a rush of warmth to spread through her. She knew her cheeks were flushed; she could feel them burning. She kept her gaze focused on the sidewalk and refused to glance up.

"You're blushing," he said with a throaty chuckle.

"I've got a sunburn," she snapped. "That's a hazard out here in the desert."

"There's another hazard here for you."

He pulled her into the shaded entryway of a small print shop. Shielded from passersby, he took her mouth with his own.

Time ceased to exist for her during those precious seconds. Her heart was beating wildly as he tenderly coaxed her lips apart and deepened his kiss. Her body came alive with sensations too enticing to resist.

All too soon the intoxicating warmth that had spread through her became a raging inferno. Passion rocked her all the way to her core.

With a soft sigh, she stepped back out of his embrace and onto the sidewalk. She had to move away now while she could find the strength to do so. As she looked up at him, she saw the storm raging in his eyes.

Her breath caught in her throat. She wanted to step back into his arms but knew she could not. Silently, she walked with him to his carryall.

"Denying what's happening isn't going to help either of us," he said quietly as they got under way.

"We can't pursue this, either. It's pointless, don't you see?" she said in a cracked whisper.

"That's only because in your heart you still don't trust me."

Instinct assured her that they would accomplish far more, personally and professionally, if she did take him completely into her confidence. But she thought of the expensive pickup she'd seen at his home, and the questions about the source of money that raised. Then there was the timing between when he'd seen the file on Katrina in his captain's office and the murders. She was certain Ashe was no killer, but there *had* been a leak, and until she could prove with one-hundred-percent certainty that he hadn't been involved, even inadvertently, she couldn't risk bringing him in on the job she'd been sent to do. Her orders and duty were clear.

Yet, by holding back, Casey knew she was risking alienating Ashe forever, and that thought weighed heavily on her. She hadn't been looking for love when she'd come out here, but that was what she'd found. What hurt most now was knowing that it was an impossible love—something doomed to die before it ever blossomed. To grow, love required trust, and that was the one thing she could not give him.

Casey stole a furtive glance at Ashe as he drove toward the Reservation. She would eventually lose him and her life would never be the same again, no matter where she went or whom she met later.

"Let's go see Elsie Benally," he suggested, breaking the silence at last. "She's a good source. Elsie teaches spinning and weaving to other women. Most are grandmothers who already know the craft, but they get together to share ideas and socialize. Everyone likes Elsie, so people often confide in her."

They arrived at the six-sided hogan in the middle of a solitary canyon an hour later. Ashe parked in direct line with the blanket-covered entrance. Minutes ticked by, but he did not even open the vehicle's door.

"Maybe she's decided to ignore us."

"No. Just be patient."

Casey was certain they were getting nowhere, and was going to suggest they give up, when Elsie came to her doorway and waved at them to come inside.

"Don't press her for answers," Ashe warned. "Let her set her own pace."

As they stepped inside the hogan, Casey was startled by the primitive conditions she saw there. A black, potbellied woodstove served as the only source of heat for cooking and warmth. The floor was hard-packed dirt, and the joints between the rough-hewn logs were filled with hardened mud. She'd meant to mask her thoughts, but something in her expression must have given her away to the old woman.

Elsie glanced at her, then waved for them to sit on sheep-skins she'd laid on the floor. "I choose to live in this hogan instead of in the modern housing at Shiprock. This is the way my grandmother and mother lived, and I feel closer to everything that makes me who I am, here. Do you understand?''

Casey nodded, silently wondering if she would have been able to withstand the hardships, year after year.

''I know why you're here,'' Elsie said to Ashe. ''Maybe I can help you. I can tell you that your foster mother was having nightmares. She was afraid of something but she didn't know what. In her dreams she was faced with a terror she didn't understand. I tried to tell her not to ignore her instincts, that dreams had power and she was sensing danger on some level. But she wouldn't listen.''

''If you hear anything that can help me find these killers, will you send word to me?'' Ashe asked.

''You know I will,'' Elsie replied, walking them to the door.

Ashe was quiet as they drove back to the highway.

''What are you thinking?'' Casey asked gently.

''Volumes could be written on what I didn't know about my family. But one thing I'm certain about—their secrets led to their destruction.''

''Keeping secrets is often what people do when they have no other choice,'' she said, knowing only too well the burden of the secrets she kept.

''We always have choices,'' Ashe answered.

She heard the warning laced through his words and understood. Her decision to hold back would eventually cost her dearly.

''I'm going to make a stop at the substation and drop you off there, if you don't mind. The coroner must be getting closer to releasing the bodies and I need to take care of that matter.''

''I understand,'' she replied, hearing the sorrow in his voice and wishing she could do something to comfort him.

After they arrived, Ashe handed her the coroner's report and got ready to leave. "There are no surprises there. Now, if you don't need me, I'll stop by my desk and then go."

After saying goodbye to Ashe, Casey went to see the captain. He was getting ready to leave for the day and seemed preoccupied, so she didn't stick around. She was on her way out of the station when she saw Ashe—still at his desk and on the phone.

It was strange how he kept glancing toward the captain's office. He seemed impatient and restless—two things that were very much out of character for him, but under the circumstances, she supposed it was understandable. He was probably eager to leave as soon as possible but wanted to talk to the captain before taking off on personal business.

It was nearly two-thirty—almost time for the shift change—when Casey left the building. As she drove back to her motel, she focused on the comprehensive reports she had to file before the end of the day. She was several miles away from the station when a vague sense of uneasiness started creeping through her. Something was wrong, but she couldn't put her finger on what was disturbing her. Remembering Elsie's warning about the dangers of ignoring intuition, she forced herself to analyze her feelings.

As she thought back on everything that had happened that day, she saw Ashe clearly in her mind. His preoccupation with the captain had seemed odd, but it was easily explained. Yet something about it continued to nag at her.

Slowly, another possible explanation for his actions came into the forefront of her thoughts. What if it hadn't been the captain he'd been focused on, but rather the man's office? The conversation they'd had with Elsie must have been just one more reminder to Ashe of how little he knew about his family. Maybe Ashe had decided to go after the one thing he thought would provide him with answers—the file on Katrina.

Casey turned the sedan around and pressed hard on the accelerator, racing back to the station. Once there, she hurried inside and asked the first officer she saw where Captain Todacheene was.

"The captain has gone to a meeting over at Window Rock. He won't be back today."

Casey's heart drummed as she hurried into the squad room. It was between shifts and the area was nearly deserted. As she glanced around, she saw Ashe in the captain's office, standing in front of the file cabinet.

Casey felt as if the floor beneath her were dissolving. She knew she had to stop him. He was putting everything on the line, including his job, to help Fox, and his sacrifice was completely unnecessary. She would have given anything at that moment to tell him what she knew, but she could not violate the trust and duty that had been placed on her shoulders.

Casey started toward the office, one thing clear in her mind. At least now she knew for sure that Ashe had never seen that file. If he had, he wouldn't have been willing to risk so much in order to look at it now. This was solid proof that he hadn't inadvertently leaked the information it had contained. But whether his curiosity had tipped off someone else was another question entirely.

Casey entered the captain's office silently and caught Ashe by surprise. "Are you crazy?" she demanded. "You could be suspended for this, or worse." She knew what his job meant to him. Only someone who shared his dedication to law enforcement, as she did, could understand that his work was his lifeblood.

"There are some things that demand obedience to a higher loyalty. I've made my choice. Now it's your turn. Will you leave and let me finish what I've started, or turn me in? It's your call."

Chapter Ten

Casey glanced around. If she tried to stop him now, he'd realize that she'd known the file existed all along. As she quickly considered her options, Casey saw Captain Todacheene appear in the doorway leading to the squad room. One look at the files covering the top of the captain's desk told Casey that there'd be no time for Ashe to cover his tracks.

"Hurry," she warned, gesturing toward the captain. "I'll buy you some time." She strode out of the office, closing the door partway.

Acting on impulse, she intercepted Todacheene before he could cross the squad room. "I have some information about Patrick Gordon we should discuss," she said, blocking his way. "I need to talk to you in private."

"Then let's go to my office," the captain suggested.

"I'd prefer the conference room where there's no phone and less chance that anyone will interrupt us." Casey stepped to the side, so he had to turn away from his office to speak to her.

"Okay, but I have to warn you, I only have a few minutes to spare. I only came back because I left some papers behind that I'll need for my meeting."

Just then, Ashe joined them. "Captain, I didn't expect to see you back today."

"Consider me gone for all intents and purposes. I'm already running behind schedule." He glanced at his watch, then gave Casey an impatient look. "Why don't you fill out a report for me on Gordon, instead? I'll get to it as soon as I can. Right now I'm out of time."

"Of course. I'm sorry I held you up," Casey said.

As the captain went to his office to retrieve the papers he needed, Casey glanced up at Ashe. "Okay, what did you find?"

"Not what I expected."

She'd never heard his voice sound so cold. Anger was clearly etched on his features. For a moment she considered the possibility that he'd discovered the real reason why she'd been sent to the Rez. If that was true, she wasn't sure what she'd do with Ashe now. He was already difficult enough to deal with.

"What's going on?" she asked, matching the coldness of his tone. Sometimes the best defense was a good offense. "And I want a clear answer. I deserve that from you. By running interference for you, I put my own career in danger."

He said nothing for several seconds. "Let's get out of here. You and I need to talk."

Once they were outside, alone in his vehicle, Ashe shifted to face her. "The file is gone. It's as if it had never been there. What part did you play in that—or in the captain's unexpected return?"

"Wait a second. You're blaming *me* because you couldn't find what you were looking for?"

He held her gaze. "Did you ask Todacheene to move the file elsewhere because you knew that I was interested in it?"

"You're not giving your captain enough credit for knowing his men," she said coldly. "My guess is that if there really was a file, he moved it himself, assuming that sooner or later you'd do exactly what you did." She paused, then added pointedly, "Keep in mind that by intercepting him, and buying you some time, I covered for you and risked a reprimand, or more."

Ashe took a deep breath and let it out slowly. "You're good, I'll give you that. But I'm getting tired of cat-and-mouse games. For whatever reason, you've chosen not to put all your cards on the table. My captain may also be involved to some extent in whatever you're up to. Don't expect me to rush out and trust either of you. Those days are over."

Casey swallowed hard. His words had hurt her more than he'd ever know. Wordlessly, she left his vehicle and strode across the parking lot. She'd done a lot for the sake of her job, but until today she'd never known what it was like to pay with a piece of her heart.

ASHE SPENT THE REST of the day making the arrangements to have his foster parents buried in the cemetery of the Christian church they'd attended. Now, as darkness covered the land, he stood alone under the full moon, his gaze resting on Beautiful Mountain. He'd come here to try to regain a sense of balance and harmony. The peace of the desert enveloped him, and he found a measure of comfort in it. He'd needed this time alone. He still couldn't think clearly around Casey. He'd never met anyone who stirred him the way she did. He wanted to be part of her, and her to be one with him. That pairing, that need to know her in all the ways a man could know a woman, was affecting his every decision. But he couldn't afford to let it hamper his ability to work the case effectively.

He thought of his brother Travis. He'd be home soon, and by then, Ashe had to have answers. Travis wouldn't play by anyone's rules, and that would add another wild card to an already impossible situation.

As a prairie hawk cried shrilly overhead, Ashe felt a fierce longing for the woman who'd captured his heart, and for the future they might have had if she'd only trusted him.

CASEY ARRIVED AT THE station at eight the following morning. Ashe was already outside waiting for her when she pulled up and parked her sedan. As she looked at him, a shiver coursed up her spine. He stood tall, proud and supremely confident. Her breath caught in her throat.

He gestured toward his vehicle wordlessly.

"Where do you want to go? Did you find a lead?" she asked.

"I've been trying to figure out why Fox's car hasn't been found anywhere, even though most of the cops have been looking for it, along with the motorcycles and the van. Fox is around here, we know that. She's probably not using her own vehicle, so it's parked somewhere hidden in plain sight—like maybe among the other cars in the Tapahonso Salvage Yard."

"What do you hope to find in her car? You know she's okay. You spoke to her."

The silence was thick between them as the moments passed. "I don't really 'know' anything at this point," Ashe finally said, then added, "What I do know is that you're *not* FBI." He held up a hand as she started to deny it. "I've been a cop too long. I know when someone's holding something back, or when things aren't what they seem to be. I do believe that you're part of some agency—

federal or whatever—or my captain wouldn't have let you anywhere near his people.''

Casey said nothing, neither confirming nor denying.

''Whatever you are, you're definitely in law enforcement. You have the right instincts. That's why I don't understand why you're holding out on me. Deep down you must sense that I can be trusted.'' He paused, then in a gentle voice said, ''If your gut feelings aren't giving you the assurances that you need, then listen to your heart.''

He pulled over to one side of the road, and shifted to face her. ''When I hold you in my arms, when I feel you responding to me, I know that there's something very right between us.'' Ashe took her hand and placed it over his heart. ''There is no greater truth than what we feel for each other. Listen to the woman inside you—the one who wants my touch, and knows how to touch me and drive me wild. She'll tell you that you have no reason to distrust me—not as a cop...or as a man.''

Casey's throat tightened. She could feel his heart drumming beneath her palm. She wanted to confide in Ashe more than she'd ever wanted anything in her life, but some decisions weren't hers to make. She reached out to him in the silence of her mind, begging him without words to understand.

His gaze held only tenderness and the need that begged wordlessly for her trust.

She took a deep breath and let it out slowly. She couldn't continue to shut him out—not when everything in her demanded she do otherwise. She considered her words carefully, then began.

''Let's say, hypothetically of course, that Fox's past is the key to this case. If that's so, then something from that past must have led the killer here. Someone betrayed her, accidentally or on purpose, and your foster parents paid a price. Fox's only chance lies in secrecy now, so she's hidden. I've told you time and again that it's best that no one can find her, yet I can't convince you of that. To you, trust means following instincts and obeying them. But would you really trust a cop who was willing to put personal feelings ahead of professional responsibility?"

"Are you talking about the Witness Protection Program?" he asked, his eyebrows furrowed. "Their job, I thought, was to protect the safety of someone, like the Secret Service."

"It's more than that. Federal marshals or treasury agents won't just baby-sit some witness or government official. They go looking for potential threats to head them off in conjunction with local agencies. Things can become terribly complicated. People like you and me aren't always at liberty to make the choices we'd like when we're out on the job."

Ashe considered her words, then started the engine and got under way. "That may be so, but from where I sit, you're still playing word games with me. When we're working a case we all have a certain amount of autonomy. It's impossible to do our jobs otherwise. The bottom line here is that you can't bring yourself to trust me completely. Until you can do that, and earn my trust in return, I'll have to follow my own judgment."

Aching regret swept over her. She knew now that there was no hope for them. No amount of wishing would ever change that. The realities of their lives would forever keep them apart. She drew into herself, trying to find some respite from the bitter sadness that filled her, but there was only a hollow emptiness where her heart had once been.

THEY ARRIVED AT THE salvage yard about a half hour later. Although she hadn't really wanted to come here, Ashe had refused to let her talk him out of it.

Casey looked around. There was no fence around the four- or five-acre field that was overgrown with old appliances, cars and anything made of metal that could be discarded.

"What is this place?" she asked. "Does he sell parts, recycle the metal, or what?"

"All of the above, and then some," Ashe said. "The man who runs this place is older than both of us put together, but he has a knack for fixing things. Sometimes it's a lawn mower or a washing machine that he restores. Other times it's a car. Then he resells it for a price people around here can afford."

There was always that on-the-edge quality to life here, and it made her admire Ashe and his people all the more. It was their indomitable spirit that allowed them to face seemingly insurmountable odds with such courage and determination.

"My brother hated living on the Rez. He said he wanted more out of his life than a daily battle for survival. He preferred an adversary he could confront directly, not one that destroyed by undermining—like poverty."

She wanted to ask Ashe more about his brother, but before she could frame her question, an elderly man stepped out of a metal portable building and walked toward them. His back was erect and his stride so filled with purpose that only the wrinkles on his weathered face attested to his advanced age.

Ashe introduced her to the owner of the salvage yard, Kenneth Tapahonso, and this time Casey remembered not to shake hands.

"Are you here looking for something to buy, or on police business?" Tapahonso asked.

"We're actually looking for Fox's car. I have a feeling someone may have hidden it here."

Tapahonso nodded thoughtfully. "You could hide almost anything here, that's for sure. People drop off stuff all the time rather than take it to the landfill. It's cheaper, and they know I'll make use of it sooner or later."

"Mind if we look around?" Ashe asked.

"Help yourself. And, if you decide you want to buy something, let me know. I can make you a good deal."

As he went back inside, Ashe looked around. "I'd normally suggest we start by looking for tracks, but the recent rains have probably washed those away. Let's just go ahead and start down the first row."

The deeper they went into the maze of old appliances, cars and salvaged parts, the more claustrophobic the pathways became. Casey felt her skin prickle as it always did when there was danger around.

She glanced up at Ashe and, with one look, knew he sensed it, too. "Anything or anyone could be hiding in all this junk," she commented.

"Yeah, but my hunch paid off. There's Fox's car."

"It's in good condition," Casey said as they approached it. She tried the passenger-side door, and it was unlocked. "There are no signs that the occupant met with violence, and there's no damage or bloodstains on the inside." She gestured downward. "What about the gum wrappers on the floorboards. Hers?"

"She chewed that brand. But why was it necessary to hide the car here, or anywhere?"

"Like I said before, I think she's trying to stay alive. It's not a kidnapping. It's more like going to ground."

Ashe looked around him. "We'll leave the car right where it is in case she's able to come back for it."

Casey stood very still, listening, her skin prickling. "Something's not right."

"Yeah." He remained close to her side, and his hand moved to rest on the butt of his pistol.

"Let's head back," she said. "That way," she added, picking a path through two rows of junkers stacked three cars high. "It's wider, and we'll have more room to maneuver if we need it."

As they approached the halfway point, Casey heard an ominous creaking noise.

Ashe instantly grabbed her hand and dived to one side just as two junked cars came crashing down. Dust and sand rose high into the air, followed by the revved-up whine of a motorcycle.

The sound of the bike faded rapidly, and a deadly silence slowly descended over the area. Ashe stood, pistol in hand, and ran to the end of the row. Casey followed his lead, going in the opposite direction, hoping to catch sight of whoever was on the motorcycle.

As she emerged from the wreckage, she saw Tapahonso doing his best to hurry toward them. "Are you two okay?" he yelled out.

"Yes, we're fine," Casey answered.

Tapahonso looked down the row at the two cars that had toppled off their pile. "How did that happen? I had to use a crane to stack them like that."

They walked back to the fallen cars, and Ashe joined them. Together they studied the ground searching for footprints, but the ones they could make out were indistinct because of the packed soil.

"It's possible that the cars shifted and toppled because the rains and erosion undermined the base of the stack," Ashe said.

Casey heard the touch of skepticism in his voice, and

noted a large, rust-covered pipe sitting behind the remaining car in the disturbed pile. It would have made a powerful crowbar. Ashe wasn't buying this as an accident, and, in that, they agreed.

They looked around but the junkyard was vast and neither of them could say for sure from what direction the sound of the motorcycle had come. The search for bike tracks proved useless.

After saying goodbye to Tapahonso, they returned to Ashe's vehicle.

"We're getting closer to finding answers. That's why someone wanted us out of the way," he said, his voice distant and thoughtful. "I noticed you saw that pipe, too. It had deep scratches in it, and was curved just a little. It was used to pry the cars off-balance, I bet. Too bad its surface would make lifting fingerprints from it impossible."

"Let's go back to the station. Maybe something's come in from my office. I asked for your foster father's military records and for a full background check on Patrick Gordon. With luck, that information is here by now."

When they arrived at the station, Casey went to the empty office she'd been using, while Ashe went to his desk. Ten minutes later, she opened the door and waved at him to come in.

"I've got a fax with pages from your foster father's military records." She placed the papers before him. "A lot of what's in here is blacked out, classified. The rest doesn't look too useful for our purposes. But I did find out that a clearance check was run on him after he left the military. Those missing years you were wondering about are no longer a mystery. Your dad was an investigator for the U.S. Attorney's office in Phoenix." Casey studied Ashe's expression. At least this news didn't pack the hammer blow the other revelations had.

"I wonder why he left that job to come here and start a school."

"The job file has a comment from the U.S. Attorney saying that your father was discouraged by the cycle of putting criminals behind bars just to have them walking the streets again."

Ashe nodded. "I can see how that would happen. He always said that what he loved most about running a school was that he was working toward the future, not just dealing with the problems of today." He paused, then continued. "I remember how he always took time for the troublemakers and gave them special attention, too. I finally understand why."

Suddenly a gunshot reverberated within the confines of the squad room, and they heard the sound of glass shattering. Ashe ducked and reached for his weapon as Casey pressed her back to the wall and peered out into the next room.

"It's Gordon," she whispered. "He's holding the officers out there at gunpoint. A light fixture is broken, so I think his shot went into the ceiling."

Ashe crept to the other side of the door. Gordon's back was to them. If they acted now, they could take the gunman before the violence escalated any further. "Cover me. I'm going in."

Chapter Eleven

Casey didn't have time to stop him. She saw Ashe move noiselessly, trying to position himself near Gordon's side, so he could get a clear line of fire. The problem was that any shot would carry an element of risk. If Ashe missed or the bullet passed through Gordon, another officer could be struck, as well.

"Drop it," Ashe said, from behind the cover of a desk. "You don't want to die, and I don't want to shoot you."

"No," Gordon replied, glancing over to where Ashe was hiding, but not shifting his pistol away from the other officers. "You're all after me. I'd rather die this way than spend my life in jail for a crime I didn't commit."

"You taught my niece, man," Nakai said. "She wouldn't have passed if you hadn't tutored her. Nobody is after you. Put your weapon down."

Gordon turned to look at Nakai, shifting his aim. "I did help your niece, and a lot of other kids, too, but I still got fired."

Casey saw that Ashe was moving closer, now that Gordon had taken his eyes off him. Gordon was suicidal, but she intended to see to it that he didn't die at the hands of an officer. Trusting Ashe's police training and her own instincts, she grabbed a coffee cup from the desk and walked casually into the squad room. She was holding the cup up as if taking a sip, while keeping her weapon inconspicuously down below desk level in the other hand.

"Who set off the firecracker?" Casey asked.

Gordon spun around, but before he could draw a bead on Casey, Ashe lunged, grabbed the man's weapon, and wrestled him to the floor. Several officers were instantly there to help, and Gordon was handcuffed within ten seconds.

"Good instincts, partner," Casey said, holstering her pistol and setting the cup down on the closest desk.

"Next time don't make me read your mind," Ashe said, hauling Gordon to his feet.

As two officers led Gordon away, Ashe stepped up close to her. Casey felt the heat from his body envelop her. The passion that continued to draw them together sang to her now. She could sense him reaching out and then drawing back, as he struggled against what they both yearned for—the passion they didn't dare to indulge.

Hearing Gordon's ranting outside in the hall, Ashe cocked his head toward the door. "The guys here can take care of booking him. Do you want to let him cool off awhile before we try to question him?"

"Yeah, that's probably a good idea. I've got to tell you, though, any half-competent attorney will be filing a diminished-capacity defense. Gordon is suicidal." They walked down the hall and out of the police building, keeping their voices low.

"In this case, I'd agree," Ashe said. "My guess is he'll be taken to a hospital for evaluation as soon as his lawyer gets the paperwork done, which will probably be in another day or so."

"None of this disqualifies him as a suspect in our case,

though,'' Casey reminded. "It even strengthens the possibility. Unbalanced people do unbalanced things.''

Ashe nodded. "That's true enough, but Gordon's pistol was a .22 revolver—not the same type that was used at the other crime scenes. What I'd like to do now is go back and talk to Walker over at the Farmington Police Department. I can't shake that feeling that he's involved somehow,'' Ashe said. "His service weapon is a nine-millimeter.''

"So is mine and yours and most of your fellow officers, as well. Could it be that you're focusing on Walker because you don't want to believe your captain or Officer Nakai could be involved in the crime? We could tie both of them to the case with a motive at least as strong as the Farmington cop's.'' She kept her tone soft.

It was a moment before he answered, but his voice came out clear and strong. "My captain, like you, knows more than he's saying, but I'm not about to accuse him without stronger proof than that. And Nakai, I'd trust with my life.''

The second comment stung. The implication, though he hadn't said it directly, was that she, like Todacheene, was unworthy of his full trust. Knowing he had reason to feel that way made it hurt all the more.

They had almost reached Ashe's carryall when District Attorney Prescott came running up to them. "I just heard what happened. Is Gordon our killer, then?''

Casey found it difficult to hide her dislike for the man. "We're still investigating. The only thing that we know for sure is that he showed up at the station, unannounced, then apparently came into the squad room waving a .22 revolver around and fired off a shot, shattering a light fixture. But none of that links him to the murders. For one thing, his firearm is not the same caliber as the murder weapon.''

"Couldn't Gordon have another pistol, though?'' Prescott asked. "Maybe he's hidden it somewhere. I need evidence I can use to convict a killer, not set him free."

"We're working on it," she said, and stepped into Ashe's vehicle, closing the door behind her.

Ashe took her cue and slipped quickly behind the wheel.

"I know he's officially on our side," she said as they pulled away, "but he makes me nervous. I get the feeling that he's going to foul up this case."

"He's annoying, but we'll both have bigger problems in another day or so. You may find Prescott's meddling a breeze to deal with in comparison."

"What are you talking about?"

He took a deep breath, then let it out slowly. "My brother will be here soon, and neither of us is going to be able to keep him out of this investigation. He's going to be everywhere at once, looking for Fox."

"I fully expect him to want to search for her, just as you've done. What's so unique about that?"

"I'll let you discover that for yourself, but I will tell you this—all of his life my brother has been in love with Fox. He'll never admit it, but I know it because I know him. When a Redhawk gives his heart, it stays given, and nothing will stop him from doing whatever's necessary to protect the woman he loves."

The power of Ashe's words laced their way around Casey's heart, filling her with such an intense longing, she ached everywhere. She would have given anything to be able to tell him everything she knew, to assure him that she trusted him as both a cop and a man. But however much she wanted to, and truly believed it would be safe, Casey could not bring herself to violate the trust that had been placed in her.

Thanks to a government contact who'd made a discreet inquiry, she'd learned via fax that morning that Ashe had purchased his truck with cash. She wanted to look into Ashe's bank records to see where the money had come from. She was certain that the answers she'd find there would finally settle her superior's doubts. But there was no way she could get permission to search those bank records without a court order, and she didn't have sufficient grounds to get one.

To simply ask him about the matter would be pointless, since she'd need more than his word to take to her supervisor. In fact, asking could do much more harm than good at this point. Ashe would never forget that the agency she worked for and her own investigation had branded him a suspect. She'd have no chance of keeping him as an ally, and the fact was, she desperately needed his help to investigate here on the Rez.

They arrived at the Farmington police station and parked in the visiting agencies' space near the rear of the building. "I think we'll have better luck if I use my official capacity to wring some answers out of Walker," Casey said.

"That's probably true." Ashe threw the car door open, and waved to a young female officer who was heading toward a police cruiser. "Let me get some unofficial background for us first."

Casey had to admit Ashe excelled at that. He had a gift for making friends, particularly of the opposite sex. As she saw the wide smile the attractive policewoman gave him, Casey felt her chest tighten. Soon she'd be gone, and Ashe would find more than one woman willing to occupy his time, his thoughts and his heart. An unbearable sadness filled her, choking the air out of her lungs as she forced herself to accept the inevitable.

"Hey, Ashe!" Casey heard the female officer's greeting clearly, though she continued to hang back. "What brings you here?"

"Still trying to get a lead on Fox, Betty," he responded.

The policewoman's expression became somber. "I'm so sorry about everything that has happened. You know I'll help any way I can." She looked directly at Casey, letting her know her offer extended to her also.

"Tell me this much," Ashe pressed, lowering his voice. "Do you think Walker knows anything about Fox's whereabouts? He likes to brag, I know, and I was hoping you might have overheard something."

Betty shook her head. "We work the same shift, but we don't hang out together anymore. He spends a lot of time working on his cycles. You know he's still with the motorcycle unit. He wouldn't give that up for the world," she said with a shrug.

"There is one thing," she added as an afterthought. "Walker has always had a thing for Katrina. He and I went out together a few times, and on one occasion we had pizza and watched 'Monday Night Football' at his place. I spotted Fox's high-school photo on his bookcase. He tried to pass it off as just a high-school memento, but it was in the center of the shelf. I think she was the first real love of his life."

"Keep your eyes and ears open for us, Betty, okay?" Ashe asked.

"You know I will."

As they headed inside the station, Casey nodded to Ashe. "Nice police work. Did you know that Walker felt *that* strongly about Fox?"

"I'm not as willing as Betty is to believe that the emotion he actually feels has anything to do with love."

"Just remember that not everyone defines love in the same way," Casey replied.

"Real love is easily defined. It's the desire to put someone else ahead of yourself. Walker wouldn't put anything ahead of his own wants and needs. To him, love is measured by what the other person can do for him. Fox would look real good on his arm.''

''I find love harder to define than you do,'' Casey said quietly. ''I'll agree that it includes *wanting* to put the person you love ahead of everything else, but the world we live in determines to what extent we're able to do that.''

Ashe shrugged, unwilling to debate the point. ''I can tell you one thing—if Walker has anything to do with Fox's disappearance, he may never get out of the hospital.''

She didn't doubt that he'd want to punish Walker physically, but she also knew Ashe would do whatever was necessary to help Fox. He'd want the person responsible tried and jailed, but violence would be his last resort. Upholding the law meant everything to him. Casey knew that when the time came for her to put all her cards on the table, her only hope would be to appeal to him from that standpoint.

Casey flashed her badge and they were ushered into the watch commander's office. Her official request to interview Walker was granted almost immediately.

Moments later, Walker and another officer came into the conference room where Casey and Ashe were waiting.

Walker looked directly at Ashe, then at Casey. ''I'd like Officer Cooper present. I want a witness who can attest to everything that happened here today, should the need ever arise.''

''There are no charges against you,'' Casey said. ''This is all routine.''

''So you won't have a problem with my request, right?'' Walker pressed.

Casey considered telling him about the tape recorder she had in her jacket pocket, but then nixed the idea. She wasn't using it for this interview anyway. The legalities were complicated, and knowing she had it at all might make things even more difficult with Walker now. "Officer Cooper can stay, though I am surprised that you feel it necessary." She leaned forward, resting her elbows on the table. "Let's get started. I have reason to believe that you were following Katrina Johnson around on campus, waiting for her after classes, and so on."

Walker nodded. "That's true, but I wasn't stalking her or anything like that. I would sometimes wait for her after class, that's all. I think she was attracted to me, but she wouldn't go out with me because she knew Ashe and Travis would be dead set against it. I wanted to overcome that reluctance of hers and figured persistence would pay off."

Casey could sense Ashe tensing up, though she wasn't looking at him. Without making an obvious point of it, she shifted her chair so she was sitting squarely between the two men. "Why didn't you tell us about this before?"

"I knew I had nothing to do with Katrina's disappearance, or the death of her foster parents. Yet, had I come to you, I would have been placed on your suspect list. I wanted to avoid that."

"You realize that failing to tell us puts you in the exact position you were trying to avoid."

"No, not really. I'm only involved circumstantially. By now you must have better suspects—those with motives."

"Your interest in Katrina, your involvement with motorcycles and your familiarity with weapons keeps you on the short list," Ashe said, biting off the words.

Though she knew Walker resented her authority, Casey held his gaze, forcing him to keep his attention on her.

"A motorcyclist features in the crimes, though I'm not at liberty to explain how," she said.

"Well, it wasn't me. I have two bikes, both big machines. That doesn't make me a criminal. Just to show my goodwill, I'm more than happy to have you compare the tire impressions of my Harleys with whatever you lifted from your crime scene. But I warn you ahead of time, there are only a few cycle shops and brands of tires available in the Four Corners area. You might find a match by coincidence.''

Casey glanced at Cooper, who was leaning against the wall in silence. The tall, dark-haired cop had not said one word, but she had no doubt that he was keeping careful track of everything.

Casey looked back at Walker. ''Thanks for your cooperation. I'll have someone take tire prints for comparison.''

''Let me know if they match. I deserve that much.''

''I'll do what I can,'' Casey replied. ''By the way, what size boots do you wear?''

''Bigger than your friend there.'' Walker grinned, nodding toward Ashe. ''Tens or bigger, depending on the brand and style.'' Walker stood. ''Anything else? It's time for me to hit the street.''

''That's it for now. We know where to find you if we need you.''

''Any time,'' he said, giving her another cocky grin and ignoring Ashe altogether.

The moment they were alone, Casey glanced at Ashe. ''Can you have someone from your department check out the tire treads on his bikes? And see if they can tell if the tires have been changed recently.''

''Sure.'' Ashe's expression remained impassive. ''I'll choose the person carefully, too. I don't want anything to jeopardize this case.''

She nodded. ''That I know. That's why I didn't object to your being here when I questioned Walker. Officially, I was stretching it, you know.''

"I'm aware of that." He paused, and weighing his words, added slowly, "It's strange how your trust works, isn't it? You trust me a little, just not enough."

His accusation hurt, but there was nothing she could say. "Let's get going. I'm going to follow up on the background checks I ordered on Nakai and Captain Todacheene. Those have been slow in coming in."

He shook his head. "I wish those weren't necessary, but I suppose you're right to do them, if only to eliminate them as suspects."

They were halfway out of town when Ashe's carryall began to pull to one side. "There's something wrong with one of the tires," Ashe said, driving up a side street and parking.

Casey got out, automatically glancing both ways to make sure there were no other surprises awaiting them.

Ashe crouched by the left front tire. "Someone let the air out of this tire. The valve's been loosened." He got into the back to get the spare. "They tampered with this one, too. That means someone entered the vehicle while we were at the police station."

Casey heard the sound of a motorcycle approaching. Instinctively, she moved her hand slightly closer to her weapon. A motorcycle cop turned the corner, coming toward them, then parked and removed his helmet.

Walker glanced at Ashe and Casey. "Car trouble?"

"A bit," Casey said coldly. "Seems someone messed with our tires. They even entered the vehicle and let the air out of the spare, too."

"Imagine that! The troublemaker must have had one of those slim jims that cops carry to help people who've locked themselves out of their cars."

As Walker strode toward Ashe, Casey moved between the men. There was no way she was going to let them square off here. Casey could see a squad car parked a block away. It had just arrived from the other direction. Whatever was going on, it was being monitored and had been carefully staged. She casually reached into her jacket pocket, having a plan in mind.

Ashe straightened and faced Walker. Both men stood at least a head taller than she did, but Casey stayed squarely between them.

"I'm sure you have patrol responsibilities, Officer," Casey said. "The problem with the tires is an annoyance, nothing more. We can handle it."

"Shove off," Ashe warned. "You're not needed here."

"I figured you'd say that. You've spent all this time trying to get the pretty agent into the sack. The last thing you need is competition."

"You're treading into sexual-harassment territory again, Officer Walker. I suggest you back off," Casey said.

"It would be your word and his against mine, baby. I can hold my own against that."

Casey smiled slowly. "You do such a fabulous job of incriminating yourself, it's a wonder you're still on the force." She brought out the small tape recorder she carried in her jacket pocket and played back what he'd just said. "It may not be admissible in a court of law, but I bet your department would still like a copy for your file."

"Give me that," he said, reaching out for the recorder.

Anticipating his move gave her the advantage. Casey grabbed his outstretched hand, pinched a nerve, and increased the pressure until his knees began to sag.

"Get going, Walker," she said releasing the pressure and moving back. Casey glanced up the street and saw the squad car pulling away. "Even your backup is gone. It's over."

"No, it's not over—not by a long shot. It's just beginning."

As he straddled the motorcycle and roared down the highway, Casey laughed. "I'll bet his pride really stings about now."

Ashe stood immobile, his expression as impassive as a stone. "The men will razz Walker about this back at the station. He's more than just one of several suspects now. He just became a dangerous, personal adversary."

Chapter Twelve

A road-service truck couldn't come to them for a half hour, so they elected to walk to the nearest gas station, only a mile away. They were halfway there, rolling the flat spare tire, when the D.A., Prescott, pulled up beside them in his county vehicle. "What on earth are you two doing out here?"

Casey glanced down at the tire, then back at Prescott. "I would say that's pretty obvious."

Prescott laughed. "Yeah, I guess it is. Come on, hop in."

"We wouldn't want to put you out," Ashe said.

"No trouble at all. In fact, I was on my way to try and find you two. You've saved me a trip." Prescott pulled a lever, and the trunk popped open.

Casey slid into the front seat of the sedan as Ashe tossed the tire into the trunk. He closed the lid and got into the back seat.

"What's on your mind, Counselor?" Casey asked as Prescott pulled back onto the road.

"I heard that you were questioning a Farmington cop today. What's that all about? If you're going to cross departmental lines, you should have had the courtesy to notify my office. This is my county."

"Counselor, I'm investigating a felony and interviewing

those who know Katrina, not interrogating a suspect. I'm not obligated to keep your office apprised of every step we take."

"No, you're not obligated, but let me explain something to you. I can't have an FBI agent and an officer from the Navajo police going after a cop from a department not linked to either service. When that happens, my office will be contacted by that cop's superiors, and I damned well better have strong answers to give them. I won't tolerate being made to look like a fool."

Casey nodded, conceding for the moment. It would serve little purpose to have the district attorney gunning for her. "We're following leads wherever they take us. In this case it was to a motorcycle cop who may have been harassing a woman linked to the crime I'm investigating." She filled him in on their history with Walker, including their encounter by the road, but didn't mention the tape.

"If that man gives you a hard time again, you let me know about it," Prescott told her. "Despite what you may believe, I'm very much on the side of justice. If the trail of evidence leads you to a cop, I'll back you one hundred percent."

"Thank you."

"Don't thank me until you've heard my warning. If you end up following a false trail and accuse a clean cop, we'll have a problem. That'll create a lot of bad blood between the departments and the heat from that's going to land on my head. Watch your step and we'll get along fine. Am I making myself clear?"

"Eminently."

Prescott pulled to a stop in front of the gas station. "Okay, here you are." He glanced at his watch. "I wish I could give you a ride back to your car, but I have a meeting I'm supposed to attend at the Farmington mayor's office."

"That's no problem, sir. It's not far," Casey said as Ashe removed the flat tire from Prescott's trunk.

As Prescott drove off, Ashe muttered an oath. "Despite the fact that he's only been on the job here for a few months, that man makes every single cop I know crazy. He's always around to soak up any good publicity, and won't take a case to court unless he's certain to win. He's first in line for anything that could show him or his office in a positive light."

"What I'm wondering is how he happened to be on this road at precisely the right time." Casey looked at Prescott's sedan, now disappearing in the distance.

He grinned at her. "I was wondering about that, myself. I have a lot of problems attributing anything to coincidence."

"Me, too. Any ideas why he'd be following us?"

"He may want to keep an eye on the people who are making loud noises, since it could end up making him look bad."

"Possibly," Casey replied, unconvinced but unable to think of a better explanation. If Prescott was involved in the Johnsons' deaths, she and Ashe certainly hadn't uncovered any apparent motive so far. Prescott was too young to have been associated with Nick Johnson in the military or during his days as an investigator.

Twenty-five minutes later, they were back at Ashe's carryall. He reached for the jack and lug wrench, and noticing the oil and grime on the tools, stood and stripped off his shirt. "Hold on to this, will you? Something happened to the rag I usually keep in here. I'd rather not get grease and dirt all over me. I don't want to have to go home and change before we go back to the station."

"No problem."

Her gaze was riveted on him as he stood there, shirtless.

He was magnificent. His bronzed skin gleamed in the fading sun. Every fiber in her body responded to him. Her hands tingled with the need to touch him. Casey watched the play of muscles on his back as he jacked the carryall up, took off the flat, and replaced it with the newly inflated spare. The sweet fire raging inside her made her feel weak at the knees.

Ashe gave her a sideways glance. "Don't look at me that way," he warned, his voice deep and taut.

"What way?" she managed.

"Like a woman who sees a man she wants."

Casey knew she should have protested, but her throat closed and the words wouldn't come.

He grabbed a handful of sand, used it to rub away the grime on his hands, then shook off the dust. Then he stood and, holding her gaze, held out his hand.

She couldn't move. If she took his hand, she'd step into his arms.

"My shirt."

"Oh—yes, of course."

Their fingers brushed as she handed it to him and the force of that casual touch sent ripples all through her.

He sucked in his breath. "Do you know what you're doing to me, and the consequences of it? When you dance near the fire, you're bound to feel the heat. And if you draw too close, it will brand you forever."

"But it's only within that heat that I feel truly alive," she said, the words leaving her mouth before she ever realized she'd spoken them out loud.

Through his open shirt, she could see the muscles on his chest grow taut as desire pounded through him. "Maybe it is time for us," he said, his voice smoky. "I want you to see me as a man—one who cares for you, one who deserves your trust."

That last word wrenched at her heart. The need to show him how she felt drummed through her. She had to reach him somehow, and this was the only way she could do it before the whole story came out and she lost him. Maybe if she could touch his heart now, a piece of her would remain with him forever.

As a car sped by, he gestured for her to get inside the carryall. "Let me take you someplace that's special to me. Maybe there you can finally see me for who I am. Then it'll be up to you to decide if I'm the man you want loving you."

The words cast a magic spell all their own. With Ashe, she was more than the career professional she'd worked so hard to become; she was a woman who wanted to be loved, and to give love in return.

THEY ARRIVED AT A beautiful place southwest of Shiprock, where the mountain foothills met the desert floor. There was a peculiar formation of red sandstone that jutted out toward the skies like a monument to the majesty of the Navajo Nation.

"When I was young," Ashe said, "my father and I would leave the Rock Ridge area and head out on camping expeditions that would sometimes last weeks. This was a favorite place of his. It's here that I learned about the Navajo ways. My father would tell me about the hero twins who fought to make the world safe. It was from those stories, handed down through generations, that I learned to love everything my people stand for and believe."

Long shadows flickered and danced around them. The temperature was dropping as the sun began its nightly descent, but the heat of passion warmed Casey, holding her in an inescapable embrace.

Ashe took her hand in his and stood with her, facing

Ship Rock, which jutted up from the desert floor like a lone sentinel standing guard over them.

He glanced at Casey, then off toward the eastern horizon. "People come to our land and see only poverty and the harshness of life within the bounds of the mountains. But the earth itself defines the Diné and gives us strength."

Casey looked at the beauty around her, wondering how she could ever have seen this desert as other than full of color and life.

"When you look with your heart, many things open up to you."

She looked at Ashe and held his gaze. "What I see is a man who is strong, but gentle in spirit, and who has shown me a way of life I never knew existed. I won't bind you by making or asking for promises. What I want is as simple as this desert that claims your heart."

Ashe drew her into his arms. "You are the one who holds my heart in the palm of her hand."

He clasped her tightly against him. She felt his chest rising and falling in deep, uneven breaths. Engulfed by emotions as primitive as the land where they stood, she held him, basking in the warmth of a love more precious than anything she'd ever known.

"We have been drawn together, though I have nothing to offer you. The riches I can share with you won't buy you the pretty things out in your world."

"All I want is your love, here and now," Casey whispered.

"If I take you and make you mine, there will be no turning back," Ashe warned her.

As he stroked her cheek with the palm of his hand, she leaned into him. "Look at the way you respond to my slightest touch," he said. "Our feelings for each other are too strong for a one-night stand. What we forge here today will bind us both. And the day may yet come when we regret those ties.''

''Never,'' Casey whispered. Standing on tiptoe, she leaned forward and pressed her lips against his. Her kiss was gentle at first; giving, yet demanding nothing in return.

She felt the shudder that ran through him as he struggled to hold himself in check, trying to slow things down. She wanted to give him pleasure, and make him as wild and as hungry for her as she was for him. As she pressed her body up against his, her fingers digging into his shoulders, she could feel the tension in him. His hand shook as he tilted her chin upward.

''Let it be here and now, then, with Mother Earth protecting us,'' he said, his voice ragged.

He undressed her slowly, revealing every inch of her flesh, then branding it with moist, hot kisses that left her too weak to stand.

''Lean on me,'' he said, dropping to his knees before her. He kissed her stomach, and then moved lower until she could scarcely breathe.

She'd never dreamed anything could be so intimate, so powerful. Shudders traveled through her, and when at last he stood, he wiped the tears from her eyes, and held her.

She couldn't speak. No one had ever loved her or held her like this. In his eyes, she was a treasure—precious and adored.

Moving away from her, he stripped off his clothing, allowing her gaze to take him in. His body was hard and ready.

Love filled her heart to aching. When he drew her back into his arms and took her mouth, his kiss was breathtakingly deep. Thinking ceased for her, and only a slow burning remained.

He lowered her gently to the ground, onto a bed made

of their discarded clothing. As the call of a hawk filled the skies, he entered her in one powerful stroke that wrenched a cry from her throat.

"Please, don't stop. Love me just like you promised."

His body was trembling as he took her mouth in another searingly tender kiss. Lights flashed before her in a kaleidoscope of color as feelings more intense than any she'd ever experienced rocked her. She could feel him deep inside her now and knew it was taking all his strength to hold back. Yet, with every second that passed, he was proving how much she meant to him.

"I want this to be special for you—not just a moment of passion that someday you'll forget, along with me," Ashe said, his voice unsteady as he struggled for control.

"It is special. And how could I ever forget you? You're the only man who has ever really touched my heart and soul."

He began moving in a gentle rhythm within her, and as she tilted upward to welcome his thrusts, he groaned like a man who had reached his breaking point. "Don't urge me on like that. I can't hold back if you do."

"I need you, Ashe. Never hold back," she said in a ragged whisper.

Her world became a rainbow of colors as he filled her, then withdrew, only to claim her again. She was a part of him now and as he entered her body, he was a part of her.

"My *sawe*," he murmured. "You're mine."

"Yes, yours," she whispered, surrendering to the magnificent fires sweeping through her.

As her world shattered, she felt him shudder and heard his own cry of triumph. Bathed only in moonlight, she clung to him as they drifted back to a world now gentled by love.

It felt like an eternity later when she opened her eyes.

He nuzzled her neck tenderly. "You gave me a gift beyond measure tonight when you gave yourself to me, my *sawe*."

"What does that word mean?"

"'Sweetheart,'" he whispered.

His gentleness soothed her, but, as he pulled his body away from hers, she suddenly felt desolate and more alone than she'd ever been.

Sensing her thoughts, Ashe drew her close to him. "You can't lose me or what we found here tonight. And no matter what surprises the road ahead of us holds, this night will be a part of us forever."

To Casey, knowing exactly what the road ahead held for them altered the assurance he'd intended to give her.

ASHE WALKED INTO THE tribal police substation alone the following morning. Casey had insisted on going back to her motel shortly before dawn. She'd pulled away from him emotionally, but he wasn't quite sure why. Instinct told him that it had something to do with the secrets she still harbored. What hurt him most was that, even after what they'd shared, she continued to hold back. Those secrets were a terrifying barrier between them.

Ashe looked for Casey, but she hadn't shown up yet at the station. As time passed and she failed to show, he tried to call her on the cell phone but she'd either turned it off, or was in a section of the Rez where communications were impossible. Ashe tried the radio then, but had no better luck.

As the hours passed without word from her, his concern grew. It wasn't like her to disappear like this, but perhaps she'd needed time to herself after last night. There was another possibility, however, and that was what worried him most now. As a law-enforcement officer working a case, it was possible she'd run into a problem. Dangerous situations cropped up when you least expected them.

Ashe called the motel where Casey was staying and was told her sedan was not in the parking area. He considered his options. He could put out an APB on her, but if she wasn't in trouble and was simply out working the case, he could do more harm than good.

He decided to try a different tack. Sometimes a low-profile approach was best. He contacted Officer Nakai on the radio and switched to a private frequency. "You out patrolling your regular area?"

"That's a roger. What do you need?"

"I need to find Agent Feist. Can you keep an eye out for her vehicle?"

"You've got it. Shall I pull a few other units on this, too?"

"Only people you trust. I want this kept under wraps."

"You've got it. My cousin is patrolling another section. I'll get his help."

Ashe was driving past the café near the hotel when his radio crackled to life. He picked up the mike and listened to John Nakai's report.

"I just located her sedan. Do you know those rent-by-the-week apartments south of the old high school? She's there."

"I appreciate this," Ashe said, changing direction for that location.

"Any time."

Ashe sped down the highway, weaving around the few slow-moving vehicles in his way. As he turned and drove up the narrow, paved road that paralleled the river, he caught a glimpse of Casey rounding the corner of the small apartment building.

She didn't appear to be in any kind of trouble. Yet instinct told him something was definitely going on. She would have checked in, otherwise. He parked a hundred yards from the apartment and approached on foot.

As he turned the corner of the building, he saw Casey walking with Fox. Surprise instantly gave way to relief as he realized that Fox was fine and safe at last. He started to call out to them when Fox moved to one side to step around a garden hose on the sidewalk.

Then he saw the gun in Casey's hand as she urged Fox forward. She was hiding the weapon between them, but there was no mistaking what he'd seen. His blood turned to ice and an impenetrable darkness descended over his soul as he faced the extent of Casey's betrayal.

Chapter Thirteen

Ashe crept forward, keeping Fox and Casey in sight. Anger twisted his gut as he remembered the woman he'd made love to only hours ago. He'd given her his heart, his trust. She'd given him her body, but nothing else.

There was no reason he could think of, except one, for Casey to be holding Fox at gunpoint. Casey must have been involved in Fox's kidnapping for reasons of her own. There was a heaviness inside him, as if his very spirit were being weighed down with stones.

The two women ahead of him stopped, and Casey suddenly turned in his direction, scanning the area. Ashe slipped out of sight around the edge of the building. Counting to fifteen, he looked cautiously around the corner again. Both Fox and Casey had disappeared.

Ashe pulled his weapon from its holster and moved forward silently, intent on finding Fox and yet uncertain what would happen next. The possibility that he might have to hurt Casey knifed at his gut. He passed by several rooms that were obviously unoccupied. Then, as he walked to the end apartment facing the parking lot, he caught a glimpse of a shadow inside the room. A figure by the window was holding a gun.

Without hesitation, Ashe kicked the door wide open, then hit the floor and rolled as one shot rang out.

The room was dark. The only light came from the apartment hallway door and from a crack in the window curtains. He moved forward by instinct, half guided by the memory of where he'd seen the figure standing.

As daylight trickled into the room, he saw Casey's outline less than six feet away, her head turned toward the doorway leading to another room. Seizing the moment, he dived forward, tackling and pinning her to the floor.

"Ashe!" Casey yelled up at him in surprise. "What the hell are *you* doing here?"

"I might ask you the same question." Casey struggled to keep her gun firmly in her grasp, though Ashe had her hand pinned to the carpet. "Let go of your pistol."

"No! No way. Not until you tell me why you're here."

"You're not in a position to bargain."

"I'm not in a position to compromise my assignment, either."

"What kind of assignment? I saw you leading Fox down the sidewalk, and you had that gun in your hand." He could feel her softness pressing against him. His body recognized and remembered hers. He bit back a groan. "Don't push this, Casey. Just tell me where Fox is. We'll settle the rest later."

"I can't tell you that. Now let me get up. This is getting us nowhere."

He saw the stubborn gleam in her eyes, and realized that she would not give him the information he needed willingly. He knew then that he had to break through to her somehow.

"You're in way over your head on this, Ashe. Believe me," she said. "You've misread the situation. I'm here to protect Fox, and that's exactly what I intend to do."

"I'm here for her sake, too. I can't let you get up while you're still armed. If you want me to trust you, then you'll have to trust me, too." He saw the hesitancy in her eyes and continued. "I held you in my arms only hours ago. I loved you in every way a man can love a woman. Yet your trust, your loyalty...those were already given to something—or someone—else."

"I'm guilty of nothing—except doing my best to keep Fox safe. Let me go and I can prove it to you."

"Drop the gun," he repeated, his voice a hiss.

"All right." She released her hold on the weapon, and as he moved away, got up slowly. "I'm a U.S. Deputy Marshal. I was sent here to protect Katrina. I had my pistol out and Katrina close to me because I heard a vehicle drive up."

As she started to move her hand toward her jacket, he tensed. "Don't," he warned.

"I'm not reaching for my backup. I'm reaching for my ID—the real one. You've suspected for a while that I wasn't in the FBI, that it was only a cover. You also knew that your captain wouldn't be foolish enough to give me access to his department if I didn't have some solid credentials." She pulled out her ID and silver badge. "I'm telling you the truth now."

"I don't care about *your* kind of truth anymore. I'm sick of playing games. Let me talk to Fox."

She shook her head. "I can't. You're forgetting something. There's a leak somewhere, and it has already resulted in the murder of your foster parents. I want to trust you, but I have questions about you I just can't reconcile. I'm under orders and as the deputy in charge of this case, I'm accountable for everything I do. I'd trust you with my life, Ashe, but this is duty we're talking about, not personal choice."

"You think I'd do something to harm Fox? Is that what you're saying?" He moved away from her. Nothing could have hurt him more. "Don't bother answering that. I'll find her myself."

As he released her and shifted to stand, Casey pulled out her backup pistol and leveled it at him. "Don't do it. I may not have it in me to kill you, but I will shoot you in the leg if I have to, in order to stop you."

He turned around slowly. The loss he felt was devastating. This was the woman he'd loved, the woman he would have given his life for; yet she didn't trust him enough to even let him talk to Fox. Half of him hoped that she would shoot and put an end to the pain tearing at his gut.

"I took an oath to protect any witness under my care. I can't break that just because my heart tells me that you're incapable of harming her."

Ashe walked up to Casey slowly. She wouldn't shoot him. He couldn't have been that wrong about her.

"Ashe, stop."

He stood directly in front of her, grasped the barrel of her pistol and forced it against his chest. "If you want to shoot, do it. It can't hurt me any more than what you've already done."

Casey tried to move her hand back, but he forced it to remain exactly where it was. "Ashe, don't." She moved her finger away from the trigger and relinquished her hold on the weapon. "If you try to go after Fox, I will do my best to stop you. But I don't want to hurt you," she said, her voice an anguished whisper. "Why do you find that impossible to believe? Only hours ago I held you and welcomed you into my body. You know me in a way that no one ever has. You're hurt, I realize that, but how can you think that doing this isn't hurting me just as much?"

"Take me to see Fox. We'll both protect her."

"I can't. As I said, there are questions about your background...." She held his gaze, pleading silently with him to understand.

He returned her backup pistol to her. "What is it that you've found that makes you question my honesty?" He'd given her his heart and she was tearing it apart. "Ask your questions, Casey, and then let me go to Fox."

With a sense of detachment he would never have thought possible, he noted the way tears filled her eyes. He wanted to take satisfaction in knowing that she, too, was in pain, but he could not. He felt empty inside, and very cold.

"You paid cash for that truck of yours," she said, her voice quivering. "That's a huge chunk of your salary. Where did you get that money?"

The veiled accusation was shattering. He knew now that this had been on her mind all along. But, without solid evidence against him, she hadn't been able to get a court order to check out his bank records. Though he wished she had come to him directly, he also knew why she hadn't. A question like that would have placed her at odds not only with him but with his entire department, compromising her ability to work the case on the Rez.

Yet, hearing Casey voice her suspicions about him now, coldly and clearly, asking that he prove his innocence to her, almost destroyed him. Each of Casey's words had sliced through him like a blade. "I paid in cash after saving the money for five lean years," he answered grimly. "I didn't always get a chance to go to the bank, so whatever money I had left at the end of the pay period I set aside. I'd make deposits whenever I could and put the money into a special savings account. The amounts were never large, but they added up. Check it out." He picked up the motel phone, got the number of the bank and dialed. After getting his bank manager and exchanging a few quick instructions, he handed her the phone.

After a few minutes' discussion, she hung up.

"Are you satisfied?" Ashe asked coldly. "If you are, then let's stop wasting time. I'd like to talk to Fox now."

"I'll take you to her," Casey replied.

She went across the apartment and stood by a closed door at the end of the hall. She knocked, identifying herself in a soft voice. An older, but tough-looking Anglo man stood at the door, saw Ashe and immediately reached for a handgun at his waist.

Casey stopped him. "It's okay."

Fox sat in an easy chair away from the windows, leafing through a magazine. The instant she saw Ashe, she stood and ran up to him. Remembering the Navajo custom of not touching, she hesitated, but then, seeing him smile, she followed her heart and hugged him.

Ashe held her for a moment, obviously relieved to have her safe at last. "I'm so glad you're okay." His voice was thick with emotion.

As he released her, Fox smiled and moved away. "I told them you wouldn't give up."

Satisfied she was okay, Ashe nodded to the Anglo man, then turned to Casey for an explanation.

"This is Bobby Hayes, my former supervisor at the U.S. Marshals Service. He's retired, and the only person I knew I could trust to take care of Fox while I was out in the field investigating. Someone compromised Fox's location, and we believe that's why your foster parents were killed. Since we have no idea where the leak is, I couldn't trust anyone inside my department—or in yours. I sent reports to my boss, but even he hasn't been told where we're keeping Katrina."

"I knew you'd be frantic," Katrina said, "and that

Travis would come back and turn the Rez upside down, looking for me. That's why I sneaked away and called you. I tried to let you know that I was okay, and that you didn't have to rescue me or call Travis back here just on my account.''

Ashe smiled at her. ''My brother should be back any time now. He wouldn't let you face this alone.''

''It *will* be nice to see him again,'' Katrina said in a soft, faraway voice. ''But I wish it wasn't under these circumstances.''

''When I realized she'd called you,'' Hayes said, ''I had to move her fast. Casey was under orders not to tell anyone—not even you—about Katrina. Since we had no idea how the killer was getting his information, the simple act of phoning you meant it was possible Katrina's whereabouts had been compromised.''

''I covered our trail every step of the way,'' Casey explained. ''I wore a black wig when we checked into a motel and I always made sure I was never too close to any of the clerks. I gave Fox the wig to wear later, because I knew her blond hair stood out too much here on the Rez. I still don't know how you managed to keep tracking us down.''

Ashe looked at Fox. ''Why are you in the Witness Protection Program?''

''It goes back to something that happened when I was just a kid. I don't really remember very much of it. But it looks like someone doesn't know that.''

Casey looked at Ashe and gestured toward the adjoining room. ''My partner will guard Fox. If we're going to work together, I need to fill you in.''

CASEY LED THE WAY INTO the next room—the bedroom— then closed the door. She knew how badly she'd hurt Ashe, but what was hardest of all to face was the coldness in his eyes. The love she'd seen reflected there only a few hours ago had completely vanished. The knowledge of what she'd lost was like bitter acid eating away at her soul.

"All right," he said in a quiet voice. "Let's hear it."

His tone was so matter-of-fact and impersonal, it wrenched her heart. Casey wanted to touch him, to show him that it wasn't too late, that their feelings were strong enough to overcome anything. Instinctively, she reached for his hand, but he pulled back.

"Don't. What we had is over. You distrusted me both as a man and as a cop. There's nothing left for us to build on."

Her heart was breaking into pieces as she saw the pain that was mirrored in his eyes. Like drops of water, her dreams were slipping through her fingers, leaving her with only an aching sense of loss.

"Tell me about the Marshals Service involvement with Fox," he demanded without emotion.

Casey took a deep breath and forced her voice to stay even. "When Fox was six years old, she was an eyewitness to her parents' murder. Fox gave the police a description of the killer and an artist sketched out a composite, but it was very rough. Then, while the police investigated, Fox was placed in a foster home. Less than a week later, there was an attempt made on her life."

"Even if she was a target, this still doesn't sound like a federal matter."

"There's more. The moment the police ran her parents' names through the computer, we learned what had happened and took over the case. Fox's biological father was in the Witness Security Program. He'd asked for protection after he testified against a group of Russian criminals working in the U.S. He had been in the WITSEC program for six years at the time of the murder."

"His enemies found him despite everything the Marshals Service had done?"

She nodded. "Despite the repeated warnings of his handler, he would play the ponies at the racetrack from time to time. Eventually that led his enemies right to him. When Fox's father and mother were killed, Fox was placed under our care. She was entitled to our protection on two counts— her father had arranged for protection not only for himself, but for his family, and Fox was the only witness to the murder of a federally protected witness."

"So you changed her identity...and my foster father, who was working for the U.S. Attorney's office at the time, must have heard about the case and offered his help. It sounds like something he would have done." Lost in thought, Ashe gazed at an indeterminate spot across the room. "Did Fox ever give you a better description of the killer?"

"No. In fact, after the attempt at the foster home, she was unable to remember anything pertaining to the murders or even the attack on her. As far as she was concerned, she'd always lived a very happy life at the foster home."

"I gather the killer was never caught, but how does this fit with the present? Someone is after her now because of what she saw? But why, after all these years? If Fox was six at the time of the murders, that was fifteen years ago. Why come after her now?"

"I can't answer that. I also can't guarantee that it's got anything to do with what happened in the past."

"Then why are you here?"

"Your foster parents took custody of Fox, moved here to the Rez, and eventually adopted her, but she remained in WITSEC. Both your foster parents had our number. When the gentleman who had been Fox's handler retired, the case became mine. Everything was quiet throughout the years. Then, out of the blue I received a call from your foster mother. She suspected that their house was being watched but she wasn't sure.''

"Why didn't she call the tribal police, or me?''

"Your foster parents did call the tribal police, but they weren't at liberty to divulge the reason they were concerned except to Captain Todacheene. He was the only person here who knew about Fox.''

"So I was right about the file I saw, and you knew about it all along,'' Ashe observed flatly.

Casey nodded, trying to block out the new betrayal and disappointment she saw mirrored on Ashe's face. "The Rez was a perfect hiding place for Fox. There was a downside, though. We couldn't monitor her very easily here, and that meant we needed someone on the inside. Captain Todacheene was our choice. We did a complete background check on him and knew he was clean. He was also in a high enough position to order any action that was necessary if there ever was trouble.''

"So he had extra patrols scheduled in the area of my foster parents' home?''

"No. He checked things out himself. He went out several times and monitored the area. But he never found any evidence that there was anyone watching your foster parents' home or Fox. Your foster father finally dismissed the matter, telling us that it was someone at school playing a prank. Now that I know more, my guess is that he had Patrick Gordon in mind. We let the matter drop at his insistence. To be honest, it just didn't seem likely that anyone had tracked Fox down after all this time.''

"My foster father could be stubborn at times,'' Ashe conceded.

"I didn't just let it drop, though. I actually called your foster mother the day before the murders. I wanted to verify that everything really was okay, and that she was comfortable with the way things had been handled. She told me in no uncertain terms that she didn't think it was a prank. Her fear for Fox's safety was real so I decided to trust her instincts, and came to the Rez to check things out for myself.''

"You arrived the day of the murders?"

She nodded. "I was on my way here when I got an urgent call from your foster mother. She told me someone had followed her and Katrina that morning when they'd gone out shopping together after Fox's first class. She assured me that Fox wasn't at all concerned. To her, it was just coincidence. But your foster mother made a real good point. She told me that a local kid tailing them wouldn't have had the skill to disappear and reappear almost as if by magic.'' Casey paused. ''I was less than a half hour away at that point. Your foster mother said Fox was at the Corral Café, so I made a stop there first, introduced myself, and asked her to come with me."

"And she went," Ashe said. "She would have trusted any badge."

"She never questioned me," Casey admitted. "Although she'd never been told that she was in WITSEC, I think that in her subconscious it was something she'd always known."

"So many secrets and too many deaths," he said softly.

The same quiet strength she'd loved in him, now kept him together, but the pain he felt was etched in his features. Seeing it there, and knowing she'd played a part in breaking his heart, made her ache everywhere.

Ashe went to the door and without looking back, returned to the adjoining room. Casey heard him speak briefly to Fox, then leave. She stood alone by the window, watching as he walked to his vehicle. Today she'd lost the only man she'd ever truly loved. As his carryall faded from her sight, tears spilled down her cheeks.

ASHE DROVE DOWN THE highway, trying to come to terms with everything he'd learned. Fox would be all right with Casey and Hayes for now. What he needed to do was put everything he'd learned into perspective.

He'd always been proud of his ability to control his emotions but, right now, all he felt was the pain of Casey's betrayal. Beneath that, there was nothing—just a cold emptiness. He wasn't sure which was worse.

He gripped the steering wheel so hard that his knuckles began to hurt. He still had a debt to pay for the Johnsons, and there was Fox, who continued to need protection. For that, he'd have to work with Casey but, first, he had to find a way to shut her out of his heart. Only then would his thinking be clear enough to make him an asset to the investigation.

Only one thing was perfectly clear to him now—there was no time for him to nurture the pain she'd caused him. There were other things to attend to. He turned the carryall around and headed back to the motel.

Hearing the cell phone ring, he picked it up, and instantly recognized the voice that came over the unit as D.A. Prescott's. The D.A. wanted an immediate progress report on the case.

Ashe was stalling, trying to find a way to get off the phone without giving the man any information, when he caught sight of a van the same color and model as the one that had tried to run him and Casey down. It was moving slowly up the alley behind the motel where Fox was hidden. A chill ran up his spine as he saw the van stop behind a tree directly in line with Fox's room.

He hung up on Prescott and called Casey as he screeched

to a stop in front of Fox's room. He had a minute or so
lead time, maybe more. If they could get Fox out of there
before the occupants of the van made their move, they'd
have a chance to get away clean.

Casey was near the door, Hayes at her side, shielding
Fox, as they urged her to his carryall.

Suddenly the olive green van emerged from behind the
tree and sped across the parking lot. As it closed in, someone inside the vehicle opened fire.

Casey pushed Fox to the ground and shielded her with
her body. Bullets peppered the wall above them as Ashe
and Hayes returned fire. The van made a sharp turn away,
then pulled around in a tight circle.

''Get them back inside the room!'' Hayes shouted to
Ashe.

Ashe pushed Fox and Casey through the doorway. He
turned to give Hayes cover fire but, at that moment, two
bullets slammed into the man's chest, hurling him backward.

As Hayes crumpled to the ground, Ashe and Casey del-
uged the front of the van with bullets, shattering the windshield. Their accurate return fire saved them for the moment; the van sped away in a shower of dust and gravel.

Chapter Fourteen

Ashe fired two more shots in rapid succession at the fleeing van as Casey ran over to where Hayes had gone down.

"You better have worn a vest, you stubborn old coot," she muttered in a strangled voice.

Hayes's eyes blinked open as Casey hurriedly unbuttoned his shirt. "Easy there, will ya? Vest or not, it feels like I got kicked by a mule."

Casey stared at the two slugs embedded in the synthetic fabric of the vest and smiled. "You'll live, but you may have a cracked rib or two."

"Man, what did they use? It feels like they almost penetrated the vest."

"They nearly did," Ashe said, studying the rounds. "They're fully jacketed nine-millimeter slugs, probably a real high-velocity load. At point-blank range, they might have done the job."

Casey gave Hayes a hand up. "We've got to get out of here *now*. They obviously know where we are, and they're still after Fox."

"No one followed Katrina and me here," Hayes said firmly. "I made darned sure of that."

"They didn't follow me, either," Ashe said.

"Just because we didn't spot a tail doesn't mean one of

us didn't have one," Casey warned. "We don't have a lot of people assigned to covering our movements, in case you haven't noticed. Or maybe management here was paid to tip off the killers, or a patrol car saw our vehicles."

"Nakai spotted your sedan. That's how I found you. But there's another possibility. Somebody might be monitoring police-radio traffic. We should start being very careful what we say over the air."

"And we have to keep Nakai out of the loop at all costs," Casey added.

"All right. But, for the record, you're barking up the wrong tree," Ashe insisted. "He's clean. I'd stake my life on it."

Ashe's faith in Officer Nakai was admirable, but years of working in the U.S. Marshals' office had shown Casey that human nature wasn't always predictable. Some of their own people had sold out in the past, and might be doing so now.

Casey turned to Katrina and Hayes. "Get your things. We're leaving here right now."

"Where to?" Hayes asked.

"Good question. I'm not really sure. I'm thinking that maybe we should leave the Reservation."

"No. Bad idea," Ashe said. "If something happens that absolutely requires fast backup without relying on either your department or mine, I can get that for us here, guaranteed. We can't count on the same thing outside the Rez."

"All right, but the problem is that it doesn't leave many motels to choose from if somebody is checking them out."

"We'll find a place," Ashe said. "But first let's check our vehicles for tracking devices. I don't think it's likely, but it won't hurt to look." A loud squeal reverberated from his handheld radio, which lay on the sidewalk where it had fallen during the shooting. He picked it up quickly.

"Be careful what you report. We've got to secure a new hiding place quickly, and it's imperative that no one know where Fox is," Casey said.

He nodded in agreement as Prescott's voice came over the radio clearly.

"What the heck do you think you're doing hanging up on me? What's going on out there? You're not answering your cell phone. I had to resort to the radio just to get hold of you."

Ashe glanced toward his carryall, where the cell phone still rested on the seat where he'd tossed it after the warning call to Casey. "A kid cut me off on the highway, and I had to drop the phone and keep both hands on the wheel to avoid an accident. Then I tracked him down and pulled him over. Sorry about the delay, but I have nothing new to report. As soon as I do, I'll be in contact. Ten-four?"

"Yeah," came the reply. "Ten-four."

Casey went outside with Ashe and, together, while Hayes kept watch from the doorway, they checked the carryall and the two sedans for tracking devices, but found none.

"We're clear," Casey said, noticing a few people standing at their windows and watching them. "Time for us to get going before more officers arrive."

As they went back into the room to get Hayes and Katrina, Casey fell into step beside Ashe. "We can't have this wall of animosity between us and still work well together. Let's settle this."

"It *is* settled. We'll do our jobs. We're both professionals. Our personal feelings don't figure into the equation— not anymore."

"If you can turn off your feelings that easily, then I'm not sure you ever understood love nearly as much as you said you did," Casey replied, hoping to force a reaction out of him. Anything was better than this coldness.

Ashe stopped in mid-stride and faced her. He started to say something, then turned away and continued into the room.

Her heart skipped a beat. It wasn't over. There was still a chance that hope would not be a cheat. For a brief instant, just beyond the pain mirrored in his eyes, she'd seen the shadow of love.

KATRINA MET ASHE the moment he entered the room. "I know where we can go. It's a place only Travis and you would know how to find. Remember the lodge?"

Ashe nodded and smiled slowly. The cabin west of Rock Ridge had been their favorite camping spot for years, and he'd looked there for Katrina the day of the murders.

"Do you think you can remember how to get there?" he asked her.

"Count on it."

He smiled, remembering that day at the lodge when he'd seen Travis kiss her. He still remembered teasing his brother about it—and taking a solid punch in the jaw for his trouble. Travis had never had much of a sense of humor when it came to Katrina.

"It'll take some expert driving to get there in a sedan," Ashe told Casey, "but you and Hayes can make it with Fox showing you the way."

"Tell me more about this place," Casey pressed as they hurried Katrina to Hayes's car.

"It's an old log cabin that my real father built. It was mine and Travis's special getaway place, but we shared it with our foster family after they agreed never to reveal where it was."

"Sounds perfect. I'll hang back in my car and make sure you're not followed," Casey told Hayes. "If anyone tries, I'll head them off."

"I'll be nearby, too, in case backup's needed," Ashe said. "I'll take a parallel road that cuts across some high ground. I'll make sure the way in front of you is clear."

Once the others were under way, Ashe drove off in his carryall. He hadn't gone far when his cell phone rang.

"Hey, little brother. I'm almost home." Travis's voice was clear and distinct. "I'll be there in another hour or two. You handling everything okay?"

Travis's question made him feel like the kid he'd once been—never quite sure of himself, and always wanting to be more like his older brother. He pushed back the feeling, annoyed with himself. "I found Fox. There was another attempt made on her life, but we took care of the situation."

Travis spat out a vicious oath. "Little Fox wasn't hurt?"

"No, I told you, the situation is under control. But we've still got a fight on our hands. Nothing's solved yet."

"I'm not far away. When I get there, we'll track down whoever's after her. It's time to end this."

"Leave this to me. I'm a cop. I want these guys, but in a way that will stand up in court."

"I don't think I can play it your way—not totally, anyway," Travis said. "But I'll try. Where can I find her?"

"You can't at the moment. Go to my place instead. We'll talk there."

"If you think for one second you're going to keep me from seeing her—"

"Just do it." Ashe hung up on his brother, then smiled slowly. Travis had to be reminded that his kid brother didn't take orders from him—and hadn't for a very long time.

ASHE WATCHED FOX AND Hayes's car on the road below. Casey was hanging back, covering their rear. She was good at her job—he had to give her that. A knife-edged loss sliced through him as he thought of her and what they'd shared. He still loved her and, like his brother, he was a one-woman man. When a Redhawk gave his heart, there was no turning back. But he wasn't sure he'd ever be able to forget that she hadn't really trusted him. He understood her dedication to her job, but the fact remained that, in her heart, she hadn't been sure enough of him to disobey orders and let her intuition lead her.

He shook his head. There was no time to figure this out now.

Once assured that Fox and her guardians were safe at the lodge, Ashe radioed Casey that he'd be along later, then turned and headed home. It was time to face his brother.

It was dark when he pulled up to his trailer and parked. Travis was standing there in his uniform, his feet braced and his jaw set. Ashe could tell he was just itching to run into someone with fists flying.

"Hey, brother," Ashe greeted, getting out of the carryall. "I hope you haven't been waiting out here for long."

"No problem. I picked the lock an hour ago and helped myself to a cold one from the fridge. Where's Little Fox?"

"It's good to see you, too," Ashe said, going to the door and flipping on the outside light. He studied the doorknob. There was a hole where the lock had been. He saw the lock resting on the bookcase inside the trailer. "The skills you pick up in the army could get you arrested now that you're back home. How did you do that?"

"Military secret," Travis answered coolly. "Where's Little Fox?"

Ashe looked at his brother, gauging his mood accurately. Travis wasn't interested in conversation. He wanted to know everything that was going on, and now.

Ashe deliberately kept his expression neutral. A few years ago Travis had tried to get answers out of him—

answers he hadn't been prepared to give. They'd ended up really getting into it, though, as usual, neither of them had come out with anything more serious than a few ugly bruises. Ashe unhooked the handheld radio from his belt and placed it on the top step. He did the same with his pistol and holster. Both of them knew what was coming.

"Still the contemplative one, little brother?" Travis hissed, taking off his jacket. "Let's stop dancing. Tell me where Little Fox is, and you can keep your face out of the dirt."

"She's safe, and in hiding. I can't take you to her right now without placing her in danger again. Someone is still out to kill her. Don't try to force the issue."

"Since I intend to find out where she is, I'll just have to convince you to change your mind." Ashe saw the flash of movement, and rolled his head back as Travis faked a left jab. He knew a right was coming instead. Travis was a skilled fighter, but Ashe had a few good moves of his own. As Travis's fist struck air instead of cheekbone, Ashe blocked his brother's arm up and drove a hard right into Travis's breadbasket.

It felt as if he'd punched a brick wall. Travis's stomach muscles were rock hard. It wouldn't be easy. "This will get you nowhere," Ashe growled, exchanging blocked jabs with his brother. They'd sparred so many times before, it was difficult for either to score with a solid punch.

"We'll see, won't we?" Travis slipped past Ashe's counterpunch, and then, grabbing his arm, threw his brother to the ground, flat on his back.

Ashe sprang up just as Travis reached for him again and grabbed Travis's sleeve in a judo move he knew his brother wouldn't expect. Falling back, Ashe threw Travis into the air. Travis hit hard, but rolled up to a fighting stance.

"You've learned a few things while I've been away, little brother."

"You haven't," Ashe retorted.

They continued to spar, both pressing unsuccessful attacks and striking only glancing blows until they were both too tired to keep moving. At long last, Ashe leaned back against the side of the trailer, trying to catch his breath, and wondering if the bruises to his arms from blocked jabs would be hurting for the rest of the week.

Travis stood with his hands on his knees, taking deep breaths as he wiped away a drop of blood from the corner of his mouth. "I'm not giving up until I get better answers," he said, advancing toward Ashe once more.

"Don't you get it?" Ashe demanded, once again on his back on the ground from a lightning-quick throw. "We're too evenly matched in a clean fight. You can't take me any more than I can take you."

Travis was on one knee, having gone down, as well. "Yeah, but it still felt good to go a few rounds."

Travis stood slowly and offered Ashe a hand up. "We need to work together, little brother." This time his voice held more emotion. "We've lost our parents again, and now it's Little Fox's life we're talking about. We can't let anyone stand against us and succeed."

Ashe nodded. "We're getting close to the killer—I can feel it. I can't prove it, but I think he's connected to Fox's past." Ashe filled his brother in quickly about the Witness Protection Program tie-in. "Casey has done her best to keep Fox safe. She's a good agent," he admitted, wondering why it hurt so much to say that.

Travis gave his brother a long, speculative look. "Well, I'll be. I never thought I'd see the day. Can I assume that your interest in this Casey is more than just professional?"

"What makes you say that?" he challenged, neither confirming nor denying his brother's guess.

"Your voice changes when you talk about her. It gets softer...almost mushy," Travis added with a grin that went crooked as the cut on his lip cracked open again. "That, and your reaction to my comment."

Ashe shot his brother an icy look. "I think you've been standing too close to the artillery and your brain's scrambled."

"Yeah, yeah, but I'm right and you know it."

Ashe shrugged as if dismissing the matter. "The way I feel about her is irrelevant. We have no future together."

"Okay, but if you ever want to talk about it, I'll listen." He rubbed his neck with one hand. "Now quit wasting my time and tell me where they're keeping Little Fox. From what you said, I gather you basically have one retired agent watching over her while they're holed up in the middle of nowhere. The other, younger one is working with you on the murder investigation. That's a good tactic in one way, and a lousy one in another. If the bad guys manage to find the place and strike at a time when the guy's asleep, he might get caught off guard completely. There's no possibility of immediate backup, either."

"And you're offering your services as a second guard, I assume?"

"Yeah, and my training can be an asset. I can make sure no one can get close to their hiding place, if they're stupid enough to try."

Ashe saw the determination in his brother's face and nodded. "I agree with you. You would be an asset, and I think Fox would like you to be there, too. It can't be easy for her to trust her life to a virtual stranger when someone keeps trying to kill her."

"Take me to her now, then."

"I'll need to clear it with Casey first." Ashe was about to do just that when a call came over his handheld radio. He picked it up from the trailer step and answered it quickly, recognizing his captain's voice.

"I want you at the station *now*," Todacheene ordered. "I have two motel employees that swear you were part of a shootout just a few hours ago. I want a full report from you immediately, including the reasons why you didn't call in for backup or file a report."

"On my way, Captain." Ashe rehooked the handheld to his belt and glanced at his brother as he picked up his weapon and holster. "This shouldn't take long. I've got nothing to tell them, especially related to Fox or her location. I'll be back in an hour, and then I'll make arrangements to take you to see Fox and introduce you to the man who's guarding her. Meanwhile, you could put my lock back on, to kill time."

Ashe arrived at the station a short while later. His knuckles were scuffed, his clothes were wrinkled and dusty, and one side of his mouth felt swollen. Had there been time, he would have showered before coming in, but experience had warned him not to make the captain wait a second longer than was necessary.

Ashe had just entered the squad room when Todacheene bellowed out his name. None of the other officers present even glanced up. When no one looked at you, big trouble lay ahead.

As he entered the captain's office, he saw Casey and Prescott already seated there. Casey's expression was set. Making a quick guess, he figured that Prescott had been trying to press her for information and had not been successful. The anger on Prescott's face supported that theory.

The captain sat in his chair, looking as friendly as one of the rock giants on Easter Island. "About time you got here, Detective. Did you know that Patrick Gordon escaped from the mental-health center lockup this morning?''

"No, I didn't. Any idea where he's gone?'' Ashe wondered if Gordon had been the one in the van today. He certainly had produced a weapon before, and was dangerously unstable.

"I was hoping *you* might know. It's time for you to start explaining what you've been up to. My patience has been stretched to the limit.'' Todacheene glanced out the window, then stood and edged closer to the glass, studying something outside. "Is that a bullet hole in your department vehicle?''

"Probably,'' Ashe replied.

"I suppose you'll tell me that it happened when you pulled over that kid for cutting in front of you,'' Prescott interjected.

"Actually, sir, I wasn't planning to tell you anything at all unless my captain instructed me to,'' Ashe said affably. "You don't sign my paycheck.'' He started to sit down, but the captain stopped him with one look.

"Don't even think of getting comfortable. Stand there until I tell you differently.''

Todacheene fixed Ashe with a glare that would have made most people flinch. Ashe stood a little straighter. "I got a call this afternoon from a terrified desk clerk reporting a gun battle at the Prairie Dog Apartments. You were recognized and identified, along with your police unit,'' he said, looking at Ashe. He shifted his gaze and stared at Casey. "So were you, Agent Feist. Now, the owners of the place are holding us accountable for the damages to their property.'' He glared at Ashe. "I want a full explanation, and I want it now.''

Ashe stared in silence at the decorative wall clock behind the captain.

"Sir," Casey said, "Detective Redhawk was assisting me on a federal matter."

"That kind of explanation is not sufficient, Agent Feist. And I'd appreciate it if you'd remain silent. I was speaking to my detective."

Anger flared in Casey's hazel eyes, but she remained quiet.

"Well?" Captain Todacheene stared at Ashe, eyebrows raised. "Are you going to talk or do I ask for your shield? You still answer to me, Detective."

"Captain," Casey started again. "If you'd let me—"

"Quiet." Todacheene's voice was as sharp as the crack of a whip. His gaze settled on Ashe. "You look slovenly, and that's a disgrace to this department. Do you honestly think you're above meeting our standards? And what on earth made you think I'd let you turn the county into a war zone?"

"It wasn't our intent to become involved in an armed confrontation," Casey interrupted. "We were protecting a civilian connected with the case we've been working."

"Who? Who were you protecting?" Prescott demanded.

Captain Todacheene glared at Casey, then got up and walked toward Prescott, until he stood only inches from the other man. "*I'm* interviewing one of *my* people. I don't want to hear one more word from anyone else in this room, including you, Counselor." He turned to face Ashe. "Spill it. I'm tired of waiting."

Ashe spoke. "Captain, we were protecting Fox. Someone tried to shoot her, and we did what was necessary to defend her."

"You *found* her?" He looked at Casey who, this time, remained silent.

Prescott looked at Ashe, then at the captain. "Wait one minute! You found the only possible witness to a double homicide, and you didn't notify my office? I want to talk to her right now."

Casey pulled out her Deputy Marshal's star. "Mr. Prescott, I was sent here on a special undercover assignment. I'm from the U.S. Marshals Service, not the Bureau," she said. "And Captain Todacheene has been cooperating from the beginning by protecting my cover. I'm sorry, but I can't let you have access to Katrina Johnson at this time. Ms. Johnson is under my protection and is safe, but her life is still being threatened. Until I'm able to find and apprehend the criminal or criminals responsible for killing the Johnsons and attacking Katrina, her whereabouts will remain a secret, even from your office."

"I'm the district attorney in this county. I'll be prosecuting those responsible, if they are ever arrested. Who has more of a right to know this witness's whereabouts than I do?"

"The only people who have such a 'right' are myself and the individuals guarding her," Casey said simply.

"You cannot withhold this information, Deputy Marshal Feist. I won't put up with this high-handed attitude. I'll take this to your superiors if I have to."

"Feel free. The number is in the phone book," Casey answered calmly.

Prescott turned to glare at Ashe, venom in his eyes. "You out-and-out lied to me."

"I did what was necessary to protect a life," Ashe replied.

"All right, that's enough," Todacheene snapped. "You're facing all kinds of disciplinary action, Detective Redhawk, and I can take your shield, as well. You owe me a full explanation, and I intend to get one. I already have the necessary clearance, and I will not allow you to continue to circumvent the regulations of this department."

"That is not my intent, Captain. I've already seen how far the men after Fox are willing to push this. It looks like they killed my foster parents trying to get to her. I believe it's in everyone's best interests if I keep quiet about Fox's location."

Prescott stood and faced Todacheene. "Take his badge, Captain. I'll make sure he never gets it back."

"I told *you* not to interfere," Todacheene growled. "This is in my hands now. I'll contact you when there is something new to report."

Prescott stared at the captain for a moment, clenched his fists, then wordlessly spun around and stormed out of the office. Todacheene expelled his breath in a hiss, then regarded the two people before him. Moments ticked by, but no one broke the silence.

"Deputy Feist," he said at last, "you were supposed to work *with* this department, not just one officer. But I do understand. We still have no idea who the leak is, or in which department he's operating—yours or mine."

"That's precisely why I can't give out any more information—not with the life of the witness I'm sworn to protect hanging in the balance," Casey said. "My supervisor and a handpicked team are searching within the U.S. Marshals Service for a leak there. It's part of my job to search for a leak here. What I'd like to do next is see if anyone at this facility has had any suspicious contacts recently. To do that, I need to study the station's phone logs for the past few months. They may help me pinpoint the individual who's been passing information."

"Only police emergency calls are logged in any great detail. The ones that come through the switchboard are simply listed according to name of caller and recipient. Checking them all will entail going through several dozen logbooks," Todacheene warned.

"I'd still like to go ahead," Casey said.

"Okay. Get started. But no holding back—not on this. Clear? I want whatever you find as soon as you have it, regardless of the direction it leads. Nobody should be considered clean without proof, including the detective and myself."

"I agree," Casey answered. "In the meantime, I hope you have officers out looking for Patrick Gordon."

Todacheene nodded. "The whole county, including the Farmington police. We'll find him."

Fifteen minutes later Casey and Ashe were closeted in the cramped records room. The table in the center was just large enough to hold the notebooks representing the past two months of daily phone logs.

Nonemergency incoming calls to the Navajo police were identified only by the telephone number of the caller. She handed Ashe the list of phone numbers she'd made. "Those are all our regional office numbers and the home numbers of our employees. Let me know if any of those numbers, or numbers from those area codes show up as incoming calls prior to two weeks ago. Also, if *any* number you see listed catches your eye for any reason, tell me about it."

Ashe stared at the stacks of papers in front of him. "This is going to take a while, and I've got an impatient brother waiting." He told her about Travis's arrival.

"I'll need to talk to him before deciding if he can join our team."

"He won't take no for an answer."

"That seems to be a trait in your family," Casey replied, with a trace of a smile.

Ashe gazed at her for a moment, noting how tired she looked. His heart twisted. He wanted to draw her into his arms, to love her, to hear her cry out his name as she'd done yesterday—a lifetime ago. But so much had happened since then. Casey wasn't the woman he'd held then. He wondered how she had been able to fool him for so long. He still couldn't understand her reluctance to trust a man she'd given herself to so completely. She could have found a way to tell him Fox was safe without compromising herself. Yet she'd held back.

Slowly an explanation came to him, giving him the answers that had eluded him until now. But instead of relief, it filled him only with pain. Casey had held back something far more precious than information; she'd kept her heart protected by barriers he'd never really surmounted.

"You look as if you've lost your best friend," she said, her voice a tortured whisper.

"I have." Ashe tore his gaze from hers, opened the first logbook and began to work.

He called his trailer and spoke to Travis, assuring his brother he would be back soon. He knew Travis was impatient, and he didn't want him setting out to search on his own.

"I recognize this telephone number," Casey said, pointing to an entry in Captain Todacheene's log. "This call came from the Marshals Service office in Phoenix. I worked there for a while. The entry indicates a call came in three months ago. That substantially precedes my active involvement in this case."

"Phoenix again. That's where my foster father worked as a P.I. many, many years ago."

"That was fifteen years ago. I don't think your foster father's past has anything to do with this call."

Ashe stood behind Casey, looking over her shoulder. "Does anyone call periodically to check on protected witnesses?"

"Yes, but they'd call the witness or her guardians, never

an outside third party—not unless there was a full-scale emergency that required police involvement."

"Let's go talk to the captain and see what he remembers about that call."

"And why he didn't bother mentioning it to either of us before," Casey added pointedly.

A few minutes later, Casey stood in front of Toda-cheene's desk and placed the phone log before him. "Do you remember speaking to someone from the Marshals Service office on that date?"

The captain leaned back and rubbed his jaw. "I remember getting a strange call about that time, now that you mention it. But the call was a very short one, certainly nothing earth-shattering. A deputy named James called me and asked if our case file on Katrina was still secure. I was told they'd had an unauthorized access into their computer system, so they were checking to see if anyone had made inquiries relating to individuals under their protection."

"It sounds like a fishing expedition to me," Ashe said, glancing over at Casey.

"Maybe. First, let me find out who James is. Then we'll know more. The name's not familiar to me, but that doesn't mean anything. We have a lot of people."

Ashe's gaze remained on Casey as she stepped out of the room.

"Be careful, Detective," the captain said, interrupting his thoughts.

Ashe glanced back at him. "Excuse me?"

"You know what I mean. Most *bilagáana* women, white women, don't stay too long on the Reservation. This place fascinates them in the beginning, but then the novelty wears off and they return to their own world."

"Thanks for the advice, but there's nothing going on between the Deputy Marshal and me," Ashe said.

As they waited for Casey to return, Ashe's thoughts remained on her. The truth was inescapable now. He knew without a doubt that Casey's first allegiance had been to her job, not to the feelings they'd shared. He could understand that to a point, but what had devastated him went deeper than the actions her job had demanded.

At first he just hadn't been able to figure out how she could have kept information from him so easily, even though she'd known how Fox's disappearance had affected him. There should have been signs, nonverbal ones, that would have told him more. But the more he saw her at work, the more he understood. Casey had kept a part of her heart out of his reach, depending on herself and her job, focusing on those as the only permanent fixtures she could count on. She'd expected things to fall apart between them sooner or later, and that knowledge had kept her behind a barrier he could never completely cross.

As Casey walked back into the room, his gut tightened. She wasn't lost to him; she'd never been his to lose.

"I've got bad news," she said. "There is no employee named James—not in the Phoenix office or in any other section of our organization. There are two Jamesons though. One is female."

The captain shook his head. "It was U.S. Deputy Marshal James—a man. I'm sure of it."

"Well, that settles it. We now know how they discovered Fox was hiding in this jurisdiction," Casey said. "All he had to do then was come to this community and start nosing around."

"Are you saying I'm the leak?" the captain challenged.

"Yes, I'm afraid so."

"If that's the MO he used, he must have made a lot of phone calls," Todacheene said.

"Possibly, or he might have followed a hunch, or a lead

provided by someone else. Either way, we're not left empty-handed. We now know that there's a Phoenix connection, if only via a phone," Ashe said.

"It makes sense, considering her background," Casey observed.

"This time I really have to insist on seeing Katrina's file," Ashe said flatly. "As a cop working on this case, I need to acquaint myself with every bit of her past history."

Todacheene nodded to Casey. "He's right. You can't expect him to be much of an asset to the investigation if he only knows bits and pieces of the story."

Casey looked at Ashe. "You have a need to know, but I'd like you to see the comprehensive file that was made available to me. A lot of her father's background, however, is classified. And none of the men he testified against are in this area. My office checked that already."

"I think it's time for us to try and jog Fox's memory. She holds the key."

"We've tried, but even hypnosis won't work."

"Maybe talking to someone who cares for her instead of a stranger will help her find the answers we need," Ashe said, thinking of Travis. Ashe had no doubt Fox would do just about anything for his brother.

"Let's talk to Fox again before making any decisions," Casey suggested.

"It might be a good idea to take Travis over to see her now," Ashe said.

"Okay, we'll stop at your place and I'll talk to him there."

"Fair enough."

They drove to Ashe's trailer but, by the time they'd arrived, Ashe's truck was gone, and so was Travis.

Chapter Fifteen

Casey searched around for signs of Travis, but the place was clearly deserted. Ashe went to where his pickup was usually parked and, as he crouched to study the tracks, she saw the anger on his face.

"What's going on?" she asked.

"My guess is that my brother ran out of patience and decided to go looking for Fox himself. He knows where I like to hide my spare key. I usually put it in a magnet holder inside the back bumper, near the license plate. He obviously found the key, and drove off in my truck." Ashe gestured at the rental sedan parked off to one side. "He knew that shiny new thing wouldn't get far on some of our roads."

"Your brother sounds like a loose cannon. Not exactly what we need on this case. Tell me this—does he have enough information to actually find her?"

Ashe considered it. "He's extremely resourceful. My best guess is that he'll figure it out, based on the little I *did* tell him. He knows it's a place I consider safe, and that it's in the middle of nowhere. Sooner or later he'll show up at the lodge. That was one of the first places I looked."

"I'll call Hayes and warn him." Casey used her cell phone and managed to communicate with the retired marshal, though the connection was extremely poor. "He'll handle it, but he won't let anyone get near Fox until she or you can confirm his identity."

"I should warn you that nothing stops my brother. It was always that way, but it's even more so now that he's an Army Ranger. I just hope no one gets hurt before the ID is made."

They were on their way toward the lodge in Ashe's carryall when a call came over the radio. Switching to a tactical channel, Ashe connected with Officer John Nakai, remembering to be careful what he said.

"What's going on?" Nakai asked. "I ran into Travis not fifteen minutes ago, and he's ready to kick some butt. He's been asking everyone if they've seen you hanging around anyplace in particular recently."

"Where was he last time you saw him?"

"Racing out of the Waterflow Café, heading north in your new truck. He was talking to Selma there when, according to her, he just dropped some bills on the table and ran out."

"What were they talking about?"

"The year the football team won the district title."

Ashe swore under his breath. "Thanks. I owe you one."

Casey looked at Ashe, her expression guarded. "What's going on? You think he figured out where we're hiding Fox?"

"I'd bet on it." Ashe expelled his breath in a hiss. "The year the football team won district, our family went up to the lodge for Thanksgiving. It was a special time for all of us."

They took a shortcut across country, which also served to throw off a potential tail. The terrain was rugged and the ride extremely rough. As she watched the way Ashe gripped the wheel, she remembered the tenderness of his hands and the way he'd caressed her intimately, igniting fires all through her. Casey drew in a ragged breath.

"You okay?" His tone was strictly business.

Loss settled over her spirit like a suffocating shroud. She'd always been a fighter, but she was just beginning to understand that some things just couldn't be forced. It was up to Ashe. If he chose, he could allow his heart to open to her again.

Everything was quiet as they reached the lodge an hour later. "Maybe I overestimated him," Ashe said. "My brother may not have put it together after all."

Casey listened carefully. "It's peaceful out here."

Ashe parked fifty yards away from the lodge in a wooded area, then waited, attuning himself to his surroundings. "It's too quiet. Something's wrong. I can feel it."

"Let's go inside, then."

Ashe hurried toward the house. They were in no danger from Travis or Hayes, if they were recognized. The only danger was to Travis himself if Hayes reacted before Katrina could ID him.

"It's always been like this between my brother and me," Ashe muttered. "When we were kids, he'd go out looking for trouble, no matter how hard I tried to stop him. I'd swear I wouldn't back him up, but he always knew that I'd be there anyway."

Casey chuckled softly. "He had you pegged."

"Yeah. But, you know, he was always there for me, too. He wouldn't fight my fights for me, but he was always around to make sure the odds stayed even."

As they drew close to the lodge, Ashe grew quiet. They could hear two people speaking softly, and he recognized both voices.

"Travis is already inside. I just heard him."

As they emerged from the stand of pines that gave them

cover, Ashe saw Hayes at the door, watching. He waved them in.

Ashe glared at his brother as he approached the door. ''You couldn't cool your jets for a little longer, could you?''

''I came a long way to see Little Fox and you were late getting back. I saw no reason to waste any more time waiting for you. Oh, and by the way, that's a nice truck, but it might have gotten a little scratched up when I took the arroyo to get here.''

''You came up that little canyon?'' Ashe asked, trying not to wince. ''It's always filled with brush.''

''It was the only way I could approach unseen. Besides, trucks like that are made for tough roads.''

''There is no road there, you jerk.'' Ashe took a step toward his brother, then stopped and looked over at Casey. ''Feel free to shoot him,'' he said, and stepped into the room.

''Let me talk to him first.'' Casey motioned for Travis to follow her outside.

It was difficult for Ashe to keep Katrina calm while Travis and Casey negotiated on the extent that Travis could be involved.

''It's okay, Fox,'' Ashe said gently. ''You know my brother. He'll find a way to get assigned to you. But let him work for it. He needs his self-confidence turned down a few clicks.''

Katrina laughed. ''It's just like old times. You two were always either fighting, or teaming up to fight someone else.'' She looked around her then, as her gaze settled on Hayes who still was wearing the shirt punctured by bullets meant for her, and she sighed. ''Well, not quite like old times.''

"You'll be okay. You know that we won't let anyone hurt you."

"I know you'll do your best to protect me, but I'm as worried about you and Travis as I am about myself."

"We can take care of ourselves."

Before she could reply, Travis came inside, accompanied by Hayes.

"Agent Feist may have agreed to let you take part in this case," Hayes grumbled, "but, as far as I'm concerned, you're the last thing we need."

"Funny thing. From what I've heard, it seems you haven't done real well on your own so far," Travis retorted.

"Cut it out!" Casey snapped, then glared at Travis. "Hayes has been working his behind off to keep Katrina safe. He's already stopped two bullets meant for her with his own body. You just got here, Travis. Do us all a favor, show a little respect."

Travis looked at Ashe, who simply nodded. Slowly the cockiness faded from Travis's expression, and he gave Hayes the once-over, his gaze taking in the bullet-ridden shirt. "I thought you were just a sloppy dresser, like Ashe. I suppose I owe you more than an apology and a handshake, don't I, Hayes?"

"I was just doing my job. Did you earn that Ranger patch? I could use somebody with those skills to provide security to spell me. Think you're up to it, hotshot?" Hayes smiled for the first time that evening, and offered to shake hands.

Travis took Hayes's grip with a firm shake, something Ashe might have avoided. "What do *you* think?"

Travis turned and gave Katrina a cocky grin. "Hey, Little Fox. I'm going to be here with you from now on. You've got nothing to worry about."

Ashe saw Katrina roll her eyes. Yet, no matter how hard

she tried to hide it, he knew she was crazy about Travis. He felt a twinge of jealousy, knowing Casey would never feel the same way about him.

Hayes's cell phone rang and, after a moment, he motioned for Casey to step out of the room with him. When Casey returned, she looked somber.

"The D.A. has been in contact with my supervisor and his boss, the U.S. Marshal for New Mexico. They've all been called on the carpet for this operation. I've been given three days to neutralize the threat to Fox or they're pulling me off the case."

"Does that mean they'll send someone else to take over?" Ashe asked.

"That's what Prescott wanted, but he'll get more than he bargained for, I'm sure. Someone else will take over the investigation, but they'll also give Fox another handler and relocate her again."

"I met Prescott a few weeks ago when I went to a political rally with Mom and Dad," Fox said. "I didn't like him then and I certainly don't now." She shot each of them an icy look. "I've got news for him and all of you. I'm not going anywhere. I'm through running," she stated flatly. "I'm not a child anymore. Whatever happens, I'll face it here."

"You can't," Travis said softly. "If you do, they'll pull their protection and you'll be an easy target for the killers." He looked at Casey. "Isn't that how it works?"

Casey nodded. "Either you play it our way, or you lose our protection."

"Then we'd better come up with something fast." Fox looked directly at Travis. "My life is here. I won't go."

"We have three days. Let's use every second of it," Ashe said.

As Casey moved away to speak to Hayes, Ashe watched

her. She worked well with the retired marshal. There was an understanding between them that was rooted in mutual respect. Ashe had wanted that and so much more for himself and Casey, but it hadn't been in the cards, and now they had all but run out of time.

As Casey turned to look in his direction, their eyes met. Desire twisted through him, hard and fast.

"Hey, little brother," Travis said, approaching quietly. "Seems to me you have unfinished personal business."

"That's all said and done. It's time to move on. But how about you?" He glanced over to where Katrina sat, then looked back at Travis. "Don't you think it's time you stopped calling her 'Little Fox'? She's a woman now, not a kid." Ashe gave his brother a knowing smile. "And that scares you, doesn't it? The rules between you are changing."

Casey came over to where the brothers were standing before Travis could respond. "So far, the killers have had us on the run. Now that we're under deadline, we're going to have to start putting some serious pressure on our suspects."

"Well, now that there are two of us here guarding Fox," Travis said, "you'll both be free to concentrate exclusively on the investigation. I can guarantee you that no one will get to her with us here on the job."

"I'll second that," Hayes said, handing Travis his backup weapon and an extra clip of ammo.

"What we need to do is start rattling our suspects— everyone from Captain Todacheene on down," Casey said. "But, first, I've got to figure out a good strategy. Cops don't rattle easily."

"You know that high-handed attitude federal agents are known for?" Ashe said with a trace of a grin. "Use it for all it's worth. If we make enough waves, there's no telling what will come to the surface.''

ASHE MET CASEY AT HER motel the following morning, then took her to the station in his carryall.

''I'm going to start by requesting access to all the local law-enforcement and prosecutor's-office personnel records,'' Casey said. ''That's bound to make people hostile. The downside is that we'll have to search through those records ourselves, and in a hurry. There's no one else we can trust to handle it. I want to check out all our key players for possible motives, intent and opportunity.''

As Ashe captured her gaze, Casey's heart constricted. He obviously still cared for her. A sweet, fierce fire spread through her, working its way to her heart. ''You're the only ally I have here,'' she told him. ''You wanted my complete trust? Well, you have it now.''

''Necessity is not the same as trust,'' Ashe replied. Sadness touched the edges of his smile. ''I never realized how different you and I are. You stand alone, no matter what you're doing, because you insist on maintaining as much control as you can. You think that I should understand that your feelings for me were real, and that holding back was part of your job. But there's more to it than that. Your feelings were genuine, that's true to a point. But the only thing you gave me without qualification was your body. You trusted me with that, but you never completely surrendered your heart.''

His words hurt, but the truth in them was what stung the most. Casey said nothing for a long time, then answered at length. ''My first reaction was to argue and say you were wrong about me—that although it's true I am independent, I did give you my heart. But you are right. I have held back, though not as much as you may believe. I was pro-

tecting myself. I knew that when you learned the whole
story, things would fall apart between us. I needed to keep
a part of myself safe from that hurt. What I held back was
my lifeline—something that I could hang on to after you
were gone.''

''It's that center you've never let me reach that will always keep you safe, but also alone,'' he told her. ''You
wanted my love, but you weren't willing to risk everything
to love me in return.''

''But I saw my mother almost destroyed after my father
left her,'' Casey said. ''She gave him everything and had
nothing to hold on to when it was over. I swore I'd never
let that happen to me. It's called survival. Love weakened
my mother and then abandoned her when she needed it
most. I swore that if I ever fell in love, it would be with
someone who would understand the need for separateness
between us. I care for you deeply, Ashe, but I don't want
to lose myself in the process.''

''You think you can be stronger by pushing people
away?'' Ashe shook his head. ''You've never even used
the word *love*—not when you speak of your feelings for
me.''

He was right and she knew it. She also understood now
that the price for reaching his heart again would be to open
hers in a way she never had before. There would be no
lifeline to hang on to. It would be a leap of faith into unknown waters. The prospect frightened her as much as the
conviction that it was the only chance they had left.

Her heart had broken once when she'd faced the consequences of her actions and the loss of a love she'd only
just welcomed into her life. Yet she'd had her work, and
that part of herself she'd never shared, to hang on to and
help her through. If she tried again and something went
wrong, there would only be pain.

They rode in silence to the station. The tension between them charged the air like an invisible force that drew them together despite the need for caution. As they walked into the squad room, Casey immediately forced herself to adopt the high-handed attitude that Ashe had suggested. She knew it well. It was mostly a defense mechanism. Local police departments usually resented it when federal agents took over a case. "The Attitude" was just a way of establishing command in a hostile work situation.

"Captain—" she strode into Todacheene's office without knocking, with Ashe directly behind her "—I'm going to need the personnel records of every officer in this substation and auxiliary personnel as well, including the district attorney's office."

"I can open our personnel files to you, but the files pertaining to county employees who work *with* this department aren't kept here."

"They're computerized somewhere. Get them."

Captain Todacheene's gaze hardened. "I said I'd cooperate with your department, but—"

"I don't have time for protocols or niceties," she said, her voice loud enough for those outside in the squad room to hear. "I'm running out of time. I want those records, and the cooperation you promised. If I don't get it, I'll bring a federal team in here and turn this place inside out. The situation is critical, and I don't have time to indulge in turf battles."

"Follow me, Agent Feist. You, too, Detective, since you're obviously working with her." Captain Todacheene strode out, anger evident on his face.

He led the way to the same crowded, windowless office they'd used before in their search of the phone records. "The terminals in here will access whatever you want. Redhawk knows the system. There are also hard-copy printouts in those file cabinets against the wall." He paused, his gaze steely as it focused on Casey. "But not one piece of paper leaves this place. Is that perfectly clear? You can access information, and you can sit here and memorize it, for all I care, but what's in here is confidential and will remain that way unless you produce a subpoena."

"Understood," Casey replied.

"Now turn your backs while I enter my access code into the two terminals."

A moment later, after Todacheene had left the room, Casey glanced around. "Well, he didn't say we couldn't take notes if we found something interesting."

Ashe exhaled softly. "There are enough files in here to keep us busy for the next year."

"Unfortunately, we have to go as fast as we can. Let's focus on new employees first—those who've been hired within the past two to three months. The trouble started recently, so let's track it that way."

Hours later, Casey leaned back in the wooden chair and rubbed her eyes. "Anything turn up on Prescott yet? I didn't realize his appointment was so recent."

"I'm still accessing that information. It's a little complicated because he's in the county database."

"I've learned something interesting about Nakai," she said. "He took a six-month leave of absence, and only rejoined the force recently."

"I knew about that, but I'm telling you, he's not our man."

"According to this, he went to Arizona for a while. Need I remind you that the call asking about Fox came from Phoenix?"

"The timing's off, though. John was already back at work on the Rez when the call came in. There's nothing mysterious about his trip to Arizona, either. His mother was in a hospital there being treated for a rare form of cancer. I remember the entire department chipped in to help him with the funds he needed for that trip.''

''You do realize that what you've said doesn't make him any less a suspect. Money problems have pushed people into doing all kinds of things.''

Ashe shook his head, then a moment later looked up from the computer. ''Okay. Here we go. I've got the file on Prescott. He is the newest employee we've checked so far. He accepted the D.A.'s post eight weeks ago, after the elected D.A. resigned to take a job with a private law firm. Interestingly enough, Prescott also has a Phoenix connection. He was raised there, but moved to New Mexico to attend college. His law degree is from the University of New Mexico. But he was serving as a legal consultant to the Phoenix municipal offices when he was appointed to take over the district attorney's job in San Juan County.''

Casey looked over his shoulder. ''Now that the captain has met Prescott, do you think he'd remember if his voice was that of the person who called posing as Deputy Marshal James?''

Ashe leaned back and stared at the computer screen pensively. ''Maybe. Maybe not. But that Phoenix connection still features everything. We have to follow it up, but we'll have to tread carefully. Prescott will sue this department— and you and me, as well—for defamation if we start asking pointed questions about his background. He wants the D.A. position here permanently. He's made that clear.''

''Okay. So we'll use kid gloves, but we can't back off. Get me the telephone number where Prescott worked. I want to compare it to the one on the phone log.''

''There's a one-digit difference,'' Ashe said, giving her the number, ''so it was probably from the same building, maybe the same office.''

Casey mulled it over. "That really sends out a red flag. It also gives a new slant on Prescott's pressuring my boss to remove me. Maybe he knows we're getting close and he'd rather take his chances with a new investigator. But this is all conjecture. Near as we can tell, he doesn't have a motive. We have to keep up the pressure on him and see what happens. We also need to find out where Prescott was when the attacks on your family and on us occurred. But I don't want to ask him directly. We can't tip him off until we have more to go on."

"Then how do you propose to get the information?"

Casey shrugged. "I can question his secretary and tell her that it's imperative that she tell no one I asked, at least for now."

"Even if she agreed, you couldn't be sure she'd do it. A lot of secretaries are very loyal to their bosses."

"Have you got a better idea?" she retorted.

"I think it would be a mistake at this point to come up with a set game plan. I have a feeling we may do better if we give ourselves room to improvise."

"Okay." She might have worried if she'd been working with anyone else, but she knew Ashe. Whatever he came up with—even off-the-cuff—usually worked out.

Chapter Sixteen

A short time later, they stood outside the building where Prescott had his office. "Okay. I called his secretary and was told Prescott would not be back in until much later today. He's in court."

"Then let's go meet his secretary."

They climbed the stairs to the second floor and walked directly to Prescott's office.

As a young brunette greeted them, Casey brought out her U.S. Marshals Service badge. The direct route was usually her style.

The secretary glanced at the badge, disinterested. "Mr. Prescott won't be available for the rest of the day. In fact, I was getting ready to leave myself. It's my lunch hour."

"I would like to ask you a few questions before you go." Casey saw the tightening around the young secretary's mouth, and knew she'd be facing some resistance. This wasn't going well. "We need some help," she said, softening her tone. "We're trying—"

Ashe stepped toward the window, but bumped the desk hard with his leg. Everything on the desktop was jolted, and some of the items went crashing to the floor.

The brunette rushed around to his side. "Are you okay?"

Ashe was doubled over, grimacing and holding his leg.

As the woman proceeded to help him to a chair, Ashe caught Casey's gaze and nodded toward the appointment book next to the phone.

Casey picked it up and stuck it in her purse while Ashe kept the secretary distracted.

"You should check and make sure you don't have a nasty cut. I've bumped that corner myself, walking by." She took a set of keys from the top drawer. "The rest room is right down the hall. Let me show you the way," she said, but the phone began to ring.

"It's okay," Casey said quickly. "I'll help him find it. We'll be right back. Can you wait a few more minutes before you leave?"

"Sure. I'll answer this call, then I have to contact the garage where my car's getting fixed anyway."

As soon as they were around the corner from the office, Ashe straightened. "Good backup, partner."

"Any information we get now won't stand up in court, but we may get answers that can lead us in the right direction, or at least save us some valuable time. That bit you pulled was a great diversion."

Ashe unlocked the rest-room door and took a quick look inside. "It's empty, and we've got the key. If we both duck in there, we can study the entries without being seen."

The bathroom was small, with barely enough space for one. Casey's back was pressed against the sink as she opened the book. Ashe tried to stand next to her and look at the book but the angle and the lighting were all wrong. Finally he lifted her up onto the sink and stood in front of her. "You read it to me," he said.

She opened the book. He was standing so close that every nerve-ending in her body tingled to life. As he placed one hand on her knee, she fought the crazy desire to part her legs and pull him to her.

As if he'd had the same thought, he glanced downward, then reluctantly moved away.

She took a deep, unsteady breath and read the entries that coincided with the times they were investigating. "That's that, then. He was scheduled for court both times. He couldn't have been involved in the drive-by shooting, or in the murder of your foster parents."

"So much for Prescott as a possibility. Too bad. This was one guy I wouldn't have minded arresting for something."

"But this doesn't completely exonerate him, you know. It just means that he couldn't have been physically present at either crime scene."

As Casey jumped down from the sink, she collided with Ashe's chest. He grasped her firmly around the waist, steadying her. "I think we'd better leave," she muttered as heated images once again filled her mind.

"Yes—before I forget what we're doing here."

His husky voice left her nerves tingling. Desire urged her to be reckless and let passion guide them. It was only as she remembered what he'd said earlier about love that she found the courage to edge around him and move away. Ashe would never accept meeting her halfway. He wanted her very soul. With a heavy heart, she stepped out into the hall.

As they returned to Prescott's office, both of them were quiet. Casey felt restless. Seeing the young secretary still on the phone, she slid the appointment book out of her purse and onto the floor beside the desk, as if it had fallen there.

"Is everything okay?" the brunette asked after hanging up.

"Yes. Here are your keys," Ashe said, rubbing his leg.

"You said you wanted to ask me something," the young woman reminded Casey reluctantly.

"I just wanted to know the best time to catch Mr. Prescott."

She looked around for the appointment book, then noticed it on the floor. Ashe picked it up and handed it to her with a smile. "He's pretty booked for the rest of this week," the secretary said after a quick check.

"That's okay. I'll be in touch next week and set up a meeting then," Casey answered.

As they left the building, Casey could sense Ashe's change in mood. He was tense, almost angry.

"What's wrong?" she asked.

"I've spent my entire life learning how to achieve a balanced life. Yet, around you, I lose all perspective. I should be focused on catching the people who killed my foster parents. Instead, I find myself fighting the urge to make love to you."

It was clear to Casey that Ashe wasn't talking about love now, only passion. She didn't answer, nor did she look at him.

There had been a time when she'd seen the love she felt reflected in his eyes; then that had turned to cold anger. To see passion there now, without any of the feelings that had once given it meaning, would have been impossible for her to bear.

ASHE MADE THE FINAL arrangements for the burial of his foster parents, then met his brother at the church graveyard, which was located in a beautiful spot northwest of town, overlooking the river valley below. It was the last place on earth Ashe wanted to be, for a multitude of reasons, but this was a duty he had to see through. Fox had wanted to be there, too, but they'd all known the risk was too great, and had managed to talk her out of it. No one had been told of the service, either, for the same reasons; they could not take the chance of someone tailing them back to the lodge.

The two brothers stood alone side by side as the caskets were lowered into the ground. They waited in stony silence as the Anglo minister said a few words.

Out of respect for the brothers, the minister kept the prayer short, and when he came up to them, did not offer to shake hands. "They were very proud of both of you, and of their daughter," he said, not mentioning the Johnsons by name. "Their love is something you'll carry in your hearts for as long as you live."

Ashe nodded, feeling his throat tighten. "Thank you. You've done what you had to for their sakes, and you've shown respect for my brother and me, as well."

Travis also thanked the minister. Then, as they walked away, he glanced at Ashe. "You and I have to finish the fight, brother. It's up to us to see that Fox is free to live her own life again. We can't let her down."

"And we won't," Ashe replied flatly. He owed that much to his foster family, and he always paid his debts.

CASEY WATCHED ASHE close up his cell phone. It was nearly eight in the evening, but neither she nor Ashe had been quite willing to call it a day. They needed each other's company now to push back the loneliness of another long night. It had been her idea to see if her department would finance a fact-finding trip to Phoenix, but Ashe's connections with the PD there had given them access to the information they'd needed without making the trip.

"Charley Benally is a good friend. He'll be able to talk to us later tonight. He also promises to E-mail us some files that'll help us. Apparently the D.A. is well-known there."

"I'm glad to hear that you're not ready to give up on the D.A. as a suspect," she said. "It's a good thing I decided to confirm the schedule on his datebook." Finding out that the court session Prescott had supposedly been attending during the time of the murder had been postponed, at his request, put a whole new slant on their investigation. "Obviously, canceled appointments are not always corrected on his secretary's desk calendar."

"Only two people we know who are involved in the current case have that Phoenix connection—Prescott and Nakai," Ashe said.

"From their size, I'd say both wear a size-nine or -ten shoe, too," Casey added.

It was past ten when they were able to get Charley on the phone. Ashe sat in Casey's office as he put Charley on the speaker.

"You told me that you were interested in Ben Prescott, so I've been asking some of the old-timers here who knew him best," Charley said. "He's well-thought-of, as I told you. You may not know this, but he was actually part of a violent street gang here when he was a kid. Then he got his act together."

"So he had a record?" Casey asked.

"Yeah, at one time," Charley replied. "Of course, his record as a minor was cleared when he turned eighteen. That's when he moved to New Mexico to attend college at UNM. I'm sending you a file via computer now. It's for your eyes only. Take a good look, then delete it before you leave the office. It's a compilation of statements from the officers here who knew him way back when, including the two cops who arrested him when he was in the gang."

Casey downloaded the file a few minutes later. Neither of them spoke until they'd both read the contents. "His background is really interesting," Casey commented.

"The information there is based on recollections and is hearsay, which isn't admissible in court. But it could make trouble for the officers who gave me those informal statements. The D.A. is now a respected member of the bar and no one wants to go up against him," the Phoenix cop reminded them.

"I'll take care of it," Ashe assured him. "The file will be deleted, and no printouts will be made."

"As you can see, Prescott was a kid with a violent streak," Benally continued. "His gang was responsible for quite a few residential burglaries."

"Where at, do you know?" Ashe asked.

Charley gave them the name of a subdivision, and mentioned the Phoenix suburb.

Casey recognized the area. Although Katrina's parents had lived in another community, it was one not far from there.

"Prescott was walking garbage when he was a kid," Charley continued. "He even got into a fight with two of our cops and tried to run one over with his motorcycle. But he did straighten himself out. He went to college, and made something of himself."

Casey studied the information, then clicked the mouse on the delete button. She knew the key points now. "Thanks for putting this file together and letting us take a look at it."

"No problem," Charley said. "I hope it helps you find the killers."

Ashe sat lost in thought after Casey had hung up. "I'm going to search through Prescott's personnel files, and I'm also going to try and access the files that pertain to the job he had in Phoenix before coming here. Let's see what I can turn up legally."

THE NEXT MORNING, ASHE picked her up at the motel. As they began the journey to the station in Ashe's carryall, Casey used her cell phone to check with Hayes, assuring herself that everything was all right.

"I called my home office earlier," Casey said. "By the time we reach the station, the file I requested on Fox should be there. You'll be able to read everything I have on her."

"About time." He glanced in the rearview mirror, noting a white van a quarter of a mile behind them. The driver kept his distance, never coming too close or falling back too far. "I think we're being followed."

She glanced into the rearview mirror on her side. "The white van?" She saw him nod. "How long has it been there?"

"Since we passed the café."

"It's not the same van that did the drive-by and tried to run us down. Have you managed to get a look at the driver?"

"No. When I slow down, he does, too. I wouldn't say he's skilled at surveillance, but he's no dummy, either."

"Do you think it could be Nakai?"

"It isn't him. I just spoke to him at the station, and he can't be in two places at once." Ashe narrowed his eyes, trying to get a clearer look at the driver.

"There are two other choice suspects. Let me check on Prescott. Gordon is out of my reach for now." Casey pulled a small notebook from her purse. She looked through it, found the telephone number she needed, then dialed.

"This is Deputy Marshal Feist. Is Mr. Prescott in his office?" She paused, then added, "Good. I need to speak to him." Casey placed her hand over the receiver. "His secretary says he's there working. She's putting my call through now."

Their conversation was brief but, from the expression on

Casey's face, Ashe knew that something wasn't right. "What happened?" he asked as she closed up the cell phone.

"Patrick Gordon, the teacher, apparently turned himself in to the medical center yesterday. He's back in custody."

"He's been out on the streets for a while, but I don't see him as part of a drive-by. Do you?"

"Not really, but I'll need facts before I'm ready to concede he's innocent."

Ashe realized then that her doubtful nature was another major difference between them, and perhaps the most important one. When it came down to business, he banked on his gut instincts, but Casey relied only on facts. That was why she hadn't been willing to trust him before. He'd met cops who went by the book; he just hadn't realized that when it came to business, Casey always played by the rules.

Ashe purposely turned up a dirt track he knew the van wouldn't negotiate easily. The van slowed, but remained behind them. "Okay, now I know it's more than a coincidence. He's following us. No way any driver would have taken this road if he hadn't been tailing us. It leads to an empty field sometimes used for ceremonials, but there are none going on now."

"I say we turn the tables on this guy and find out who he is," Casey said. "We can't arrest him—he's doing nothing illegal—but we can roust him and see what kind of game he's playing."

"I was hoping you'd say that." He slammed on the brakes, spinning the carryall around to the opposite direction in a moonshiner's turn. "Now we're in business." He pressed down hard on the accelerator, racing through the cloud of dust they'd raised, heading straight toward the van.

Chapter Seventeen

Ashe hurtled up the gravel road at high speed. The carryall fishtailed on the unstable road surface and bounced Casey around despite her seat belt. Ashe was a skilled driver on this type of terrain, but every bump jarred her all the way to her bones.

The driver of the van tried to make a last-minute turn-around, but his skill was no match for Ashe's. The man overcompensated, and skidded off the path into a shallow arroyo. The van's rear tires quickly bogged down, and the vehicle came to rest on the sandy bottom.

Ashe brought the carryall to a skidding stop and ran to the driver's side of the van, gun drawn. "Put your hands where I can see them," he ordered. "Then get out."

Casey stood to one side of Ashe, her weapon in hand.

"Hey, guys, what's all the fuss?" Delbert Spencer reached through the rolled-down window and with both hands, opened the door from the outside. Then he got out of the van. "Getting a little jumpy, aren't we?"

Ashe spun him around against the side of the van, then frisked him. "Suppose you start by explaining why you've been tailing us."

"Tailing you? You're crazy. I'm delivering flowers.

Take a look at the back of the van. It's loaded with floral arrangements.''

Casey walked to the vehicle, carefully opened the rear doors in such a way as to avoid being ambushed, then gave Ashe a nod. Unwilling to leave it at that, she used her cell phone and called the florist shop listed on the card attached to one of the arrangements. A moment later, after verifying Spencer's story, she closed the phone and approached Ashe. He had a strange expression on his face, as if the very act of her calling the florist had confirmed something in his mind.

"The florist said Spencer works for them, but he's also not where he's supposed to be. He does have a delivery to make on the Rez, though nowhere near here."

"Hey, what is with you? You guys bored and looking for excitement? Why are you making trouble for me with my new boss?"

"Tell us why you were following us," Casey pressed.

"I wasn't following you. I just happened to be on the same road you were."

"And then you just decided to take the scenic route down this dirt track that leads to no house or business right after we turned off?" Ashe said.

"Oh, *that*, I admit, was a mistake. I got lost and just happened to turn here because I was looking for a place to park and check my map."

Casey knew the man was lying, but there was no way for them to prove it. She studied the prints left by Spencer's shoes. They were ordinary, inexpensive canvas sneakers— not a match in size or type to the boots found at the crime scenes.

"Now, are you going to help me get this van back onto the road? It's your fault I'm stuck here, you know. If you hadn't headed straight for me, I wouldn't have had to scramble to get out of the way.''

Ashe studied the van's position, then shook his head. ''You can get out of this yourself. You'll have to do a little digging, and maybe put some brush in front of your tires to get some traction, but you're in good physical shape. You can handle it. Besides, you can always use the dispatch radio in there to call your boss for help.''

Ashe strode away, with Casey behind him. As they drove back toward the highway, Casey glanced behind. ''He's okay. He's almost halfway up the road again.''

''Too bad. I was hoping he'd have to work at it longer,'' Ashe muttered.

''I know he followed us for a reason, but I think it was just to harass us. He must have known we'd spot him,'' Casey said.

''Now that our suspect list is getting shorter, maybe the crooks have decided some form of payback is called for.''

When they finally arrived at the station and Casey saw Nakai at his desk, questions came unbidden to her mind. Although she knew Ashe was completely closed to the possibility that Nakai might be guilty, she wasn't quite so willing to dismiss him as a suspect. Like Prescott, he'd had the opportunity to see the file on Katrina. He'd also had an association with two other suspects who had featured in the case—Walker and Spencer. If Ashe had grown up with Walker, it was likely that Nakai had known him, as well.

Ashe sat down at Casey's desk as she opened the confidential envelope her supervisor in the Marshals Service office had sent her. She glanced at the contents, then handed the envelope to Ashe. ''This is Fox's history. Everything we know about her is in here. There's a lot about her parents that isn't there, but even I don't have access to that.''

He studied the file before speaking. "You're right. There are some big gaps in the information you have on Fox's parents, though the murder is documented extensively."

"I know, but this file is about Fox and the murders she witnessed. She was only six when her father and mother went into WITSEC. She had nothing to do with her father's case."

"But her enemies may come from her father's affiliations," Ashe answered.

"I know, and I've tried to get that other file, but I've been told that the key players in her father's case are either dead or in prison. We need to deal with the threat that's here now. I say we zero in on Spencer. We can start by paying his parole officer an impromptu visit."

After getting the address, they drove to Ruth Austin's office. They were ushered in immediately.

Ruth stood as they came in. "I've already heard about the incident with the van, and I've got to tell you it took some fancy talking to keep the flower-shop owner from firing Delbert. I'm beginning to suspect that Spencer's right, and you're out to nail him."

"He tailed us for quite a while. Did he tell you that part?" Casey asked, realizing that Ruth didn't exactly seem to be a fan of Ashe's. There was no telling what Spencer had told her.

"I spoke to him. He said he got lost and had the misfortune of going down the same road you'd taken. That makes sense to me. Why the heck would he follow you?"

"To give us something to worry about," Casey answered.

"Did he threaten you in any way?"

"We're not inclined to assume that a parolee tailing us has only our best interests at heart," Casey said.

"Trying to get him fired won't help—you or him."

"That's tough," Casey replied. "Spencer was looking to stir up trouble and he succeeded. The problem we now have is trying to determine just how hungry he is for revenge on Detective Redhawk and how far he'd be willing to go to get it."

Ruth Austin leaned back in her chair. "Okay. Let's lay this out on the table. What do you need from me?"

"Information," Casey said. "How many jobs has Spencer had since he was paroled?"

"Four, including the one he has now. His first job was working at a feed store. Spencer was supposed to help them rearrange their inventory, but he was too slow and breaking open feed bags by handling them too roughly. They let him go. His next employer was a grocery delivery service here in town. Nothing was delivered on time, so they fired him. Then he worked for a janitorial company on the Rez. They clean office buildings, mostly for the tribal government. He stuck to that one for a while, but when he failed to show up a few days in a row, they fired him. The fourth is the one he has now."

"Wait. You said he worked cleaning tribal offices?" Ashe interrupted. "Does that include the police substations?"

She nodded. "Yeah. He seemed to be doing really well, but then he started drinking and disappeared for two days. A police-officer friend of mine found him in a Farmington alley and called me to come get him."

"Who's the cop?" Ashe asked. "It's possible Spencer said more that day than he'd intended, and we might find some of that information useful."

"It was Officer Jerry Walker, a motorcycle cop on the Farmington PD. He's a good man, and he's been kind enough to help me out now and then."

Casey looked at the other woman thoughtfully. She had

a very hard time seeing Jerry Walker as a Good Samaritan. It didn't fit the man she'd met. There was a key piece missing from the puzzle.

"I know what you're thinking," Ruth added slowly. "You're wondering what my connection to Jerry is."

Casey nodded. "Yes, I am."

Ruth looked at Ashe, who stood quietly, then back at Casey. "Jerry and I are good friends. He knows a lot of people in this area and he's helped me find jobs for some of my parolees. He really cares about people, not just about making arrests."

It was her tone of voice that alerted Casey. Ruth was in love with Walker. It shouldn't have surprised her. Walker was a good-looking man, even if he was a creep.

"Okay, Ruth, I have no more questions for you right now. Thanks for your help," Casey said, standing.

"Any time." She looked over at Ashe. "And if you have a problem with any of my people out on the Rez, Detective Redhawk, just let me know. I'll handle it."

"I'll do that," Ashe said.

As they went back to the vehicle, Ashe glanced at Casey. "I think you already know Walker is *not* the man she thinks he is."

"That's a given. At least not for you or me. What's your take on this?"

"Worst-case scenario?" Ashe saw her nod, and he continued. "Walker's using the ex-cons in some kind of operation, helping them out so they'll help him out. On the other hand, there's a slim chance he's not the dirtbag I think he is and he is actually doing something for someone else out of the goodness of his heart. Or maybe he's just setting some of the parolees up to become his snitches."

The sun was high in the sky and the desert comfortably warm as they drove back to the station.

"You know, there's another possibility. I believe that Ruth is seriously attracted to Jerry Walker. It was the way she spoke about him, and her tone of voice. If he has any feelings for her, then it would be natural for them to want to become a part of each other's lives."

"There was a time when I thought that you and I had that. As cops we understood each other like no one else could. As man and woman, we knew love."

A yearning more powerful than any she'd ever known filled her. "It could be that way now if you'd accept that there are things I don't know how to give." She looked at him and saw the flash of pain that crossed his eyes. She had no desire to keep hurting him, or herself. "You want me to love you completely, to not hold back anything from you. But even if I did, what hope of a future can we ever really have? This land defines you, but it will always see me as an outsider. You belong here, but I do not."

Ashe parked by the side of the road and shifted to face her. "Look around you, *sawe*. This is no longer an alien place to you. It's the Dinétah, the land of a people you've come to know and whose ways you've grown to value. Don't you know that it has already started to become a part of you?"

He'd only used the Navajo word for *sweetheart* once before, when they'd made love. Feelings tangled with desire and flowed through her body. His words and the gentleness in his eyes sang seductively to her woman's soul, urging her to surrender to love.

"Once we close this case, we'll both be free to take what life has offered us, or walk away," Ashe continued. "But regardless of what we choose, neither one of us will ever be the same again."

Casey knew now that love didn't need anyone's consent to exist. She'd thought she could run from love, but it had become a part of her. No matter how far or how fast she ran, it would always be there, locked within her.

Suddenly a vivid image of her childhood days came unbidden into her mind. She remembered her mother crying in her room alone at night. Love had tempted her mother to believe and trust, then almost destroyed her.

"I used to think that love disrupted harmony, that it would only bring confusion into my life," Ashe said slowly. "And in some ways it has done just that. But the Navajo Way also teaches that only by pairing can a man and a woman be complete."

Pairing. The word made a delicious shiver course up her spine.

Ashe cupped Casey's face in his strong hands. "I see longing in your eyes, but fear is there, too. Maybe someday I'll only see love. Then I'll know that the time for us has come."

Having said that, he moved away from her, started the vehicle, and pulled back onto the highway. Casey understood. His message was clear—the next move would be up to her.

Chapter Eighteen

They sat behind closed doors at the station. Ashe knew the plan Casey had come up with was risky, but he couldn't think of any other that was better or safer. They were almost out of time.

"Fox will be fine where she is," she said. "Hayes and your brother will stay with her at the cabin until this is over.

"Meanwhile we'll leak information that will assure Prescott, Walker, Spencer, Nakai, Captain Todacheene and even Gordon, that Fox is being kept at her own home. 'Hiding in plain sight,' we'll call it. I'll wait inside the house, wearing Katrina's clothes and a blond wig. If any of the suspects come to check things out, they'll be able to catch glimpses of a woman fitting Fox's description."

"We can't use you as bait for this trap without backup."

"I could get more deputies here but they'd stick out like sore thumbs on the Reservation. Can you find six officers or trustworthy individuals to work this detail with us without alerting the captain?"

"Yes, but there's going to be hell to pay afterward. The captain is innocent, and when he learns about the way we handled this, heads are going to roll."

"I'm sure he'll see that we had no other choice," Casey said.

"Maybe, but I'm not counting on it, nor can I make that promise to any of the officers who choose to help us out."

"Fair enough. I'll take care of leaking the news to Prescott and Captain Todacheene. Gordon is in the psychiatric facility, but I'm going to make sure one of the nurses slips him the information. I want him included in this roster. Spencer and Walker are going to be trickier to contact without tipping our hand, though," Casey admitted.

"I can make sure Walker knows by having another parole officer drop the information to Ruth Austin. I'm sure she confides in him, if you're right about their relationship," Ashe suggested.

"That leaves Spencer, but we can rule out Ruth Austin for that. I don't think she'd want him knowing something that could lead to more trouble for him," Casey said pensively.

"He lives just off the Reservation and rents a place from a Navajo family I know. I can make sure the news reaches him."

"Once the word is out, our backup team will have to keep all the suspects under surveillance so we can monitor whatever action they take."

"Then we'd better get busy. Tonight's the night."

ASHE HANDPICKED THE TEAM—his two cousins and four former classmates and students of the Johnsons he'd known for years. Only two were not cops, but both had military experience. After giving his team their instructions, Ashe drove out to see Katrina and his brother one last time.

Tonight he'd be Casey's closest backup. If the killer managed to get into the house, he was prepared to do whatever was necessary to protect her, no matter what it cost him. Casey would be alive to see the next morning, he'd see to that. But he didn't lay the same odds for himself. Too many things could go wrong.

Travis met him some distance away from the lodge and Ashe filled him in on Casey's strategy. Travis regarded his brother thoughtfully for several long moments before he spoke. "It's a good plan. By tomorrow, Fox should be free again. But take a hint, little brother. Don't let Casey walk out of your life after this case is closed. If you do, you'll regret it."

"I do love her, but what happens next is up to her."

"So you're bowing out so she can make the decision all by herself? That's mighty big of you, but a woman likes to hear a man admit how much he needs and wants her. If you really love her, speak plainly, then you can sweep her off her feet."

Ashe looked at his brother in surprise. "You're making a lot of sense, for a change."

"Don't be so shocked." Travis laughed. "Life's taught me a thing or two along the way."

Ashe followed Travis to the cabin and visited with Katrina for a few minutes. If something happened to him tonight, he thought she should know that he'd died doing precisely what he'd wanted to do.

Though he was careful not to give her details of the plan because it would only make her worry, he could see that she was already concerned.

"Promise me you'll be very careful. You're not the same tough-as-nails cop who used to live for the job. You've changed. There's something gentler about you lately. It's like your heart has been opened..." Her voice trailed off. Then, suddenly, she smiled. "It must be Casey. Are you in love?"

"Yeah, I guess I am," he said in a quiet voice.

Katrina sighed softly. "I wish you luck." Lost in thought, she glanced across the room at Travis for a moment.

He knew Fox was thinking about herself and Travis. But the feelings between them were ill-fated. Travis would never settle down. He was like the wind, finding purpose only in movement.

"After tonight, if all goes well, you'll have your life back," he said. "Think of that."

"But it will come at a price, too," she said. "Life seems to be that way a lot. You gain something, only to be asked to give up something else."

"You've turned into a very smart lady," Ashe said.

She gave him a familiar smile. "I was always smart. Now go do whatever it is you have to. And watch yourself."

CASEY PACED NEAR THE window of the Johnson-home living room, wearing the long blond wig. Anyone who approached the house would easily mistake her for Katrina.

"It's still quiet out here," Ashe told her, speaking through a cell phone instead of risking the radio. He was just inside the door of the garage. From there, he could see the front of the house.

"Someone will make a move soon." There were two police-uniformed mannequins beside windows—one in the kitchen, and one at the back of the house—positioned as if they were keeping watch, and with enough backlight to make them only barely visible. This was the security that the attackers were supposed to see in order not to suspect a trap.

"I just heard from three of my people," Ashe said. "Prescott is on the move, and so is Spencer. Walker is at a coffee shop in Farmington."

"Let's see what they decide to do."

Casey continued moving around the room, making herself visible at random intervals, without turning herself into an easy target.

If her hunch was right, by daybreak, they'd have all the answers they needed. The thought weighed heavily on her. Once the case was officially closed, she'd have no reason to stay on the Rez. Ashe would no longer be a part of her life.

There had been a time when the excitement of an operation like this would have been enough for her. Her job had been her life, her passion. But now, it seemed like a poor substitute for the kaleidoscope of emotions she'd found in Ashe's embrace. Love had redefined her life.

Ashe reported in, interrupting her thoughts. "We need to stay sharp now. One of my cousins just called in. Spencer and Prescott went into the mall on the west side and, although their cars are still outside, both men have dropped out of sight. Neither he nor the guy tailing Prescott has seen either one for over a half hour."

"I wonder if Prescott made Spencer a parole offer he couldn't refuse," Casey grumbled. "Ashe, do you hear a truck?"

"Yes. There's a postal-delivery van coming up," he warned, urgency in his voice.

"Great. Just what we need. Innocent bystanders."

"No, I don't think so. There are no mail deliveries in this area. You have to pick up your packages at the post office."

"Then it's showtime," she said.

Casey pulled out her pistol and felt for the spare clips in her pocket. Reassured that they were in easy reach, she held the weapon down by her side so anyone spotting her behind the curtain wouldn't notice it.

"I'm calling in our troops now, but I don't think they'll be here in time to help. There are two figures in the van, though I can't make an ID yet, so the odds aren't bad."

As the van pulled up, Casey closed the cell phone, placing it in her pocket. Now she purposely stayed well back from the window as she walked past it so they could see that she was inside. Moving quickly toward the part of the room where the light was subdued, she stopped and peered out the side window. Prescott and Spencer, dressed as deliverymen, were carrying two boxes to the door.

Casey moved into the darkness of the kitchen as they knocked. "I saw you come up and unlocked the door. Come on in." She wasn't ready to tip her hand, and prayed her voice had been so soft they wouldn't recognize it.

She wanted them inside, their plan evident, before she made her move. As the men entered, she saw Ashe pass by outside the window, moving into position behind them to block their exit.

"Packages, ma'am," Prescott said, looking around the room to see who else might be present.

It was their signal, apparently, because both men reached inside the boxes, bringing out automatic pistols.

Casey dropped to one knee and aimed, using the doorjamb as partial cover. "Federal Marshal. Lay down your weapons."

Prescott cursed, then snapped off two rounds at her as he scrambled for the front door. Casey flinched as the bullets struck the wall just above her head. The D.A. was halfway outside when Ashe ambushed him. He struck Prescott hard with the butt of his pistol, and the man dropped like a sack of grain.

Spencer, seeing Prescott go down, panicked and dived behind the couch, firing wildly at Ashe. Several bullets struck around the entrance, and Ashe had to flatten himself against the concrete floor of the porch.

Casey rushed into the front room to take the pressure off Ashe. She hit the floor and directed her pistol toward the far end of the couch. But Spencer appeared at the other end, at point-blank range, aiming at Casey. Ashe crouched and fired two shots. The man clutched his chest and crumpled to the floor, his gun slipping from his hand.

Ashe stood slowly and went to Casey's side. "You okay?" he asked, gently helping her up. His gaze caressed her as he made sure she was uninjured. "Great work, partner."

"Looks like we came through for each other once again," she said quietly.

Casey knelt by Spencer's body, then checked the pulse point at his neck. She shook her head, answering Ashe's unspoken question. "He's gone."

Together with Ashe, she went to where Prescott lay. Ashe crouched next to him, noting the regular rise and fall of his chest. "He'll live, but he'll have one heck of a headache."

Hearing Prescott moan, Ashe handcuffed him quickly and made sure he didn't have any weapons still on him. "Time to wrap this up," Ashe said, hearing the wail of approaching sirens.

As Ashe went outside to meet their backup, Casey looked down at Spencer's body. His life had amounted to nothing more than a waste of the time he'd spent on earth. He had touched no one, and no one had touched him. Now he lay alone in death.

A chill touched her soul. Life came with a ticking clock that could stop at any time. Without reaching out for a dream and having the courage to make it come true, life amounted to nothing more than an endless parade of days.

Ashe came up to join her. "We have to go to the station now. I have some explaining to do to my captain, and I want him to hear what happened here from us first. I owe him that much."

"All right." Later there would be time for them to talk. Love bound them together and, if it was as strong as she hoped, surely it would guide them now.

HOURS LATER, AT THE police station, Travis, Katrina and Hayes sat in the conference room while Casey and Ashe filled the captain in on everything that had occurred.

"It wasn't Detective Redhawk's decision to leave you out of this," Casey explained. "It was mine, but I think you can clearly see my reasoning."

"I understand what prompted your decision, but I'm glad to hear that it wasn't the detective's choice. I'd hate to think one of my own officers felt I couldn't be trusted."

Ashe looked at the captain. "I never believed that either you or John Nakai were involved, and it wasn't just a matter of loyalty to another member of the tribe, or to the force. It was because I know you two well. Unfortunately, I couldn't find any hard-and-fast evidence to support that belief before we put the sting in motion."

Ashe saw the tension ease on Todacheene's face, and knew that eventually they would work things out.

"Prescott is back in his cell, stewing," the captain said. "But he's a crafty one. Don't expect him to give you squat."

"We raked him over the coals for some time, but he won't admit to anything. A confession at this point would be tidy, but it's not necessary," Ashe said. "The lab has identified his weapon as the gun used to kill my foster parents. There was also a stocking-cap mask in his possession, and the fibers from that look like a match for the ones found at the crime scene. Then there's that dirt bike in his garage. He was so cocky, he didn't get rid of any of the things that could put him behind bars. I bet we'll find his size-ten boots, too. With that much evidence backing us up, the charges will stick.''

''What about motive?''

''We believe we also have a handle on that,'' Casey answered. ''The Phoenix connection and his affiliation at one time with a violent gang there is the key. That gang committed a lot of residential burglaries in the general area where Fox's parents lived. My guess is that, at one time or another, the gang expanded their territory and Prescott ended up killing the people he'd come to rob. Fox, who'd seen it all, became his target, but he failed in that attempt at the foster home. Then, after he became an attorney, Fox loomed as an ever-present threat to his career and political ambitions. But he couldn't track her down. Once he was able to determine she was in New Mexico, he came just to see if she still remembered and could recognize his face after all these years. He had other incentives, too. Shortly after he got here, he was presented with a wonderful political opportunity—he was appointed to take over for the D.A. who had left that post. He had to find out quickly, then, how dangerous Fox was to him and take care of that matter once and for all if she seemed to recognize him.''

Fox exhaled softly. ''I guess I must have prompted him to act after the political rally I attended with Mom and Dad several weeks ago. I was introduced to Prescott and I mentioned that he looked familiar somehow. He said that it was probably because he'd been in the papers so much, and I believed him. I guess he didn't want to risk me remembering any of the details later on.''

Casey nodded slowly. ''From that moment, he knew he had to kill you and everyone else, like your adoptive parents, who might link him to the murders. He had no way of knowing how much the U.S. Attorney's investigator—your adoptive father—had been told or, for that matter, what you'd told them.''

"I think I know now why Prescott wanted Casey off the case, too,'' Ashe said. "I bet he was hoping Fox would refuse to be relocated, and then she'd be an easy mark. On the other hand, if she did relocate, then it would have been to someplace so far away she would have stopped being a threat to him anyway.''

"It explains a lot of things, but I have a feeling…'' Todacheene shook his head, and smiled. "Never mind. This case is now closed. Since your witness is no longer under any threat, I suppose you'll be leaving the Rez?'' the captain asked Casey.

Casey avoided looking at Ashe. "The time has come for me to face new challenges,'' she said, avoiding a more direct answer.

After Ashe and Casey left the captain's office, Katrina, Travis and Hayes came up to meet them.

"It's really over, isn't it?'' Katrina asked.

Ashe saw the sadness that flickered in her gaze for a moment as she looked at Travis. He understood what the end of the case meant to Katrina. Travis would be gone again within days, maybe hours. And if Ashe didn't do something soon, Casey would be gone from *his* life, too.

Ashe saw Travis place a gentle hand on Katrina's shoulder. "It's time for me to go rejoin my unit, Fox. But you'll be okay now.''

Hayes came up and abruptly grabbed Casey's hand to shake it. "I'll be packing up and heading out now. I'm retired, remember? I'll call you later to see how things are going.''

Casey thanked Hayes, and together they strolled to his

car. Ashe started to go after Casey when Captain Todacheene approached him. "I don't know where you think
you're going, Detective. I need you to sign a statement."

Ashe took care of the necessary paperwork in the captain's office as quickly as he could. Minutes later, he rushed
out, but as he reached the door, Travis blocked his way.
"Easy, little brother. Take a breath. I knew you'd want to
talk to Casey, so I made sure she'd stick around."

Ashe's eyes narrowed. "What did you do?"

"Let me put it this way. Casey's not going anywhere—
not in that car of hers, anyway," he replied, flipping a
distributor cap over to Ashe.

He caught it with one hand. "Thanks." He was still grin-
ning when he reached Casey's vehicle. "I'm glad you're
here."

"Doesn't look like I'm going anywhere. I came out to
move my car so that the DWI van could get into the garage
area. But the car has other ideas."

"So did my brother," Ashe said, holding up the distributor cap.

Casey smiled. "That's conspiracy."

"Yes, but it's for a good cause." Ashe took her hand
and gently pulled her out of the car.

For the first time, as he gazed into her eyes, he saw no
trace of fear reflected there. "Our time has come, *sawe*.
Our cultures are different, but we've both proven that the
feelings we share are strong enough to help us find com-
promises. We can work anything out as long as we have
each other. Will you marry me and share a future together?"

Casey wrapped her arms around him and pressed herself
against his chest. "Convince me," she said, nuzzling him
playfully.

"Sawe!" The whispered caress reached her a second before his hungry mouth descended over hers.

From somewhere behind him, Ashe heard Travis's laughter mingling with cheers from people at the substation.

* * * * *

Don't miss Aimée Thurlo's
exciting conclusion to
THE BROTHERS OF ROCK RIDGE,
REDHAWK'S RETURN,
coming next month
from Harlequin Intrigue.

THE BROTHERS OF ROCK RIDGE: Bound by blood, and steeped in the traditions of their heritage, these sexy brothers live their lives by their own rules—and love against all odds.

They're brothers by blood, lawmen by choice, cowboys by nature.

THE COWBOY CODE

The McQuaid brothers learned justice and honor from their father, the meaning of family from their mother. The West was always in their souls, but now it's the past they have to reckon with. And three women hold the keys to their future.

Don't miss this exciting new series from three of your favorite Intrigue authors!

McQUAID'S JUSTICE
Carly Bishop
January 1999

A COWBOY'S HONOR
Laura Gordon
February 1999

LONE STAR LAWMAN
Joanna Wayne
March 1999

Available at your favorite retail outlet.

HARLEQUIN®
Makes any time special ™

Look for a new and exciting series from Harlequin!

HARLEQUIN Duets ™

Two <u>new</u> full-length novels in one book, from some of your favorite authors!

Starting in May, each month we'll be bringing you two new books, each book containing two brand-new stories about the lighter side of love! Double the pleasure, double the romance, for less than the cost of two regular romance titles!

Look for these two new Harlequin Duets™ titles in May 1999:

Book 1:
WITH A STETSON AND A SMILE
by Vicki Lewis Thompson
THE BRIDESMAID'S BET
by Christie Ridgway

Book 2:
KIDNAPPED? by Jacqueline Diamond
I GOT YOU, BABE by Bonnie Tucker

2 GREAT STORIES BY 2 GREAT AUTHORS FOR 1 LOW PRICE!

Don't miss it! Available May 1999 at your favorite retail outlet.

HARLEQUIN®
Makes any time special.™

COMING NEXT MONTH

#509 THE BRIDE'S PROTECTOR by Gayle Wilson
Men of Mystery

When CIA agent Lucas Hawkins rescues a bride-to-be from assassins, his only thought is to get the beautiful Tyler Stewart to safety. Now Tyler is the only person who can clear his name, but only if he can keep her alive....

#510 REDHAWK'S RETURN by Aimée Thurlo
The Brothers of Rock Ridge

Travis Redhawk had sworn a blood oath that he'd always be there for Katrina Johnson in times of need. Now that danger surrounds Katrina at every turn, is Travis strong enough to be the man Katrina needs—and wants?

#511 LOVER, STRANGER by Amanda Stevens
A Memory Away...

Who was Dr. Ethan Hunter? The greedy, selfish man others described, or the strong, honorable doctor standing before FBI agent Grace Donovan? Grace's investigation—and her life—depended on Ethan regaining his memory. But if he did, would she lose the only man she could ever love?

#512 HIS SECRET SON by Jacqueline Diamond

Joni Peterson woke up next to the body of her ex-husband, with no memory of killing him, although the evidence against her was damning. She turned to the only man she could trust, Dirk Peterson, her husband's estranged brother—and her son's secret father....

Look us up on-line at: http://www.romance.net